Let Sleeping Gods Lie

Ben Schenkman

Caffeinated Terrier Press

ISBN (eBook): 978196732604-4

ISBN (Paperback): 978196732605-1

ISBN (Hardcover): 978196732606-8

Cover design by Getcovers

Chapter art by Kat Gruhala (@KinTheCryptid)

Author's Note

It's impossible to write about the legends of the Indigenous people of the Americas without also acknowledging the harm done to them.

In honor of their struggle, I will donate 10% of all profits from this book, in all formats, to Not Our Native Daughters (NOND). Please consider supporting their mission: https://notournatived aughters.org/

Land Acknowledgement

I want to take the time to acknowledge the stewards of the land where I write from, as well as where this story takes place.

My home sits on the unceded lands of the Agawam and Nipmuc peoples, and I also write from the traditional lands of the Pocomtuc and Nonotuck tribes. My characters walk the lands of the Mohegan, Mashantucket Pequot, Eastern Pequot, Schaghticoke, Golden Hill Paugussett, Niantic, Quinnipiac, and other Algonquian speaking tribes and nations.

I honor the stewardship these tribes have and continue to provide, pay my respect to elders past and present, and thank them for their stories.

Chapter 1

I hadn't expected someone to jump off a building that night. I especially hadn't expected that someone to be me.

I hung in the air, time standing still. How had I gotten here? Less than an hour earlier, I found myself walking the streets of downtown New Haven. It was a college town, and the stone buildings of Yale gave gravitas to an evening stroll you couldn't find in the more suburban parts of the city. It was outside of my territory, but something drew me to the ivy-strewn lanes.

I didn't like walking the streets of downtown. There were too many dead zones and areas devoid of life. Yale was an odd mix, where the stone buildings had the weight of history. But the history was outdone by the bones buried beneath.

I tended to trust my intuition, which had gotten me into trouble and out of it in equal measure. I'd say I was minding my own business, but following my gut was part of my profession. Though I guess it was an avocation because no one paid me for it. "Do what you love, and you'll never work a day in your life," was the adage, but I could verify that whoever said it had a weird definition of "work."

So, there I was, walking along College Street near Vanderbilt Hall, when a flash of movement in my peripheral vision caught my attention. I sharpened my focus on a patch of shadows in front of two buildings. Glaring back at me was a raccoon, the shine from its eyes glowing white in the dark. It was a chonk of its species, easily twice the size of whatever a person imagined when they thought of a trash panda. New Haven fed its denizens well, apparently.

Some things existed solely in the physical realm, others only in the spirit world, but some straddled both. In Native myths, there's often a single animal that's the representation of all. "Raccoon" would be one creature, and yet every raccoon. This specimen was closer to its namesake. It was rooted in the spirit world as well as the physical, and I could see it regardless of which sets of eyes I opened.

If you had the talent, naturally acquired or otherwise, you could see through the veil between the worlds.

In addition to being rotund, the animal was also full of energy. There were two worlds, the physical one we always experienced, and the spirit realm which existed as a kind of overlay on top of that. Like nesting topographic maps, they took up nearly the same space but were just sideways of each other. Some areas were richer in spirit life than others. Connecticut had a long Indigenous history, and the gods and myths of the local tribes walked the land long before Europe came calling. New Haven had been the traditional homeland of the Quinnipiac, but they were almost lost to time.

We stared at each other for a solid minute. I was curious, but it had the frozen stillness of a prey animal assessing a potential predator. Ever so slowly, it stretched a black hand behind its shoulder into a wide crack between the buildings. It barely qualified as an "alley" because no human could have fit more than their leg into the space, but the raccoon backed itself against the opening, its bulk covering the gap.

"Hey, friend," I said in a quiet voice. "I'm not here to hurt you." I broke eye contact and reached into a canvas hip bag tied around my waist and thigh. I brought my hand back out, holding a pinch of tobacco. Concentrating, I pushed a tiny bit of my essence into the dry leaves.

Magic was a complicated thing. Traditions existed for hundreds of years, varying in intent and practice. Some were about inner peace and enlightenment. Others took sacrifice and turned it into a quest for power. But if we were going to talk about real magic, and I mean true magic, we had to go back to the beginning.

If you looked at the earliest cave paintings, many of them were effectively spells. Our progenitors manifested the intentions of their hunt for the next day or told stories of the gods and goddesses they needed to protect them. Fast forward to today, and not a lot changed.

It boiled down to intent and the fuel that powered it, the energy around and inside us. Most indigenous religions were animistic, meaning there was a spirit living in everything. Practicing magic meant figuring out how to take that essence and do something with it. It was like martial arts. There were only so many ways a body moved, so there was a commonality among the mystic arts, even if they all boiled down to the same thing.

So, what I was doing now was taking the tiniest piece of my soul, and presenting it to this nature spirit as part of a traditional offering of tobacco. Smoking might have become mostly extinct in current times, but tobacco was a cultural crop in Connecticut even to this day. The Indigenous people considered it sacred and used it as part of their spiritual practices, and it meant something to the creatures of the land.

The raccoon's nose perked up as it sniffed the air. It tasted not only the perfume of the dried leaves on the wind but the scent of my energy mingling with it. Removing its paw from the wall behind it, the raccoon took a tentative step toward me. I returned the cautious gesture and put one foot off the sidewalk onto the grass between us.

We were making progress, and it was important to get a move on. This was what had called me here. These streets weren't always safe for pedestrians, but they were even less so for creatures like this. The local residents, often spoiled rich kids coming from affluent families, weren't raised with respect for the beings who lived here before they did.

I guess you could call me a conservationist. My ties to the land and the ancestral people who lived there were complicated. But regardless, I had no desire to see more innocent lives, human or otherwise, sacrificed to the machine of modern invention. I said no one paid me to do what I do, but it mattered, and it was worth my time.

The gentle snuffling of the raccoon's nose halted immediately when the crack of a stick, broken underfoot, shattered the silent tableau. I turned to my left and found I was not the only night walker with an interest in the local fauna. A dark shape, a slender person clad in a black hoodie and jeans, crept toward my small friend. Their slow movements had the feel of a hunter stalking prey. They took one step past the snapped twig, then another, until the raccoon launched into frantic motion.

The tiny hand snapped back to the bricks behind it, and the raccoon stuffed itself unceremoniously into the crevice between the outer walls. It reminded me of a mouse, which could compress itself to fit under nearly any crack, and this rodent of unusual size demonstrated the process in macro.

"Gods damn it," I muttered under my breath.

I hadn't expected the stranger to hear me, but they turned in my direction. I couldn't make out a face in the deep shadows of the hood, but their body radiated unwelcome surprise. They broke into a sprint, but the raccoon was already in motion, climbing upward like a striped ninja. I lunged forward, dropping my meager offering, but the furry target was already halfway up one-story and climbing through the gap toward the courtyard on the other side. Their pursuer ran past me, rounding the corner with a hard left to go around the building.

Chasing after them both, my feet slapped an uneven beat on the pavement. When I made my turn, a black iron gate came into view. It swung wide onto the sidewalk, likely flung open by the person I followed. I barreled through it into the courtyard, which was poorly lit by lampposts spaced evenly along the outer edge. The center had no lights, and the shadows cast by the trees stretched into darkness. The scrabbling of claws on flagstones reached my ears but faded into the distance. As far as I could tell, the creature had fled down the center path, which was also the darkest.

Concrete paths crisscrossed the grounds in a geometric pattern. There was no sign of the stranger who had pelted after their quarry so readily, and I made my way cautiously along a lane splitting the middle of the yard. My boots scuffed loudly against the stone path, so I moved off onto the grass, paralleling it. I started slightly at a figure looming in the distance, but my heart calmed as the sitting form of Theodore Woolsey, a bronze statue rather than a living man, came into focus.

A hiss filled the air, to the left of the paths where they crossed in an X, and I nearly leapt out of my skin. Looking up, two shining eyes met my gaze, the raccoon's plump rump hanging over the notch in one of the larger trees in the courtyard, about twenty feet off the ground, along the outer walkway. No one else was visible, and I made a circuit around the tree to confirm I was alone. Either the raccoon's pursuer was hiding in the shadows or had given up the chase when the poor thing climbed too high to catch.

"I don't have time for this," I complained to no one in particular. The hiss that answered was short, as if to say, "me neither." My assumption was if I left the raccoon in its predicament, whoever was hunting it would come in for the kill. A creature like this would be a reasonably powerful source of magic and a rare enough find in the confines of the campus.

I sighed, adjusted my hip bag, dropped my larger satchel, and fished a large canvas sack out of it. Then I did what any irrational human would do. The rational thing would have been going home and getting a good night's sleep, but instead I scaled a tree. I had practiced climbing enough, and my footwear was a reasonable combination of flexibility and support, to make it a more reasonable choice than you might think. My side work took me on all sorts of adventures, and I liked to be prepared.

Shimmying up the tree was less complicated than I feared, and I had the encouraging hisses above to guide me. I was about halfway up the trunk when leaves and other debris fell from the branches overhead. The raccoon's claws scrabbled along the tree limbs as it went higher, releasing bits of plant matter in its wake. I slid downward a foot before catching myself, raising one arm to shield my eyes from the falling cruft.

The sound of claws on wood was replaced by the click of them on slate. The furry idiot had managed to move from the trees to the roof next to us. The limbs above would never support my weight, so I needed to adjust my plan. If the pursuer had given up, then maybe–

A loud bang split the night, and light flooded one small corner of the courtyard as someone threw a door open.

"You have got to be kidding me." This person was persistent, and I was halfway up a tree. I slid down as quickly as possible, doing my best not to scuff my hands too much in the process. My feet barely touched the ground before I was off again, grabbing my bag on the run. I scanned side to side as I bolted for the entrance, dead patches of grass appearing grayer than the surrounding spots in the dark.

When I reached the door, I managed to catch it before it closed. The heavy security knob surprised me, but then I made the connection. The trouble with a lot of these younger practitioners was that the allure of magic overrode any sense of preservation, self or otherwise. A person could draw power from the environment around them, but doing so was an act of brutality. Ripping energy from the ground itself would fuel a minor spell, but it would kill that bit of the land. The groundskeepers of Yale wouldn't appreciate the vandalism, but they wouldn't understand the harm it did on the other side of the veil. A lot of this area was a dead zone for a reason, usually tied to people hell-bent on claiming more of the urban wilds for their use.

Old Campus was made up of multiple long halls set in a square around the large courtyard. The stairwell snaked upward, and I ignored the landings leading to other floors as I made my way up the stairs. Eventually, I came to a hatch overhead labeled "roof access." My quarry must have been running on empty because the padlock that secured it wasn't unlocked as much as it was bashed open. I climbed the short ladder and swung the hatch up cautiously before sneaking onto the roof.

As I stepped onto the slate, I gave a silent prayer, thanking all that was holy it hadn't rained. I glanced toward where the raccoon had clambered up and stalked silently in that direction. There was a standoff happening fifty feet toward the middle of the long roof. I didn't want to break out the flashlight I kept with me. Drawing attention to myself on the roof would have meant a quick call to the police and a lot of explanation on my part.

Enough games. "Hey!" I hissed as I approached the pair. "I don't know what you think you're doing, but that is *my* raccoon." It sounded stupid when I said it out loud, but I needed to get their attention.

They turned their head toward me and sized me up. I wasn't the most physically intimidating figure, but at five foot eight, I would have better reach over their slightly shorter stature. I rolled my neck from side to side, popping it, and settled into a fighting stance. They must not have liked their chances, because they held up their hands and backed away. This took them toward the raccoon, which skittered toward the edge of the roof.

I rushed forward, and the hooded figure fled, theoretically, to another access hatch at the other end. They weren't my problem anymore. *My* dilemma was the fat furball sliding precariously closer to a gutter overgrown with weeds and one tenacious dandelion. It wasn't over the edge yet, and I grabbed the sack out of my pack again. It eyed me with suspicion, despite the fear also present there as it lost its footing.

Creeping toward the creature as calmly as I could while still moving quickly enough to close the distance, I assessed my situation. If I reached the overgrown squirrel in time, maybe I could stuff it into the sack without getting bitten before we both fell off the roof. My furry roof-mate wasn't having any of it and continued to back away, its feet sliding on the smooth stone shingles.

"Come on, friend," I said, managing a soothing tone. "Get in the fucking bag."

With a hiss, the raccoon turned and leapt from the edge of the roof. Trees lined the outside of the buildings as well, with one a reasonable distance from where we were. Raccoons, however, were apparently bad at physics because its mass-times-acceleration didn't equal enough velocity to get anywhere near the closest branch.

"Shit!" I yelled, and in two steps I launched myself off the same patch of roof toward the flying raccoon, sack held open in two hands. My momentum was much greater than theirs, and I closed the gap in a heartbeat. The oversized rodent twisted in the air, trying to avoid me, but it had nothing to maneuver with. My luck held, and the bag enveloped my target, its teeth snapping inches from my hand before it disappeared into the canvas.

Time slowed down when you were doing stupid things midair, and a large branch of the nearest tree rose in front of me. I let go of the bag with one hand, holding onto the drawstring with the other. Hooking my arm around the approaching limb, I willed it to support our combined weight. My elbow burned from the friction of the sudden stop, but there was no snapping sound signaling my imminent demise.

I breathed a temporary sigh of relief and adjusted my grip on both the tree and the bag. The scrape of feet on slate alerted me to a presence above, and the moonlight cast a shadow over my position. My unknown adversary, hood still covering their face, stood staring down at me. They crouched and placed their hand over the flower in the gutter. A small thread of energy leapt from the head of the dandelion to their hand, the plant withering as its life was drained away.

There wasn't much in a flower, all things considered, but I didn't know what they planned. Glancing around wildly I found some bushes below, offset by about five feet from where I was currently destined to land. If I could just–

Pain blossomed through my elbow, like someone shoved a red-hot needle into it. I turned my gaze upward, and the person on the roof held something against their own arm, though I couldn't make the item out from where I was.

Magic wasn't only about energy but also about sympathy. The world wanted to operate in a certain way. You could either work with it or against it. Working with your environment made everything simpler, consumed less energy, and caused fewer problems with the rest of the ecosystem. Against it? It used up resources more quickly. Sympathy made connections between your actions and the intended outcome.

I had to assume a needle was in that asshole's hand, that they were pressing it into their own flesh through a layer of clothing. The smile under the hood was almost palpable, a wan light glinting vaguely off dazzlingly white teeth, which were the only things I could make out.

The invisible spike twisted in my joint, and I grunted in pain, my grip around the tree loosening. I had maybe five seconds before I would drop straight down, and nothing would cushion my fall except a sack full of raccoon. Swinging my feet back and forth to build as much momentum as I could in a short time, I let go before the pain became unbearable. I angled my feet toward the bushes, and the air rushed past my ears. Time became meaningless as I waited for the impact, holding the sack to my chest.

Chapter 2

"What the hell, Corbin? Why do you look like you fell out of a tree?"

My head snapped upright from where I had been leaning, body slumped akimbo in a rickety wooden chair at Mamoun's Falafel Restaurant. A half-eaten pita sandwich and fries sat cooling in front of me, and a sack squirmed under my chair, making vague chittering noises. I eyed Nour Haddad with a long-suffering stare. "Do you have any ibuprofen?"

Mamoun's had been a Middle Eastern fixture of the city since 1977, and I had been eating there for the past twenty years. Nour had worked at the restaurant for a few years and had become a constant during my visits. My regular patronage, combined with our mutual disinterest in dating, led us to be more than casual friends. She also had a large streak of social justice in her and volunteered as a medic at local protests. She had stitched me up after brawls more than once, which led us to getting closer.

Nour's long, burnt umber hair fell in waves to the middle of her back and shook as she wrinkled her nose at me. She towered over my prone form, but normally I stood a head taller than her. I thought she liked the high ground. "I'll go check." She turned and made her way back through the tiny kitchen, leaving me with my aches.

The restaurant wasn't exactly in my territory, which I considered "anything not Yale," but it was on the edge. Howe Street was one of the dividing lines, and nobody was going to give me trouble on the outskirts.

I let my head loll back again, thankful I hadn't suffered a concussion from the fall. My own calculations had paid off, and I'd landed directly in the center of a friendly bush. Other than my ass being sore for a few days, I would survive relatively unscathed. I flexed my arm, the abrasions raw and bright from the earlier abuse. The damage from the kid's spell was temporary, unless they had dropped more energy than I observed, but I expected it to be mostly better by morning.

A hand slapping two orange pills onto the table broke my reverie, and I sat up again, eyeing the tablets. "That's not sanitary."

She clucked her tongue at me. "I clean these tables, jerk."

I laughed, popped both in my mouth, and dry-swallowed. Grimacing, I washed them down with a large sip of Turkish coffee. It was late, but that much caffeine wouldn't do more than carry me to bed.

The chittering got louder, and I plucked a fry from my basket, leaning over to offer it to a small hole in the side of the sack. A tiny snout poked through, tasting the air, then retracted, and a small black hand replaced it. I put the food into its little palm, and it snatched the morsel into the sack. Satisfied noises replaced the former complaints.

Nour eyed my makeshift carrier. "You can't bring pets in here."

"That's fine. It's not a pet."

She narrowed her eyes at me, and I narrowed mine in reply. This was not the weirdest thing I had ever brought into the restaurant. Thankfully, she gave me a pass. I hadn't done anything to lower their health rating thus far, so she must have trusted me not to start now.

"You should at least feed it some salad."

I rolled my eyes but took a piece of lettuce from my sandwich and held it to the tear in the bag. The nose poked out again, huffing the greenery before retreating. Fingers reached out through the hole to take the offering, but they were much slower than before.

"I think it likes the fries better."

"There's no accounting for taste." She shrugged, tossing a kitchen towel over her shoulder before crossing her arms. "Don't stay too long. I don't want fleas."

One large bite of my pita, chased with the dregs of my coffee, and I was done. It was what I needed, a pick-me-up after the evening's escapades, but I had other things to do before I could sleep. I picked the sack up gently, the form inside still moving but only orienting to being airborne, and strode outside. Before I left this part of town, there was something else I needed to check on.

Throughout human history, people found ways to send messages to each other. Especially before the advent of electronics, communication over even short distances was complicated. If you were talking local, you had more options. Before the online ones, towns had bulletin boards, where you could post a message for someone. But what if you didn't want anyone to know what the message was? Cyphers existed for ages, and writing in secret languages was more common than you might realize. Go back even further, and you were talking about pictographs. Carvings on trees and cave walls, symbols that said simple things like, "danger."

I walked me and my furry friend down the block to a lamppost near where I had parked my car on Edgewood Ave. Popping my trunk, I placed my squirming passenger inside and left it open as I walked ten feet back to the post. I knelt, my knee cracking in complaint with a twinge of pain for spice. At the base of the light, scratched into the paint, was a combination of sigils.

I couldn't take credit for my choice of symbolism. Early in my studies, in a course on United States History, I learned about the "hobo code." It was a collection of markings tramps used to communicate with each other, often when traveling on the railways between towns. They would leave them surreptitiously, where others in their itinerant brotherhood would know to look. It was relatively simple, for what it was, but included the basics.

The two symbols I used along the border of Yale were for "keep away" and "unsafe area." They looked like a combination of lambda and three diagonal scratches, and I carved them into urban fixtures in a rough square around the outer edges of the campus. This lamp post was one of many sporting my minor vandalism. Or at least that was what should have been there.

Those marks weren't there for other people. Humans could decide for themselves whether entering the confines of Yale was good for their health. Remember what I said about sympathy? Magic wanted to follow natural pathways. I tied small pieces of energy to each of my scratchings, feeding them with magic that would say, "flee, unsafe, danger," to anything even minorly sentient.

If you were going to create a spiritual signpost, it helped to use symbols. The Norse had runes, the Indigenous people had their own written language and sigils, but I wasn't going to steal from them when I had perfectly serviceable American history to draw from. The added benefit was most people would think it was random graffiti and leave it alone. Norse runes ran the risk of being mistaken for hateful iconography, and using Indigenous markings was appropriative at best.

I didn't have either of those problems right now. Mine was that someone had scratched out my warnings with clear intent to disrupt them. "Well, shit," I said to the lamppost, which thankfully didn't respond. I took a pocket knife out of my bag and snapped it open with a sharp click. A minute later and they were replaced, once again stark gray aluminum shining through the green paint. I gathered my focus and placed a hand over the icons, closing my eyes and steadying my breathing. For those with talent to see it, a thin tendril of silver ran from my heart down through to my fingers. I pictured an angry, snarling dog as I fed bits of myself into the warning sign.

I didn't know who was messing with my work, but I understood why my little friend had wandered inside the limits. Animals couldn't read, but they could feel the intent I left at each signpost. On any normal day, he'd have had to be starving to risk crossing that invisible line in the sand, and from carrying it around, I suspected this particular robber-rat hadn't missed any meals. My hackles were up, considering someone intentionally ruined my work, but there wasn't anything I could do besides reset it.

Satisfied, I stood and brushed my hands on my pants, then wandered back to my car, closing the trunk on my way past. One more thing to do and I could rest for the night.

It was a short ride home to Westville, a suburb of New Haven where the state college and my apartment both were. A park was nearby, as good a place as any to relocate one large raccoon. I didn't want to chance being stopped by the police, so I didn't enter the park proper. I parked behind my building on Blake Street and approached Edgewood Park on foot holding my protesting passenger.

"Give me a break, we're almost there," I said aloud. The low growls I received in response from the bag weren't encouraging. I found a convenient large bush to sidle up to and placed my cargo on the ground. Loosening the drawstring, I jumped back as the grumpy mammal came hissing out of the bag.

"Easy, now."

It glared at me and appeared to be contemplating fight or flight, when I brought up my hand holding a single soggy french fry. The change was immediate, hisses replaced by curious trills.

"I thought so." I laid the fry on the ground and retreated a few steps, but the fry was gone before I made it two feet. The raccoon turned tail and trundled into the bush, loudly chewing its prize and leaving me standing alone.

"You're welcome!" I called after it but left the "conversation" there. Raccoons didn't understand sarcasm, based on my limited experience, so even the last word wasn't worth it.

There was something to be said for experiencing New Haven in the wee hours, outside of the stark streets downtown after midnight. I relaxed my eyes and let my vision double, taking in the gently waving branches above me. Concentrating on the ripples at the edge of my vision, I shifted my perception to the spirit world beside me. Like opening a nesting doll to find something nearly identical, yet wholly different, inside. Everything was softer. The greenery was lusher, the moon fuller. Hints of color traced the sky, brilliant with stars that would have been obscured by light and air pollution. A saw-whet owl's call reached my ears, with a hint of *the* owl, as if one small bird spoke for all that ever existed.

That was also part of the magic because no owls stalked the night in this area on my usual side of the world. My inner senses drank in what was otherwise imperceptible. It was always a treat seeing a spirit of the land cross paths with someone, a hint of the animal's existence passing over their foot or brushing their ankle. The innocent person would turn and look, trying to find the cause, but nothing would be there. Not for them to see, anyway.

That was what my hooded assailant didn't understand, what none of the cronies learning the teachings of white wizards descended from men who took what they wanted from the land instead of learning to listen to it.

I breathed the night air, redolent with the scent of cut grass damp with early dew, my night's endeavors weighed on me as the ibuprofen failed to compete with my earlier fall. I sighed, checked my watch, and despaired when it read three o'clock in the morning. I still had to work the next day—scratch that, today. No rest for the wicked.

Walking back down the sidewalk and across the street, I let myself into my apartment building. "Building" was a stretch. Not that it wasn't one, but it wasn't a typical residence. My place was above an antique and curio shop, Bits and Baubles, on the corner of Tour and Whalley Avenue. They catered to a varied clientele, serving genuine articles to upscale patrons. I knew they were the real deal because I helped the owner, Harriet, verify them.

I probably should mention that I was an archaeologist by training, if not by trade. Harriet gave me a good deal on rent and some pay on the side. Antiques weren't ancient artifacts, but the same eye I developed in some early field work translated into verifying some of the older pieces that landed in the shop.

I trudged up the sharply inclined stairs. The setup there was complete well before any code requirements would have dictated a more reasonable rise and run. My joints ached with every step, and I looked forward to collapsing into bed even if it was only for a few hours. Two other rented rooms flanked the hallway leading to my door, and a third led to their shared facilities. It was a tiny place, all things considered. It was only three units, and mine was the only full apartment in the building with its own bathroom. Unlocking my door, I pushed into the foyer of my apartment.

It was much nicer on the inside than it appeared from the street, though some of that was due to the sweat equity I had put into renovating the place before moving in five years ago. Beyond my handiwork, the location was odd and lent itself to more affordable rent. My space was split level, and I had turned the entry into an office. Diplomas, maps, and other official cruft adorned the walls. A battered desk held my middle-aged laptop and monitor setup. The walls were covered with an odd assortment of secondhand bookshelves, packed to the gills with tomes of various sizes.

I unclipped my hip bag and dropped it into the chair before tromping up the stairs to the main floor of the apartment. The one big open room gave the place the feel of a studio loft. Knickknacks and keepsakes from various travels were strewn across all available surfaces. A Lakota ironwood carving of a bear here, a pair of Māori poi balls with brightly woven leads there. None of that was as important as the weight bearing down on my eyelids. Bypassing the fridge, I collapsed onto the bed, despite a growl from my stomach reminding me how close it was to breakfast.

It was four hours later when I finally came back to my senses. My phone's alarm rose in volume as I ignored it. I slapped the nightstand next to me until I touched the screen with a flailing hand and groaned into the comforter. Falling asleep in my clothes was bad, but I hadn't been unconscious long enough to transform into the disgusting mess that would normally make me.

I stumbled into the kitchen and fumbled a saucepan out of the cabinet, filling it halfway with water and dropping it onto the stovetop. The gas lit with a "foomp" and I brewed some cowboy coffee while I grabbed a lightning-fast shower and changed clothes. Years ago, I spent a summer working on an organic farm in Ledyard, Connecticut. The older gentleman who ran the place loved his coffee but couldn't be bothered to brew it any other way. I picked the habit up from him, especially when I was short on time. The coffee strained easily into a dented NPR travel mug, and I was on my way.

Somewhere in my preparations a chill passed through me, and my nose started to run. That was one of the other problems with burning your personal reserves and why many practitioners used external resources. It took a toll on your body to burn your own stores, but the impact on the surrounding environment? Siphoning that kind of energy became obvious really fast.

I hadn't done much magic at all, but here I was with the first hint of a cold. It wouldn't last the day, as long as I took care of myself and replenished the reserves my system needed. It was a crapshoot whether or not that happened, given I tended to burn the candle at both ends.

My stomach roared, trying to be heard since I had ignored it before going to bed. I needed something to eat, and as I stood in front of the open door, my mostly empty refrigerator glared back at me. It looked like it was going to be another bagel morning, and I was going to be late for class. Again.

Chapter 3

"Can someone give me a reason for the Pequot War?" I asked the class, using the question as a shield to take a bite of my breakfast sandwich.

A few scattered hands raised, and I waved at one of my mediocre students in the middle of the room. Michael was enthusiastic but needed to work on the details of the things he was excited about.

"Capitalism?" he said with an uplift at the end, turning it into a question rather than a statement.

I laughed and nearly choked on my mouthful. A wave of chuckles ran through the class. Washing it down with a sip of crude coffee from my mug, I nodded graciously in his direction. "If you're going to use a hammer that size, you should blame organized religion too. English Puritans made up one side of the colonists in conflict."

"Sorry, Professor Pierce," Michael said with a grimace.

I waved his apology away. "You're not wrong. I'm just being a pedantic pain in the ass. A lot of it had to do with the fur trade, and the alliances between the Native American tribes and the various settlers, specifically the Dutch and the English."

He rewarded me with a beaming smile. Sometimes you needed to take the time to encourage the shyer ones.

"Now," I continued, "what was one of the long-term effects of the war? And if you've been paying attention to my lectures, it's a continued theme we've been discussing."

Another hand shot up in the front. This time it was Beth, another promising student. "It eliminated the Pequots and distributed them among the allied tribes."

"That's right, Beth. Someone's been reading the assignments."

She blushed but with a hint of pride in her eyes.

Her pleased expression turned sour when a voice came from the back of the room. "And now they have a casino."

My course was part of the transfer program for the state college's history programs. Not everyone who registered for it had a keen interest in anything other than satisfying their core requirements for graduation. It was a mixed bag.

I turned to eye John Fitch, one of the less interested members of the class. He sat with a smug look on his face, as if he had said something particularly insightful. I placed my coffee on the metal desk with a heavy thunk. "Personally, Mr. Fitch, I wouldn't want to wait over two hundred years for that kind of payoff. The Pequots were almost wiped out in the war, though we'll learn as we move through the course it doesn't take armed conflict to lose a people to history."

I let a moment of silence grow, leaving a touch of drama no one chose to interrupt. "But that's enough for today. Check your syllabus for the required reading for next class, and the first drafts of your papers will be due soon. Ticktock, people."

The students left in a clatter of books and backpacks, some breaking into small social groups before exiting the room. I stowed my notes in my messenger bag, which was adorned with the Gateway Community College logo. Despite my credentials, I was an adjunct professor there. It had more to do with my schedule, or lack of desire for one, rather than being independently wealthy and able to live on an adjunct's stipend.

I was actually three side gigs in a trench coat, considering my teaching, working with Harriet at the shop, and some freelance grant writing I did. Add a small trust from my father, the only good thing he ever did for me, and I was surfing enough above the poverty line that I was comfortable with it.

Teaching at GCC was mostly due to my love of history and a favor I owed another faculty member here for helping me out with a legal matter a while back. My Greenpeace tendencies had gotten me into trouble on multiple occasions, not strictly related to the spiritual side of things. I had been arrested during a sit-in protest, and one of the other people in the holding cell with me was an ecology teacher at the college. With her help, a little *pro bono* advice from her lawyer, and a promise from me to teach a course, I managed to get community service and a slap on the wrist.

Sometimes it paid to go to jail with the right people. As the students filtered out, a figure I hadn't recognized at the beginning of class remained. I had arrived late but by less than ten minutes, so the class hadn't abandoned me yet. There were always plenty of adds and drops early in the semester, and we were only two weeks in. I couldn't talk to him before getting the lesson started and hadn't wasted too much thought on it.

He was shorter, about five-foot-five, with sandy brown hair and bright blue eyes. "Doctor Pierce?" he asked in a tenor.

His polo shirt and slacks were a little formal for the community college vibe, so I placed him as possible staff. "It can't be evaluation time this early in the semester."

My statement must have thrown him off because his expression went from curious to confused. I reevaluated my brief assessment. Despite a face that appeared to be closer to thirty than twenty, maybe this was a student. Community college was a great equalizer. You saw professionals transitioning their careers attending the same classes as the eighteen-year-olds who recently graduated high school. I was a little quick to judge, but I'd been in enough situations to make snap decisions a habit.

"No, sorry, I'm not on staff–ah, I'm not an administrator." A slight blush rose in his cheeks, but he thrust his hand out. "Sorry, I'm bad at this. I'm Taylor Reed."

I shook his hand and did my best to put a disarming smile on my face. "Nice to meet you, not-administrator Reed. What can I do for you?"

His blush deepened with my small dad joke. "I do work here, Professor Pierce. I mean, I'm also a student, but I started working for the tutoring center. My manager told me to speak with you. I'm supposed to be helping students that need assistance with their history classes."

"I don't recall you going through my class before. Which ones have you taken?"

Taylor fidgeted in silence, but I let it grow until he spoke again. "I...had an aborted attempt at college a while back. I passed a few one-hundred level history and anthropology courses before taking a break from school. It's why I didn't have to register for yours as part of the transfer program."

"Not a terrible start," I said, nodding. "But with those under your belt and pursuing the transfer degree yourself, what do you need me for?"

"No, but everyone talks about how you approach your class, and I wanted to get some perspective on how you're teaching. I figured if I sat in a few times, it would help me understand how to better help the students who are struggling with the material."

It made sense, I supposed. Not to oversell my teaching ability, but I tried to turn history a living subject for the students I taught. There was so much to cover, but without tying it to something real and present, some students had a hard time understanding the *why* of events. I hated classes that expected nothing but rote date memorization and fact regurgitation.

"All right, Mr. Reed–" I said, before being interrupted.

"Taylor, please."

"Only if you call me Corbin. If you're not taking my class, we can dispense with the formalities."

"Sure thing, Prof–" The blush, which had disappeared, returned with a vengeance as he caught himself. "Uh, Corbin."

A smile crept across my face. "I'll give you the same challenge I put to all my students, though, if you want to understand where I'm coming from."

"What's that?"

"History is a tough subject, and since you've already taken some anthropology, I hope you've seen the connective tissue there."

Taylor's brow furrowed. "I'm not sure I follow."

"Our choices are inextricably linked to our culture, and when we look back at our past, we need to remember that."

Taylor nodded along as I spoke. "That makes sense."

"But here's the challenge. Go live some of it in the making. Besides history repeating itself, it's important to engage in the present to understanding how it becomes the past for our descendants."

His eyes widened slightly. "That's...an interesting concept."

"Right?" I grinned. "It's one thing to acknowledge that student protests happened in the seventies, like Kent State. *That* changed the course of history. It's another matter to take part in protests happening right now and experience what it feels like. Or how these events connect our current culture with our actions."

"I...I'll think about it?"

I chuckled but raised my hands when Taylor started looking offended. "I'm not laughing at you. My example was one that turned violent for the students, I'll admit. There are other ways to experience history in the making, even on a micro scale."

He let out a breath. "That sounds like a better choice for me."

I eyed him appraisingly, considering my schedule for the next few days. I only taught classes two days each week, and something coming up might be more his speed. "Do you have classes tomorrow, around lunchtime?"

"I've got a decent break between things, depending on where I'd need to be."

"Tell you what. If you're serious about understanding some local history, come volunteer for a few hours downtown with me."

"Doing what?" he asked.

"It'll be a surprise, but I promise there are lessons to be learned. Meet me on the Green tomorrow at twelve o'clock, over by the war memorial."

Taylor clearly went through some internal processing, his eyes darting back and forth before responding. "Sure, why not?"

I slung my bag over my neck and clapped him on the shoulder. "Great. Now, if you'll forgive me, I need to head out to meet with my other boss."

"Other boss?" He cocked his head in confusion.

"The glamorous life of an adjunct professor." I winked at him before walking to the door. "Stay in school and you, too, can achieve greatness like this."

As I walked through the front door of Bits and Baubles, letting the door close heavily behind me, the first words out of Harriet's mouth were, "You look like shit, Corbin."

"My body is a temple," I replied, knocking back the rest of my ginger shot before tucking the bottle into my pocket for later disposal. Liberal application of caffeine, anti-inflammatories, and vitamins had me feeling better than when I woke up, but I imagined it hadn't helped my appearance. I approached the counter and leaned against it heavily.

"One of those ancient, haunted ruins, maybe," Harriet said, her voice a calm drone. The humor behind the words made her delivery all the sharper in a flat affect. If she weren't sitting behind the counter, she'd stand five-foot-four, with a light golden hue to her skin. She had a broad nose, sharing the facial cast of her ancestors, with long brown hair hanging in braids to her mid-back. Pushing middle-aged or thereabouts, her face held some shadows from lines the years had etched on her strong features.

Her outfit was simple, an old army jacket over a band T-shirt, whose name was lost to the wash. She wore her usual faded blue jeans and boots with square toes. On the lapel of the jacket was a round pin featuring a rainbow feather pointing at "she/her" written on the circle, next to another "he/him."

According to her, she was Indigenous enough to be discriminated against but not enough to lay claim to any of the benefits afforded the casino-operating tribes. "Wrong side of the conflict," she'd say, referring to her Golden Hill Paugussett and Quinnipiac roots, rather than the Mohegan or Mashantucket Pequot tribes and their history with the colonizers. She was a respected member of the Paugussetts and made a decent living owning the shop. That was enough for her by all accounts.

On top of that, she was two-spirit, which didn't make her popular with the more conservative locals or even other tribes that hadn't accepted two-spirit folk. She wasn't particular about pronouns day to day. Embodying both the male and female spirit, being two-spirit wasn't the same as being trans or genderfluid. It was called a "third gender" in many tribes. In practice, being two-spirit was more about her place in the community, like Harriet filling a traditionally "male" role in a ceremony or event. The pin wasn't a facet of tribal culture, that was more expressed through how she interacted with people of her tribe. Harriet told me she had decided to adopt the visual cue from the local LGBTQ community in solidarity.

I glared at her. "Hilarious. But you're not wrong, given the night I had."

"I'm only teasing, cousin. What'd you do? Get into a fight with someone on the Green again? Did Nour have to patch you up?"

Harriet wouldn't stop calling me cousin, no matter how many times I'd asked. She started back when we first met, and I thought I had some Quinnipiac heritage myself. My mother raised me with Indigenous stories, swearing up and down that my great-great-great grandfather or something was a Quinnipiac elder. She told me about Keitan and Hobbomock, great spirits of the land and the people. How Hobbomock stamped his foot and shifted the Connecticut River and how Keitan placed a sleeping spell on him, which led to the "Sleeping Giant" in Hamden, the mile-long mound of stone in the shape of a sleeping man. Mom shared tales from other tribes too, like how Coyote created man and about Raven with his big magic pot. Even how the heron got his colors, from Alaskan Indigenous myths.

She loved it all and shared it with me. So, I loved those stories too. They got me interested in anthropology and archaeology. I'd go digging in the backyard for arrowheads, claiming every pointy piece of flint or stone was a treasure. She would humor me, despite knowing better. We'd tie them onto makeshift arrows, and I'd play hunter stalking through the bushes.

We didn't have any records of our family history, so having Native ancestry wasn't anything I stood on too heavily as far as my identity, but I always hoped it was true. As I moved forward in my career, I held onto the possibility as an internal compass. It guided a lot of my choices, trying to make good on what I felt was a responsibility to my would-be ancestors. Given what I knew, it was easier to accept I wasn't going crazy when I started seeing double, in my early twenties, and had my mind cracked open by the reality of the spirit world atop our own.

Eventually I moved into the apartment above the shop, and Harriet took my stories at face value. That's when she started calling me cousin. Instead of feeling validated, her casual acceptance made me paranoid I had been standing on the shoulders of people I shouldn't have. I quietly purchased one of those DNA tests and sent my spit off for analysis to lay my worries to rest, one way or the other. The results? Less than one percent of my DNA was from the "Northeast region" of American indigenous haplogroups.

I remembered the day I trudged down the stairs to the shop and laid the printout of my test on the counter. Harriet put her reading glasses on and peered at the graphs before pronouncing, "Well, I guess you're a really distant cousin. City needs your kind of medicine, otherwise you wouldn't be here." She crumpled up the paper and tossed it in the trash, then looked at me over the rim of her glasses, daring me to argue. We never talked about it again.

Harriet cleared her throat, startling me. By her stare, I realized I had been lost in memory, zoning out across the counter. I was more messed up from my late night than I thought.

"No, Mom," I said with a laugh. "I didn't get into a fight this time." She was right to assume the possibility. I had spent more than my fair share of protests getting into scuffles with the locals on the wrong side of whatever argument we were having. "I had to save a raccoon from a would-be poacher."

"What, it went downtown?" She clucked her tongue in disapproval. "Thought you said you set up some warning signs even the animals would pay attention to."

I huffed out a breath. "Someone messed with them."

"Bummer," she said, in clear understatement. "What did you do?"

I related the story of the night before, not leaving out any details about chasing the raccoon and the poacher both. My ass twinged in pain when I got to the part where I fell into the bushes, and Harriet winced in sympathy.

"He wasn't exactly a willing passenger, but I made do. I let him go across the street in the park, so if you see a fat raccoon, that's him."

Harriet nodded sagely. "Did you sing to him?"

I grinned. Music played a huge role in native legends. In many of the old Algonquian myths, there were secret melodies for controlling or speaking with animals. "No one taught me the song to make Raccoon obey. Are you holding out on me?"

Harriet returned my smile. "Oh, I doubt there's a tune in the world to make that rascal listen. But if there was, I hoped you'd have already learned it so you could teach me. No one's told me either."

I thought about the night before and snapped my fingers. "You know what? I may have learned something just as good."

"Yeah?"

"This one likes french fries, if you're looking to make friends."

Harriet nodded again, as if I spoke an obvious truth. "Powerful medicine, those. Put an entire country in its thrall. No surprise it worked on Raccoon, especially if it was those curly ones."

I laughed, my mood lightening despite my aches stalking the edges of my perception. "Ah, no such luck, but the ones dusted with sumac seemed good enough." I pushed back from the counter and stretched my neck from side to side. "Have anything for me, boss? I need to get some rest, but I wanted to check in before passing out for a couple of hours."

Harriet wasn't exactly my boss, but the word made the explanation easier for other people. "The person who paid me under the table to identify artifacts she resold to bougie white folk" was a much bigger mouthful and only led to more questions.

She sucked her teeth in disgust. Harriet hated it when I called her that. We were more friends with a business arrangement on the side than anything else. She had a dim view of managers and hated the idea of being one for anyone other than herself.

"Your timing's good, even if your jokes aren't," she said, getting off her stool and walking into the back room only to return a few moments later holding a black box. It was at least six inches square, the kind of thing you'd see in jewelry stores for displaying necklaces. Harriet opened it and turned the display to face me. "It's a rosary. Came in yesterday, but I don't know much about it…"

Harriet continued to explain, but the words faded into a monotonous noise in the background as the artifact in front of me consumed my attention. Malevolence rolled off it in waves, covering it in an almost tangible black haze.

The beads were made of stone and another natural material. I looked closer and determined the small disks were almost certainly bone. Polished tiger's eye beads lay in between the ivory segments. The necklace portion connected to a tarnished silver charm shaped like a curled huntsman's horn. A cross carved from antler hung below the horn on another section of beads.

"Corbin? Corbin, you still with me?" Harriet's voice broke through my reverie, and my gaze snapped up to hers. She had a vaguely disappointed expression on her face, probably from me missing whatever the rest of her explanation was. She wasn't sensitive to magic the way I was, so it shouldn't surprise me that she hadn't seen the same thing.

I shook my head to clear it and swallowed a dry lump in my throat. "Sorry. I, uh, tell me again where you found this?"

"Estate sale, some family heirloom no one wanted anymore. They were worried it was ivory, since you can't sell that anymore. I got it as part of a lot, figured it'd move easy. I knew it wasn't elephant tusk, that's for sure. What's up? You look spooked."

Gingerly, I placed my hand above the rosary. As I did so, small black tendrils rose in wisps from the bones, curling around my fingers. There was a gentle pull, and tiny silver threads left my fingertips slowly to weave their way toward the necklace. I jerked my hand back, like I had touched a hot stove. I cleared my throat. "This is trouble."

"I'm going to assume you mean bad trouble. You never tell me about the fun kind."

"It's a Hunter's Rosary," I said, closing the lid on the box again.

"Yeah, I saw the horn. Figured it had something to do with St. Hubert."

I raised an eyebrow at Harriet. It was a good deduction. "You're right, nice catch. This one's different, though. Or special, I should say, but not in a good way. When the colonists were first trying to convert the tribes to Christianity, they would give gifts. Sometimes it would be rosaries like this. The beads were valuable in themselves, but St. Hubert was the patron saint of hunters. Priests would lie to the natives and claim St. Hubert would give them luck in their hunts if they prayed to God with the rosaries."

"Interesting story." Harriet frowned. "But I don't hear any reasons not to put it in the case yet. I've got a couple of regulars who are really into religious antiques."

"Yeah, because you haven't let me finish telling you that this thing's enchanted, like a fetish. There were mages among the scholars and the priesthood, even then. They used tchotchkes like this to steal power from the locals. I don't want to touch it, but it started trying to drain energy from me as soon as I got close to it."

"Well, shit," Harriet said. "What do I do with it now?"

I gave her a gentle side eye. "Knowing you, you'll make plenty back on whatever's in the rest of the lot. Though, given this trinket, let me go through your haul once to make sure this is the only malicious antique you managed to acquire. I can hold on to the rosary, better with me than lying around waiting for someone to accidentally start wearing it."

"That sounds like a good plan. I'll get it all laid out tomorrow."

"You should also make an offering. You're lucky you hadn't done more than handle it a few times." I rummaged around in my leg bag, looking for a pinch of tobacco to sprinkle on top of the box. My hand came away empty, and my frown deepened as I investigated further to find I had lost the small pouch that carried it. Must have been somewhere between downtown last night and this moment. "I'm empty though, so you'll have to fend for yourself."

Harriet gave me a wink. "I'm sure I can scrounge something up."

I popped the necklace box into my satchel. A few layers seemed to be enough to keep it quiescent for now, but it was hungry when

Harriet had opened it earlier. I'd need to do some research and figure out what I was dealing with.

My next stop was a date with my pillow. The barest hint of a sore throat reared its ugly head, accompanying the return of my congestion. Some rest would be enough to keep me on the right side of functional, or at least I hoped it would.

Chapter 4

A few hours of sleep later and I was steady on my feet again. When I woke, the box Harriet had left with me sat like a dark beacon on my kitchen table. She truly was lucky to have kept it out of reach, though I didn't know if it would siphon energy from a non-practitioner. Better not to have found out yet. I stashed the trinket in the drawer of a side table on the far side of the room for good measure. Thinking about Harriet's safety and an offering of thanks, I recalled I still needed tobacco.

I dressed in my usual going-out attire, a pair of faded blue jeans and a long sleeve Henley shirt, a green and black flannel over top of it. Engineer boots, scuffed and worn with age and abuse, complemented the outfit with my leg bag strapped around my hips. I wouldn't win any beauty pageants, but my style had its own flair. I had my usual everyday carry items, a pocketknife and a multi-tool, weighing my bag down along with my wallet and keys.

My plan was to go downtown and replenish my stock. Yes, I could have gotten generic tobacco from anywhere in the city, but the local spirits responded best to the "good stuff." Connecticut broadleaf tobacco. It was primarily used in cigar wrappers, and no one would smoke it by itself, but that wasn't the point.

Broadleaf had been grown in the Connecticut valley since the 1600s, followed later by shade tobacco. The connection to the land was undeniable. How famous was the Connecticut leaf? Even Cuban cigars could be found wrapped in it. If I had offered my fat friend a pinch of discount tobacco last night from the local smoke shop, he'd have likely turned his nose up despite my personal energy in the mix. But I only carried the local leaf because, for my purposes, it was better than anything else available.

My budget didn't pad my wallet enough to get a panini at the Owl Shop, so I hit the corner store for enough fixings to make some simple sandwiches. Once I filled my protesting stomach, it was time to enter the enemy territory of Yale campus. The Owl Shop had been in business since the early 1900s, evolving from a cigar and tobacco bar to a more full-fledged hangout. It still sported dark wood, brass, and a solid atmosphere, but it also had a bar, outside seating, and fancy sandwiches. You had to move with the times or they'd move on without you.

It was on College Street, a few doors down from both the Music Hall and the Shubert Theatre, smack in the middle of Yale's domain. I wasn't unwelcome, per se, but some characters would prefer I never set foot within the city limits, let alone one hundred feet of the campus itself. The building the cigar bar was in wasn't even technically part of the campus, but if you drew a line from one Yale building to another, many folk thought anything that fell on the path was theirs too.

These weren't even metaphysical lines, more like poorly drawn assumptions. Either way, I ran the risk of bumping into people I had no desire to see. Given someone was actively messing with my warning signs, I wanted to be stocked up in case I needed to lure another little cousin out of the area.

I drove downtown and parked on Chapel Street, right off the New Haven Green. The Green was an interesting landmark, created in 1638 to be a marketplace and gathering spot. As if we needed a reminder of how rabid the Puritans' faith was, it was al-legedly engineered to accommodate exactly the number of people expected to survive the second coming. That was right, the Green would hold all the people waiting to get raptured into heaven. And people thought polytheism was weird, but I guess there was no accounting for taste.

I jaywalked my way across the street and headed down College to the shop. The sun was setting, already dipping below the city skyline. The streets were growing thick with shadows, and the mood of the crowds was moving from daytime pedestrians to eager night owls tasting the crisp air.

Despite the cooler temperatures of fall, a small boisterous crowd camped at the outdoor table, smoking fat cigars. I smiled at them as I passed, not noting any regulars. The interior of the building greeted me with the warm glow of lamplight on dark oak, the old, heavy bar sucking up half the light.

I strode to the bar and flagged down the owner. Rick was a large man, a football player in his prime, but that was many years ago. He hadn't run to fat, but the composition of his muscles had changed his body shape from a triangle to a rectangle. The man was still built like a refrigerator, and the paw he held out to shake enveloped mine like I was a doll. Where I had a head on Harriet, Rick had one on me.

"Tell me you're at least here to buy a drink," Rick said, grinning. I had made it a habit to show up, purchase my tobacco, and leave, though over the last couple of years Rick had done his best to nail my feet to the floor for a conversation here and there. We were as friendly as we needed to be, on a first-name basis, but he didn't actually care whether I stayed. The place was going to be busy enough without my patronage, and we both knew it.

But he liked the small talk, and I was raised to nod politely and listen when the people in charge talked to you. It didn't hurt that he special-ordered my broadleaf and sold it to me in dribs and drabs. What would I do with a pound of tobacco? He used some of it for house-rolled cigars, so stocking it was a bit of a win-win.

"Not tonight, Rick," I said, shaking his hand firmly. "I've got places to be."

"Let me at least show you my latest acquisitions. We just got in some amazing imports."

"You know I don't smoke." Well, I didn't, unless it was the occasional weed or part of a ceremony for ritual purposes. Which he understood, but salesmanship was part of his patter.

"I'm practicing my pitch, Corbin. You gotta give me *something*."

I shook my head with a smile. "No, I don't–" I stopped dead, movement out of the corner of my eye catching my attention. A familiar shape in a black hoodie passed through my peripheral vision toward a semi-private nook in the back of the shop, half hidden by a wall and fireplace. "Hold that thought," I said, turning to follow the hood.

From behind, I could only see their hair, short cropped, spiky, and raven black. As he turned, a young man's face, whip thin and smooth, greeted me. He apparently heard my heels striking the wooden floor on approach, and his brown eyes widened in recognition. The smile on his face, a match to the one grinning at me in the moonlight last night, faltered. That was all the confirmation I needed.

"Hey, friend," I said in a low and dangerous tone. "We need to talk."

"I'm sorry, do I know you?" he replied. His grin returned with knowing bravado. He was young, but the beer in his hand told me he was at least twenty-one. Rick didn't put up with fake IDs. I'd seen younger kids get tossed out during my visits.

Stepping closer to him, I left barely more than a foot between us. "I think you do. I don't appreciate being *needled* by someone like you when I'm out on an evening walk, if you take my meaning."

"Look, old man," he said, placing a hand on my right shoulder in what he must have thought was intimidating camaraderie.

That was his first mistake. I grabbed his fingers with my left hand, then moved my right hand to his elbow. Twisting my hips, I swung him around and slammed his face firmly into the wall. His pint went flying, crashing to the floor with an explosion of wet shards of glass.

The organic farmer I spent a summer with? He was also an aikido *sensei*, and after a hard day in the fields, we would practice for hours. You could debate aikido's usefulness in a proper fight until you were blue in the face. Unless you were practicing *rondori*, multiple assailants against one defender, with Sensei Burns, that is. He taught me to go for the throat and set your opponent off-balance. In this case, fingers would have to do.

"What the fuck, man!" Spittle flew from his lips.

I used my forearm to press him harder into the plaster, and the screech of chairs being shoved back from the table nearby reached my ears.

"First off, I'm thirty-five. Second, you and I are going to have a–" I began, before a calm British voice interrupted me.

"Now, now, Mr. Pierce," the man said.

I closed my eyes and leaned my head back with an exaggerated sigh. "Shit."

The Owl Shop wasn't only a popular smoker's hangout. It was also a regular meeting place for the shadowy cabal that ran the only real secret society at Yale. There were eight societies, total. You couldn't really call them "secret" if everyone knew about them, can you? The most infamous, Skull and Bones, subject of much romanticism and media attention, was also the longest running. The cabal, who named themselves "The Hand," consisted of five members at any given time. One leader and four of his most promising pupils in the occult arts, all members of the public-facing Skull and Bones.

How did I know this? Because the leader was a pompous asshole who liked to pontificate when he'd been drinking. I'd had the displeasure of running into Alexander Hughes early in my return to New Haven. It wasn't uncommon for those with the predisposition to magic to find each other. The universe could have a sick sense of serendipity, and our paths crossed here at the shop. The problem was, he had a lot of power and influence. He was a professor at the university with deep connections to the city administration and could make anyone's life a slice of hell if he so chose.

Hughes also came from old money, which separated him from the common folk even further than the Ivy League did. He wasn't an unpleasant person, for the most part, but he held sway over this part of the city in a way that made me uncomfortable. I chanced a glance in his direction, still holding one of his latest proteges to the wall. "Hughes," I said, struggling slightly as the young man under my elbow squirmed.

"Why don't you let young Geoffrey go? I'm sure we can come to an understanding like gentlemen," he said in a syrupy sweet voice, made all the more fatherly by his accent. He managed to sound both patronizing and genuine simultaneously, a feat that almost impressed me.

"Your student here nearly killed me."

Alexander chuckled with what seemed to be real mirth. "Boys will be boys. You were his age once too, fresh with your power. He probably assumed you were as invulnerable as he felt. Isn't that right, Geoffrey? You didn't mean any harm, did you?"

"No, sir," Geoffrey said, his voice muffled by the deformation of one side of his face.

"Come, Corbin," Alexander said. "Have a drink with me, and we'll talk."

My stare traveled from Geoffrey to Alexander. They outnumbered me, and we were in public. Rick wasn't likely to call the police unless our little altercation escalated, so it was on me to decide whether that happened. Sitting in a holding cell waiting for Harriet to bail me out wasn't high on my list of things to do for the night, so I released the hold I had on the young man and stepped back.

Geoffrey moved swiftly toward me, but Alexander laid a calming hand on his shoulder. "Get yourself another beer. On me."

The student's eyes narrowed, but he eventually broke his gaze and stomped to the bar with a huff. Rick was giving me the hairy eyeball but quirked an eyebrow in my direction in a way that read, "is there going to be trouble?" I gave a small shake of my head, and Rick nodded, turning to Geoffrey as he reached the bar to make another order.

Alexander gestured to a pair of leather chairs flanking a small table, and we both sat. The small group, which had been standing around a table after my little show, settled themselves and focused their attention on their beverages.

"What're we drinking?" I asked, lounging as casually as possible.

"I was enjoying a Midleton Very Rare, if you'd care for one."

Whiskey wasn't my drink of choice, but I knew enough to place a bottle like that over one hundred dollars. I could fill my gas tank twice with the cost of one glass here. "Slumming it, I see."

"Well, these local haunts do have their limits." Alexander signaled to the table, and one of the other attendees, a young woman in a plain black dress, brought a tulip shaped whiskey snifter and left it on the table beside him. "Thank you, Amanda."

"If you're buying, I'm drinking."

Alexander raised his hand in the direction of the bar, catching Rick's attention. He motioned to his glass and held up a finger. Rick, knowing which side his bread was buttered on, had a quick aside with one of his servers. The pompous man sitting next to me in a tweed jacket with leather patches on the elbows dove even deeper into the stereotype by taking a pipe and tobacco pouch from his pocket. He busied himself with the ritual of packing the bowl, gently lighting it, and puffing contentedly until a whiskey glass appeared at my elbow.

I raised the curved vessel to my nose and inhaled the rich aroma. Vanilla, spice, and leather hit the back of my palate. Normally I would savor an expensive tipple like this, but given the source and the point I wanted to make? I downed it in one go. I set the empty glass on the table with a single word. "Smooth."

The twinkle in Alexander's eye told me he understood the game I was playing, and he declined to rise to the bait. "Now," he said, "what's all this nonsense about you chasing Geoffrey onto the roof of Welch Hall?"

"He was interfering with my nature walk."

That earned me another laugh, puffs of smoke leaping from his mouth. "I don't normally expect my students to engage in pest control, but the way he tells it there was a particularly interesting rodent he wanted for a school project."

"You know my stance, Hughes. That animal shouldn't have even been within the campus boundaries. Someone has been tampering with my–"

"Ah, yes." He interrupted me. "The tin cans on strings you leave littered about the place."

My face burned with a mixture of anger and embarrassment at my magic referred to like that. "You say the sweetest things, Hughes. It's no wonder I haven't joined the ranks here."

When I first appeared on the scene in New Haven, before taking any local teaching jobs, I ran into Alexander. Full disclosure, I was no stranger to Ivy League bullshit. My undergraduate degree was from Princeton, where I went on a merit scholarship. I didn't own a silver spoon, let alone had one in my mouth. My masters came from a school with less creeping greenery. I had enough highbrow academia to last a lifetime, but when Hughes found out I had a prestigious beginning, he offered to grease the wheels to get me into a doctoral program at Yale.

Needless to say, I declined. He was more than a little put out, in an understated British way. Other than needling me about it when the opportunity permitted, we never spoke about it seriously again. He looked down on me and my choices, but just because I'd laid in the ivy before, didn't mean I belonged there.

He sipped from his snifter and grinned. "Oh, Corbin, that was a one-time offer, and you know it. Spurn me once, and that's all the chance you get."

I stuffed my frustration down. This conversation was getting away from me. "I don't want to get into semantics. Your apprentice attacked me, plain and simple."

Alexander raised an eyebrow at me. "And you were chasing him. Onto the roof, no less. How was he supposed to believe you didn't mean him harm?"

"Because when he attacked me, I was hanging by one arm from a tree. He was quite safe, I assure you."

Alexander shrugged, nodding at Geoffrey as he walked by with a fresh pint. Geoffrey only had eyes for me, and from the daggers he shot from them, he had no positive intentions.

"Be that as it may," Alexander continued, "it sounds like a messy situation."

"I want an oath from your boy there. That he won't interfere with my spells."

The casual conversation from the table next to us died, and my neck flushed hot from the sudden attention turned on me. It was less for my insulting Geoffrey, and more about what I demanded. Oaths were not small things. Promises are all well and good, but *oaths* held power. For those with magic, they were even more potent.

The stories of old, regardless of culture, included many references to oaths. Keep them, and you were probably the hero in a saga. Break them? More likely you're part of a cautionary tale. If using your personal stores of energy reflected in the body, broken oaths showed up in other ways. It might be physical health, but it might also be a streak of bad luck or something equally intangible but wholly caused by the betrayal of your vow.

"Is that really–" Alexander began before I interrupted him.

"Yes." I let the single word hang, heavy in the air. Hughes didn't have to humor me, but it wasn't in his best interest to upset the balance in his part of the city by making me more of an enemy. We weren't friends, barely professional acquaintances, but we mostly left each other alone. As far as I knew, we both preferred that.

He continued sipping his whiskey. I'd have done the same but had wasted mine in a mostly useless gesture. It was still worth it, but damn, that was good whiskey. I wouldn't have said no to another tipple, but I wouldn't lean on the goodwill of the man I was strong-arming.

"I will admit some rashness in my student's approach," Alexander said. Geoffrey stood and opened his mouth to object, but Hughes waved him to silence with a casual hand. "No, Geoffrey, Mr. Pierce is right. While it made for a good story, it was unnecessary. What are your terms, Corbin?"

Geoffrey grumbled loudly but didn't join the negotiation. He didn't sit, either, his body tense and waiting.

"He vows to not interfere with my magic. If there are spirits on the other side of the veil under my protection, he leaves them alone."

"Broad but acceptable–" Hughes began, but I wasn't finished. The trick of an oath, much like tales of Djinn or other wish-granters, was you couldn't leave wiggle room.

"Past, present, or future," I added. If Geoffrey had agreed to an open-ended oath like that, he could say he fulfilled it by not engaging with any of my preexisting spells. The universe, whatever laws governed this sort of thing, wasn't terribly specific. This wasn't contract law with well-established precedent, but it was an agreement bound by our own power.

"For a year and a day?" Hughes offered and gave me a heavy wink. He was a stickler for the theatrics of tradition. In pagan circles, agreements often held for a year and a day. Though that was as much for engagements and handfasting as the more esoteric bargain we were striking.

I didn't have any particular desire to keep a barrier between Geoffrey and myself forever. Maybe the kid would learn some balance by sophomore year. Given his mentor, I wasn't going to hold my breath, but a guy could dream. "Done."

"Splendid!" Hughes boomed, genial as Santa Claus, though no one would have taken the spindly professor for a lookalike. "Geoffrey, do come and settle this so we can get back to our discussion."

Geoffrey extricated himself from his companions and strode heavily over to stand in front of me, looming before I had a chance to get up. I stood, and it turned out we were eye to eye when I wasn't pressing his face into drywall. He waited, staring, until I cleared my throat.

"Well?" I asked, not trying to hide my grin.

"I swear to not interfere with your magic or the spirits under your protection," he said tersely.

I didn't respond but nodded as if to say "and?"

He sighed dramatically but added, "Past, present, and future. For a year and a day."

I held out my hand and pushed power into my palm, focusing on the concept of an oath. Steadfast. Binding. Heavy with purpose. A bright moonlight glow of silver emanated from below my skin, waiting.

Geoffrey mimicked my gesture, his own a light winter blue, as frosty as his mood.

When our hands met, the colors swirled and changed, combining to a brilliant cobalt. The sensation of an oath tying two people together is not comfortable, even for the one receiving it. A sense of pressure settled heavily in my bones, like diving deep into the ocean where the water itself began to crush you. It was brief but intense and then gone.

Geoffrey's eyes went wide. This was clearly an unfamiliar experience for him.

"First time?" I winked at him, pulling my hand away and shaking it. It wasn't the pins and needles of an extremity falling asleep, but the sensation wasn't far off. I looked at Hughes. "I think we're done here."

"Excellent, we wouldn't want to bore you. We were just getting to know each other. Some of our new cohort hail from some of the oldest and most storied families. Nothing that would be of interest to you." The malicious glint in his eyes told me the dig was intentional.

The talent could be hereditary, and Hughes came from a long line of mages. Casual elitism rolled off him in waves. What was his family like? I wasn't saying that when he was younger he did coke with the disciples of Aleister Crowley, but I'm not *not* saying that either. The few times we spoke, he made it a point to quietly disparage the fact that I was new blood. He put a lot of stock in legacy, which I neither had nor wanted.

"Sounds awful, I'll pass." I stood and walked toward the bar, planning to apologize to Rick before leaving with one more thing than I had planned to take with me. The tobacco and an oath.

"Do come see us again," Alexander called from the table as I went. "I was just telling them how important it was to keep up their studies, and you're a wonderful object lesson."

"Fuck you too, Hughes," I muttered under my breath as I walked out without looking back.

Chapter 5

The encounter from the evening before wrecked my mood for most of the morning. I didn't care about the insults, but the fact another young cohort of mages was going to be groomed into little Alexanders set my teeth on edge. One of the things I enjoyed the most about teaching was molding impressionable young adults. I wasn't so far away from my undergraduate studies to forget how stupid I had been when I was eighteen.

I didn't have a class to teach, so I let myself wallow in remembrance, both of last night and the more distant past. Sometimes there were lessons for us to learn from. Personal history was a topic not taught much in school, and the momentary self-reflection was almost welcome if a little uncomfortable. In the end, I put the worry for this new class of students away. There wasn't much I could do to compete with the likes of Hughes, which is why I didn't try. We had different audiences and goals. I would have to hope the kids would eventually come to their senses about what kind of man Alexander Hughes really was.

My dark cloud brightened when I remembered it was Wednesday, and I had a plan to influence another mind in what I hoped was a positive direction. If he showed up, that was. Taylor would not be the first student to take me up on my challenge only to leave me hanging when it came to putting in the effort.

With my morning ablutions handled, I took myself downtown. I parked near-ish to the Green and walked to the war monument. It was a tall flagpole honoring New Haven residents who lost their lives fighting in World War I. It was also a popular leisure spot due to the seating, fountain, and other amenities of the Green. But there was something more important, at least as far as current history was concerned, about this spot near the memorial.

"So, what's the all-important lesson I'm supposed to be learning?" Taylor said, approaching from the opposite direction from where I'd arrived.

"Lunch," I said, without elaborating. I turned and strode toward a set of plastic folding tables set up near the metal fencing surrounding the Green. On it were polystyrene clamshells, like you would find at any restaurant for takeout.

That "slap on the wrist and community service" got me involved in some of the local homeless outreach. A church nearby sponsored a weekly lunch service on the Green for the ever-present homeless population. New Haven was a prosperous city, but like many, it had plenty of people with housing and food insecurity. When I was given my choice of charities, I picked something that would get me involved with the locals.

If there was one thing traveling to various countries and visiting extremely varied populations did, it taught you there were always people who needed help. When I was working as a research assistant on small archaeological digs or other projects, I would always try to get involved in whatever was happening nearby. It was the constant balance between the lessons of history and the teachings of the now.

To his credit, Taylor followed me without complaint. When we reached the tables, I shook hands with one of the organizers, a Sikh man named Karan. He and Jasmine, a black woman who stood a head shorter than me, ran the operation. The church sponsored today's meal, and tomorrow it would be covered by a different organization. I only volunteered on Wednesdays, but they kept the whole thing running smoothly with a constantly shifting roster of volunteers and voluntolds like I had been.

"Fresh meat, Corbin?" Jasmine asked. She shook hands with Taylor after a brief introduction.

I laughed and smiled at her. "Don't scare him off, Jas. I brought him here under omission rather than pretense. Blame yourself if he doesn't come back."

We quickly fell into a rhythm, Taylor doing his best to mix following instructions and copying our actions. He was largely successful, and the service continued over the next hour without much of a hitch. I knew about half the people by name, a diverse cast of characters who were mostly regulars. Plenty of fresh faces joined us too. The economy, being what it was, had changed a lot of people's circumstances.

As we wound down, only a few cartons of food waited to be claimed, with most of our beneficiaries sitting around on the grass and benches enjoying the curry that was today's offering. Taylor had remained fairly close throughout, and we chatted among ourselves as well as with the folks waiting in line.

Taylor handed one of the last few boxes to a young woman and her son, then turned to me. "So, what's the lesson?"

"Why don't you tell me?" I shot back.

"Very Socratic. You're right, though. I said I wanted to observe and learn more about how you teach, so I guess it's fair to throw it back at me." He tapped his fingers against his chin in obvious contemplation. "If our present is someone else's history, then...it's like looking at prior world events that affected the middle and lower class–"

"Working class," I interrupted.

He raised an eyebrow but then seemed to consider. "Fair point. Was I being classist?"

I couldn't help but laugh at the real concern in his eyes. "Don't worry, next week I'll have you telling the other students to seize the means of production. No, you're fine. That's partly it, though. Something I expect we'll see, reflecting on this part of history, is the stark divide between the working class and the current bourgeoisie."

Taylor looked off toward a clump of middle-aged Hispanic men, sitting together and eating their lunch. They were laughing and talking. Anyone would think it was a picnic by choice if they didn't know any better. "I *think* I get it?"

"You don't need to digest it all now. Just consider it. I'd love to hear your observations, and especially if you want to come do this again. We can always use the–"

"Corbin!" a voice called from behind me, cutting across the end of my impromptu lesson.

I turned, and Jake, an older homeless man who was one of the regulars, walked toward us. He was rail thin, but it was the kind of skinny that was eighty percent genetics. Life had hit Jake sideways years ago, and he had ended up on the street. I never got his story. He was a private man, but he slept rough most nights except for the rare times he got into a shelter. His skin was dark, both from ancestry and from regular sun exposure. His clothes were stained but relatively clean.

"Jake!" I cried. "Let me introduce–"

He ignored my attempt at pleasantries and launched immediately into another question once he had my attention. "Has Clyde been here yet?"

Clyde would have been another familiar face and Jake's best friend. They had met at one of the lunch services and were thick as thieves ever since. My enthusiastic greeting fizzled when I took in the look on his face. Jake was a fairly laconic man, not prone to outbursts or powerful expressions of emotion from what I'd seen. The naked concern in his eyes worried me, and I shifted from social to crisis mode like a light switch.

"No, I haven't," I said. "When did you see him last?"

"It's been days," Jake said, brushing his hands against his jeans in an anxious gesture. "It's not like him to miss a meal, and I didn't find him at any of his regular spots."

"We're about done here, and I've got some time," I replied. "I can take a walk around and look for him. What are his usual haunts?"

Jake rattled off a few different locations, all within a few blocks of the Green, though in multiple directions.

"I can help. What does he look like?" Taylor added, sidling closer to us both. Jake eyed Taylor a little suspiciously, but Taylor thrust out his hand and introduced himself. That seemed to mollify Jake, who grasped Taylor's firmly in response.

"Old white guy, gray hair, 'bout my age." Jake sniffled and dragged his arm across his nose to itch it. "Idiot insists on wearing a Yankee's hat. Don't know what else he'd have on, but he'd *never* take that off."

One of the most endearing things about Jake and Clyde's relationship was the near constant bickering between them about their favorite baseball teams. Connecticut was a weird place when it came to sports geography. Stuck between the New York Yankees and the Boston Red Sox, everyone had to pick a side, and fans frowned on neutrality.

Jake was raised in southeastern Connecticut, where people tended to support Boston. Clyde, on the other hand, grew up in the western part of the state, closer to New York. Eventually, they both ended up in New Haven, with very different stories of how they got there. But each brought their baseball allegiances with them.

"We'll find him, Jake," I said, putting my hand on his shoulder. I turned to Taylor. "You're welcome to come with me, but we'll be faster if we split up."

Taylor's eyes shone with concern, but he didn't argue. "I'll head toward State Street and check those areas."

We traded numbers so we could contact each other if or when we spotted Clyde and set off in separate directions. There were some regular haunts Jake pointed us at, and I took the area west of the Green while Taylor headed east. Some were favored panhandling areas while others were preferred hangouts, where restaurants were friendly to the local homeless population. You could get a cup of coffee without being hassled and set out on a stoop where nobody would roust you.

I knew a lot of the locals and found some as I went, none of whom had sighted Clyde in the last few days. One guy named Ronnie, who was a bit of a character, told me he'd seen Clyde the day before. He offered to tell me more if I bought him a pack of cigarettes, but when I explained it was an emergency, he gave up on the light grift. I got him a coffee instead, and he told me the last place he set eyes on Clyde was a pizza place on Crown Street, southeast of the Green. The only problem was it was actually *two* days ago. I grabbed my phone to text Taylor this shred of information.

Check out those spots on Crown, one of the people I spoke with bumped into him there a couple of days ago. Not a substantial lead but the best I've got so far.

On it, I'm just north of there.

A two-day-old piece of intel wasn't enough to change my course of action, and I headed northwest into the campus. Ironically, I traversed the courtyard where my encounter with Geoffrey had been. I passed through without incident this time and ended up as far as Howe Street, checking my warning posts again while I was at it.

Crouching beside the light post near Mamoun's, my phone buzzed in my pocket. Instead of stopping with one, for a text alert, it was ringing for once. I could count on one hand the number legitimate phone calls I'd received in the past two weeks, so I took it out. Taylor's contact info flashed on the caller ID.

I didn't waste time with pleasantries. "Did you find him?"

Taylor's voice on the other end of the line was flat. "You need to get over here. Thirty-eight Crown."

"What did you–"

He cut me off before I could finish. "I already called the police, but I don't know how long it'll take them to get here."

"On my way." I swore under my breath as I ended the call. It took longer than I wanted, even if I was only fast-walking seven blocks. Jake was coming out of the Green as I went by, and I flagged him down, telling him to follow me. We trudged in silence for the last few blocks until we reached our destination.

Taylor stood at the mouth of a wide alley between buildings which had been turned into an open-air entryway, leading to a set of glass doors. The wrought iron archway spanning the two brick frontages proclaimed "38" in large black filigree. There wasn't anything out of the ordinary as I approached. The concrete path had waist high railings, and when you reached the swinging doors, a ramp on either side headed back toward the street.

Taylor motioned to the left-hand wall without speaking. Jake and I moved to the railing and peered over into what was an area for a trash can and sewer grate. Time slowed as I glimpsed something red and took in the scene in front of me. Opposite the trash can, a still form wearing a battered Yankee's hat lay prone atop a faded and ratty sleeping bag.

"You said you already called the cops?" I asked Taylor.

His face was ashen. "Yeah—uh, yes. I did."

"What did you say?" I didn't mean to give him the fifth degree, but I needed to know what to expect. If the police thought there was an active situation with one of the homeless, they might come in looking for trouble. I wasn't trying to get wrapped up in paper-work today.

"Well, I went down there and checked on him. He wasn't breathing from what I could tell, so I said there was a homeless man and he might be dead."

I cocked my head but didn't detect any sirens incoming. "I'm guessing they'll send some EMS and a cop to write up a report." With that, I hopped the railing and dropped to crouch beside the bedroll. If I didn't examine him closely, I'd have assumed he was asleep, but there was an unmistakable stillness in death.

"No," Jake breathed beside me. "You dumb son of a bitch." I hadn't even heard him come up next to me.

Leaning over, I lifted the cap to reveal the familiar face of Jake's best friend. I reached past it and checked for a pulse, but there wasn't one to find. Fall wasn't in full swing yet, so it wasn't likely he died from hypothermia.

"What do you think happened?" Jake asked with a hitch in his voice.

"Unless he's doing drugs you didn't know about, I'm not sure..." I trailed off, taking in the details. He wore a medium-weight jacket, tattered but solid enough to fend off the weather, especially considering the sleeping bag.

"Never," Jake said, firmly. "He didn't touch the stuff."

I rose and dusted my hands off. "Well, I can't say. I'm no doctor, and I doubt anyone will spring for an investigation of a homeless man passing away in his sleep. Does he have any family around here?"

"Got a daughter he doesn't talk to–well, doesn't talk to him. No way to reach her. Maybe the city can."

"Was he sick?" Taylor's voice surprised us both. He had been standing silently above us on the walkway.

"Not that he told me," Jake replied.

Something about the scene bothered me. I shifted my senses, and any commentary I was about to add got stuck in my throat. Yale might have been a "dead zone" for the land, but it wasn't dead-dead. It was only mostly dead. Everything had some amount of energy, even if there wasn't much to speak of. If the forest sang, the campus hummed low in the back of its throat.

Clyde's body was devoid of any residual essence. Whether or not you believed in the soul, even after death, there should have been *something* left. Some vestigial spark that would return to the land when they eventually buried or cremated him, consigning him to the earth.

Instead, there was nothing. A void or blank space, like a black hole devoid of light. An involuntary shiver raced up and down my spine. The lack of presence unnerved me. I had never encountered anything like this before. Sirens finally broke our reverie. Jake stooped and rifled through Clyde's pockets until he came away with a battered envelope.

"For his daughter and her kids. I promised him I'd mail it if anything ever happened to him. Never expected it to though. It's got an address out of state but no phone number." A tear rolled down his cheek and fell, dripping onto his hand rather than the paper. He knelt one more time and gently took the hat from Clyde's head, touching the dead man's forehead with reverence. "They'd just throw it out."

I nodded and, in unspoken agreement, we gathered on the sidewalk and waited for the ambulance and police cruiser to arrive. Taylor ended up giving a statement to the officer since he had been the person who made the call. I knew the paramedic in charge, a woman named Elisa. Nour had introduced us at one point. It always paid to be friendly with the local EMS crews if you were involved in any social or political action.

We waited patiently until they wheeled the gurney up the path and rolled it into the back of the ambulance, closing the door behind it. I approached Elisa, who smiled when she recognized me.

"What do you think happened?" I asked her.

"Couldn't say," she replied in a light Hispanic accent. "Doesn't look like he suffered any injuries or trauma. No tracks or any immediate signs of drug overdose. Maybe he had a heart attack? There's no crime other than loitering, so they're not gonna do an autopsy or anything."

"Yeah, I expected that."

"Shit happens, I'm afraid to say," she said to me then turned to Jake, who had come up behind me. "I'm sorry for your loss."

Jake nodded solemnly but didn't respond. Elisa gave me a small wave, then slapped the ambulance door and walked to the front. The police had finished with Taylor even before Elisa was done handling the body, and he came over to meet the two of us as we watched the ambulance drive away with dull lights and a silent siren.

We headed to the Green, Jake splitting off to go tell the other locals about what had happened. Taylor and I sat at the base of the war memorial in silence for a few minutes before I checked my watch and realized how late it was. "Hey, thanks for skipping class to help me look for Clyde."

"No problem, Corbin. Sometimes I get caught up in things when someone needs help. I'm not scheduled to work until later, anyway." He chewed his lower lip in obvious contemplation for a moment before adding, "Can I ask you an odd question? Promise you won't think I'm weird?"

"Go ahead, I doubt it's going to make my day any stranger."

"There was...something wrong with Clyde," he said.

"Well, yeah, he was dead." I couldn't keep the sarcasm out of my voice.

"No," he said, sounding exasperated. "I mean, yes. Of course he was. But not like that. It was like I could see his body, but at the same time, nothing was there. You know those old movies, where they'd have it all black and white but introduce a character who was in color? The opposite of that. It was like a shadow was where he should have been."

Well, shit, I thought to myself, *that made my day stranger, after all.*

Chapter 6

Taylor stared at me over a pint glass in Delaney's Tap Room a block away from my apartment. We had met for drinks and a bite after his short shift at the tutoring center that evening.

"I'm sorry, what?" he asked, after I finished my explanation. "I don't have better words for it. You've only taken the basics of anthropology, but I'm guessing you've read enough about world religion to encounter animism before, yes?"

"You mean how everything holds a spirit? Like, rocks and trees and stuff," he said with a tone that could only generously be called dismissive.

I took a deep drink from my glass. I had ordered a rich stout that was on its way to dulling the edges of my nerves. "Yeah, but say it without sounding like an asshole." Some lessons are straightforward.

He had the decency to look embarrassed. "Sorry. Okay, but that's what 'magic' is?"

"More or less. It's like martial arts. Our limbs only move in so many ways, so each art is working off the same base–the human body. Aikido works with the same physiology and physics as judo, karate, or Muay Thai, but they each apply them differently to similar ends."

"Similar, but not the same," Taylor said, catching my drift.

"Right. So magic is just applied physics with the stuff of the universe. Most religions, especially the oldest, come from an understanding of the spiritual world. There are more modern interpretations and offshoots, but a native shaman smudging a space to cleanse it of evil spirits is a different side of the coin to a Catholic priest using a censer to purify and sanctify a church."

Taylor held up a hand. "Wait, so what about other mythology? Like...faeries. Are they real?"

"Sure," I said, without a pause. "But go deeper. If spirits are tied to the land, what about faeries?"

Taylor drank more beer, clearly deciding sobriety wasn't going to help him in this conversation. "Then...they're connected to the land too. Like, house-spirits being part of the houses they inhabit. Or naiads living in their rivers."

"Bingo." One big concept we had skirted around so far was how it all worked with the migration of people over the ages. I wanted to see if he would make the connection himself or if I'd need to draw it for him.

"So...are there Indigenous faeries?"

Well, I guess we were going to have to call it close enough. My empty glass next to the pint he was currently working on helped me give him the benefit of the doubt that he'd have figured it out eventually.

"Not exactly," I said. "People bring their spirits with them. It's not entirely about the land, some of it is belief. But yes, there are faeries mixing it up with crow spirits in the forest at times. But they're weaker here, less prevalent."

Taylor eyed me suspiciously. "What do you mean 'here?'"

I hadn't expected to launch into a dissertation on the effects of European colonization on indigenous species, but here we were.

Maybe there was an easier way to explain the biggest pieces of this brave new world.

"Let me show you something." A half-eaten basket of French fries was next to Taylor, from which I plucked a small handful and wrapped in a paper napkin before shoving them into my flannel's pocket. I dropped some bills on the table and walked out the door of the establishment, Taylor following close behind with a bemused look on his face.

Without commentary, I led him a few blocks over to Edgewood Park, where I had relocated my furry friend the other night. Instead of standing on the periphery, I strode in among the trees along the border of the park, crunching through the light coating of fallen leaves preceding the piles that would accumulate later in the season. Taylor trailed at my heels without question, which I appreciated, until I found a convenient tree stump.

Kneeling next to the flat surface, I held a fry in my hand and lightly pushed a touch of my essence into the food. It wasn't tobacco, though I had replenished my stock, but I figured my demonstration would be easier this way.

"What do you see?" I asked, placing the tidbit down and stepping back from the stump.

"A soggy french fry," Taylor replied but cocked his head to the side, taking a second glance. "No. There's...something. Like, a sliver of light."

"Once the floodgates open, it's hard to close them," I said, grinning. "That's part of my spirit, and I'm inviting someone to join us for a treat."

We waited in amiable silence until claws scratching in the leaves intruded on the stillness. Taylor's lips parted as if he was about to say something, but I held up my hand, motioning him to silence. I gestured for him to crouch; he towered over both me and the makeshift offering plate. He complied with a grimace, muttering something about, "this is how you get ticks."

I opened my awareness, and the colors returned to the park in the early dark of a fall night. "I want you to try something," I whispered. "Shut your eyes but then imagine opening them again. Then, keeping that visualization in your mind, *really* open your eyelids."

Taylor shrugged, but the faint light of the moon shone on his face. A few moments later, moonlight glinted off his corneas. He fell backward and landed on his ass in the leaves, mouth wide in amazement. "Holy shit!"

I chuckled but held a finger to my lips. We waited, Taylor's head swiveling as he took in the aurora above him, until the scratching sound drew closer, and my fat friend from the previous night tentatively approached the stump. The glow of his eyes preceded the rest of his bulk as he crept cautiously forward until his nose was inches away from my infused morsel.

He looked from the fry to me and back again before reaching out to grab it and shove it into his mouth, chewing greedily. Taylor sat transfixed, staring at the raccoon as if he had never seen one in his life. In some ways, he hadn't.

"What the hell is that?" he whispered.

"*That* is the closest you'll get to seeing Raccoon anytime soon." I hoped he could hear the capital R when I said the name aloud, but he didn't question my statement.

With no more French fries in the offing, our friend scampered deeper into the park, leaving us in contemplative silence until Taylor said, "Jesus Christ, Corbin, you weren't joking."

I spread my hands as if to say, "you're welcome." Rising, I motioned for him to follow me out of the park. "Let's go for a drive." When we reached the sidewalk, Taylor was still looking at everything around him, his head panning like a movie camera, taking everything in slowly.

"Corbin?"

"Hm?"

"I'm getting a headache."

"Oh, right. Turning it off is a little easier. Just close all your eyes," I said. It sounded simplistic, but anyone who I'd ever taught the trick had few issues putting their perception back in a "normal mode." It was the opposite that was the trouble in the first place. He nodded, closed his eyes, then opened them again. He shook his head slightly but followed me more swiftly down the concrete.

We walked across the street, past my apartment, and behind the building to where my car sat in the small parking lot. I unlocked the doors and gestured for Taylor to get in and went around to the driver's seat to settle myself. We were pulling out of the side street and onto Whalley Avenue before anyone spoke.

"I know this is all a shock to your system, but once you told me you saw what happened to Clyde, I figured it was better to throw you into the deep end than beat around the bush."

"What *did* happen to Clyde, Corbin?"

I chewed the inside of my cheek, a bad habit I'd never lost from childhood, and considered my answer. We made good time heading downtown. The main drag was less populated this late at night. As we passed graveyards, the streets gave way to multi-family houses. I figured now was as good an opportunity as any.

"Can you turn the sight back on, like I told you before?" I asked.

"Sure, what am I supposed to be looking at?"

"Just tell me what you see, compared to what I showed you before."

I glanced at Taylor as he closed his eyes, took a calming breath, and then opened them again. The surprise on his face was subtle, his mouth compressing into a thin line.

"There's a lot less going on here..." he said, trailing off as he scanned our surroundings.

I laughed. "That's true but vague. Give me more."

"Yes, *Professor* Pierce," Taylor mumbled sarcastically but continued. "The living things are more vibrant, and the buildings are muted. Some have brighter colors than others–"

I interrupted him to explain. "Probably gardens or someone who loves plants."

We drove through a few more lights and approached the borders of the campus. This was mostly commercial space, some grocery stores and restaurants, fast-food joints, and other shops.

"Oh...it's really dead here."

"Not dead," I interjected. "Try again."

"Maybe dormant is a better word? Only the trees are shining. There are splashes of color where there's no pavement and some animals scurrying around, but that's about it."

"All right, Mr. Would-Be Historian. What happened?" I kept the car moving slowly into the belly of the beast as Taylor did his best to respond.

"We did, I guess. People, I mean. Jesus, this is crazy. If everyone could see this, maybe they would–" He cut off abruptly as we passed into York Square.

I didn't have to open my inner eye to know what he was seeing. Similar to the shopping areas we had passed through, this was a mostly dead zone, but it had the added bonus of the Hand's involvement. Alexander and his predecessors had been busy these past years draining the area in and around the campus of its vital essence. They couldn't take every drop, though. It would be hard to explain why no trees or grass would grow within the campus bounds, but the Hand did their best to ride that line.

"What–what happened here?" he asked, breathlessly.

I sighed, parked the car in an open spot on Elm Street next to Trumbull College, then turned to Taylor. "You wanted me to tell you about what went down with Clyde? Well, it was worse than what happened here." I pinched the bridge of my nose. This was all moving too fast. "This is your point of no return, friend. Last chance to opt-out on the inner workings of the universe. This isn't a fairy tale where I can wave my magic wand and wipe your memories if you end up regretting your decision later."

"You have a magic wand?"

I opened my mouth, but the shine in his eyes told me he was serious, and I put away my snarky comment. "Yes. It's a ceremonial artifact and doesn't do anything special. But *this*," I waved to encompass everything around us, "is very real. Are you in or out?"

"Magic wands aren't real, but spirit raccoons who eat glowing french fries are? I need some time to think about it before I make a decision. Is that fair?"

I nodded and put the car back in gear. "You probably want to turn your sight off before you get a migraine."

The wrinkled lines on his forehead said he was already working on one, but he did what I suggested and closed his eyes again. I fished in the center console for some ibuprofen and handed it to him. "Sorry, I don't have any water, but if you can dry-swallow pills, these will help."

He shook two into his palm and tossed them into his mouth, grimacing as he choked the tablets down. "Thanks."

We took a few one-way streets to make our way back to my apartment. Taylor was the first to speak into the heavy silence.

"I thought you were a history professor."

I gave a chuckle, shaking my head. "That's true, I am. I just have a really complicated hobby."

"Which is…"

Despite doing this for a while, I hadn't needed to explain myself to anyone in a long time. I tapped the steering wheel in thought. "Think of me as a spiritual activist and conservationist."

"Makes as much sense as anything else, I guess."

"I'll take that as a compliment. There aren't a lot of us who can see across the veil, you should know."

It was a quiet minute before he replied. "Is that why you're telling me all this?"

"One of the reasons."

I pulled around into my parking lot, killing the engine once we had stopped. I got out of the car, and Taylor followed suit, then we walked back to the corner by the taproom where he had left his vehicle. We stood around awkwardly as he fumbled for his keys, but I stopped him before he opened his car door.

I cleared my throat. "Look, Taylor. I haven't done this before."

"Had a beer with a student?" He had a disarming grin and was clearly giving me shit.

"Very funny. No, introduced someone to the mysteries."

"Is that what it's called?"

"Sometimes. But there's a lot you don't understand. You wanted some time to think about it, and it's not fair to ask you to make a decision without enough information. I wanted you to know if you decide you want to dive into this, I'll be here to help. I had a mentor once, too, when I found my talent."

"Thanks, Corbin. I'll keep it in mind."

With that, he took his leave. I waited until he drove away before heading back to my apartment. I had class to teach the next day and some thinking to do. My thoughts strayed far and wide before

I finally slept. I had lived in interesting times before, and this all had the feel of a beginning.

How would it end? That was the question.

Chapter 7

I woke the next morning to a text from Taylor accepting my offer of mentorship. He said in his note he wasn't sure what he was getting himself into but didn't want to miss out on the possibilities of whatever this new talent of his was.

I didn't blame him. If I were in his shoes, I would have jumped at the chance. I did at one point. My mentor, an agreeable man named John Coughlin, came into my life in a much more tumultuous period than Taylor's seemed to be. I had just graduated from my undergraduate program and was going through some of the stages of grief regarding my professional prospects.

I believed I was stumbling through "anger" when he and I met, during an interview for a research position on an upcoming dig in the southwestern US. He was a research fellow, assisting the leader of the project with securing the talent they would rely on during the weeks we'd be spending in a remote part of Arizona.

One reason for my angst was the awakening of my own powers. I didn't recognize what they were at the time, but I couldn't reconcile what I was seeing with the world as I understood it. John came along and changed that. We didn't start working together in the magical sense until two weeks into the expedition, but our relationship continued for years afterward. We were still in touch, keeping each other abreast of what was happening in our parts of the world, even if I didn't reach out much anymore for advice.

It's not because I knew it all, far from it, but I tended to experiment before asking for help. If I ended up needing his advice on my apprentice, I'd make a call. Until then, I'd muddle through as best as I could.

The rest of the week continued much like any other, but I could feel everything diverging from whatever my normal had become. I wasn't opposed to the change, but these kinds of events came in threes. First, it was Clyde's death, which I still hadn't come up with any convincing theories about. Second, Taylor's burgeoning talent. I could have counted the Hunter's Rosary as the first, but it wasn't too out of the ordinary, all things considered.

Harriet had me go through the rest of the lot she acquired, but I didn't find anything more menacing than antique blades in vintage razors. We were both up on our tetanus shots, so even that risk was miniscule.

Class finished for the week, with Taylor sitting in but taking off as soon as it was over to keep up with his own schedule. I spent some of Friday wandering downtown looking for leads. A dark cloud hung over the mood of the itinerant members of the community around the Green. Clyde's death and Jake's deep mourning cast a somber tone over the locals. Everyone I encountered had been willing to talk about Clyde, share an opinion or two, but otherwise had no new information. No one knew anything regarding his whereabouts before he went missing, and no one had seen him for two days before his dramatic reappearance.

I walked by thirty-eight Crown more than once, but no residual essence remained. Every being held a unique signature. My energy was different than Taylor's, which was distinct from Jake's. Clyde didn't have a trail to speak of, and the minimal energy in the downtown area led to any excess bleeding away before too long. The concrete path where his red sleeping bag used to lay was bare to all my senses.

I even took a chance and checked in with the building in case they had security footage. The receptionist wouldn't speak with me without showing credentials proving I had the right to ask. After a few passes, I spent most of the afternoon in the area. One of the other employees showed a little empathy and told me there wasn't anything to find. Their security cared about the building itself and not the walkway. The self-interest didn't surprise me. It was a long shot to begin with.

I checked in with Jake one last time and grabbed a sandwich with him before heading home. He told me he had mailed the letter to Clyde's daughter but otherwise was out of sorts. Jake was a survivor. He'd get through it, but I felt for him. Losing your best friend, when it was one of the few positives in your life, was hard.

Friday nights in New Haven were busy, but there were two reasons I decided to have a slow evening in. One, I wasn't feeling up to socialization. I'd had a lot of that digging into Clyde's disappearance, and the solitude of my apartment with a book and a glass of whiskey was more my speed. Two, I had plans the next day that resting myself for wouldn't hurt.

"Why...are we...doing this...again?" Taylor huffed and puffed beside me as we hiked along another switchback.

"It's good for the soul," I replied, sweat trickling down my spine despite the coolness of the morning. I wasn't in the best shape, but I had apparently been keeping up my cardio more than Taylor because I wasn't hurting nearly as much as he appeared to be.

I had texted him at the end of the week, proposing his first activity as my apprentice. Despite me being vague, Taylor was game for "really experiencing nature." We met at the parking lot of Sleeping Giant State Park, off Mt. Carmel Avenue in Hamden, and walked in together. We fell into a rhythm where I talked and he listened while making unhappy panting noises.

"Okay, but seriously," he replied, wiping his brow.

He was obviously too miserable to take in the scenery with his newly enhanced senses, but it wasn't important that he work himself into a headache before we reached the vantage point I wanted him to see.

"You're lucky I'm aiming to get to the Tower today. This is the 'easy' trail."

"Easy, my ass," he replied but straightened his back and breathed a little easier. He might have been exaggerating, but more likely, I'd stung his pride by calling him out.

"All right, fine, let me tell you a story. You know what this place is called, right?"

"I don't live under a rock. It's Sleeping Giant."

I laughed and nodded. "Good, but *why* is it named that?"

He opened his mouth to answer but nothing came out. I waited, and his eyes darted side to side before he shrugged.

"Taylor, let me introduce you to Hobbomock." I slapped a nearby rock with my palm, making a meaty thwack.

"Is the air thin enough that you're hallucinating?" Exertion seemed to bring the sarcasm out of Taylor.

I kept walking and ignored the barb. "Hobbomock was a giant and a great spirit of the Algonquian people. The Quinnipiac, specifically, believed he threatened this land because he was jealous of the worship given to other deities and not him. There's a bend in the Connecticut river attributed to his mighty foot stomping the ground and changing its course."

We continued our path up the hill, and I gave Taylor a minute to consider the story.

"What happened, if that's who the 'Sleeping Giant' is?"

Smiling, I paused and turned to him. At least he had been paying attention.

"Hobbomock wreaked havoc until the people called on Keitan, another powerful spirit, to deal with him. The details vary among storytellers, but the result is the same. Keitan cast a spell to put the stone giant to sleep, and here we are, walking on his neck."

Taylor was silent for a long while as we continued hiking but eventually asked, "Is it real?" His voice held a reverence I hadn't expected.

"Wait until we reach the top and ask me again."

The trail wove higher and higher up the hillside, and we followed. Eventually, we made our way to the summit. The lookout tower was situated on the "hip" of the giant. It was a large stone edifice built in the 1930s, complete with stone arches serving as windows. We trudged up the steps to reach the top of the lookout, which was also the highest point in the park. The view was stunning, even to the naked eye. The reds and yellows of fall, not even at their peak, were breathtaking. Taylor and I stood, surveying the forest below us and breathing the crisp air.

"I get why you wanted me to see this. It's beautiful," he said.

"Now." I paused, dramatically. "*Really* open your eyes."

His look of appreciation turned into one of shocked awe. I shifted my own vision to enjoy the sight for myself. It didn't matter how often I trekked there; it was always worth taking in the whole picture at the tower.

The forest nearly vibrated with color, blending in a riotous kaleidoscope of overlapping waves. The sky was a clear blue, made of vibrant crystal on the spirit plane. Even the stones of the tower held more magic here than the brick and mortar of the campus. Years of footsteps wearing paths in the rock itself, hands touching the stone balusters, leaving small imprints over time. The tower had been invasive once but no more. It had been there long enough and served no purpose other than to be part of the park itself.

Rarely were storms violent enough to cause significant damage in the northeast, but tornados and microbursts had periodically rolled through. One year, a particularly dangerous storm caused a massive amount of wreckage but left the tower unscathed. I took it as a sign it had been accepted, its stones now part of the earth itself.

"So, is it real?" I asked, a grin plastered on my face.

We gazed west across the park, to where the rest of the giant lay. The outline was clearer with our hidden vision. Not distinct in the way of a chalk outline, but how a topographical map made it easier to notice shapes and patterns.

"I don't know if it's a giant," Taylor said, swallowing heavily. "But it's amazing."

Clapping him on the shoulder, I turned to survey the southern part of the park, appreciating the trail we had climbed. Birds coasted on thermals, a red-tailed hawk trailing a cascade of fiery energy behind it. Turkey vultures circled, majestic in their own right. I had never been a huge fan of the birds, but they served a purpose like any scavenger in the food chain.

"Hey, Corbin! I can see East and West Rock from here!" Taylor's enthusiasm was infectious, and I shifted to take in what he was talking about when an anomaly caught my attention out of the corner of my eye.

I had a television with a dead pixel a while back. It was only one off to the side where a person could ignore it when most happened near the center of the screen. But when you moved your head or the action shifted suddenly, you almost *had* to focus on it. Like a compulsion, I'd notice it and get frustrated that it ever existed. A minute later, I'd forget it again until the next time.

It was like that. Something was missing due south, near to where the buzzards were buzzing. I turned my head back and forth, to capture it again, but I lost it in the shifting palette of the forest. No angle made it pop out again, but I was sure I hadn't imagined it.

"Corbin–" Taylor's smile faltered as he approached me, trying to get my attention again. "What is it?"

"I'm not sure...but we're going to find out."

My feet echoed in the stairwell as I led the way back down the tower. There was no need to bushwhack. I knew the park well enough to follow the red triangle trail south. The foliage was still thick, but I sighted the vultures periodically and confirmed we were still heading in the right direction. This path was steeper, but I barreled along it with the sure footing of a mountain goat. Taylor was going to have to keep up.

We found ourselves at the intersection of the red and yellow trails, the left hand leading to a bridge crossing the Mill River. Sighting my flying signposts, I made the turn, boots soon clomping over the wooden planks. I activated my sight again, scanning for the anomaly. Once across the bridge, I spun and surveyed the riverbanks, stopping dead as I took in the shadow near the footing on the far side of the bridge I had come from.

Taylor's heavy footfalls alerted me he had reached the platform.

"Wait!" I called out, and he skidded to a stop. Retracing my steps back over the span, I went around and scrabbled down the short riverbank to the edge of the bed below. Tangled around the nearest concrete support was a dead body. I guessed it wasn't a live one because nobody would willingly lay face down in the river in September, no matter how nice a day it was. And because they couldn't breathe underwater.

Regardless of how obvious it might seem, I still rolled the body of the woman, as I found out, out of the stream and onto the riverbed. Checking for a pulse I doubted would be there, I examined the waxy face. She was middle-aged and heavyset with stringy blonde hair and an assortment of mismatched clothes. My first deduction was she was homeless, given the layering of her outfit from various sources. A skirt over blue jeans, multiple tops and a jacket, that kind of thing.

There wasn't much of an odor, even though I expected the stench of death. The coolness of the season plus the flowing water contributed to there being only a slight rancid smell once I crouched next to the body. I wasn't a medical examiner, but it probably hadn't been there for too long either.

"What the hell..." Taylor trailed off, having found his footing to join me below the overpass.

"Tell me what you see," I said, knowing full well this was another victim of whatever had drained Clyde's essence. The stark black and white Taylor had used as an analogy was apt. It was like a line drawing of a person sketched with definition only on the outline.

"Oh, wow, it's the same as before. Isn't it?" His voice shook.

Taking out my phone, I snapped a quick picture before calling 911. She wasn't familiar to me, but maybe someone else would recognize her. I glanced down, and track marks dotted on the inside of her elbow. This would be another open and shut for the boys in blue.

It was too bad my investigation was just heating up. Once might be a hell of a coincidence, even if I didn't believe in those. Twice was the start of a pattern. If this wasn't the third thing I had been tensed for, we were in for a hell of a surprise.

Chapter 8

The visit from the Hamden police didn't take significantly longer than the one in New Haven. They asked more questions, like "How did you find the body?", "Did you know the deceased?" and "What brought you to the park today?" In the end they took my statement, but since I was the one to call it in, they seemed to tag me as a Good Samaritan.

I hadn't rifled through her pockets, but the cops didn't find an ID on the body, which meant no new information for me. The officers offered to drive us back to my car, which I accepted if only to not make them suspicious. I didn't need the hassle if they decided I was being cagey. Taylor and I rode to the parking lot in a silence that finally lifted after we were safely out of the police cruiser and ensconced in my vehicle.

"What's going on, Corbin?" A frustrated edge was in Taylor's voice. "First, we found a dead body in New Haven. That was bad enough, but now we discover one in *the woods*. And the thing that's freaking me out is that none of this is freaking *you* out!"

Sighing, I gripped the steering wheel until my knuckles turned red. "You haven't been around a lot of death, but I've seen my fair share."

"Is that supposed to make me feel better?"

I started the car, backed out of our space, and pulled onto the road, heading home. "I'm trying, anyway. In my line of work, I handle a lot of what mortality gives us. Dead people's possessions, the artifacts of lives, lived and gone. Our culture doesn't prepare us for dealing with any of this in a healthy way. Usually people fear death because it's what we're raised to do. Some believe we came from the stars and will return there after we pass on. If there wasn't so much light pollution, you could see the Milky Way at night, a road guiding people to the spirit lands when they die."

"I don't see–"

My calm cracked, but it wasn't his fault. "I'm not freaking out about finding two dead bodies, because *that's* not the problem. People die every day, and if we weren't so messed up about it in this country, you'd be looking at the problem the way I am. Because it's not *what* happened, it's *why*. And the only reason I'm *not* losing my shit about finding two dead bodies drained of any hint of their essence is practice and faking it. Because I'm too distracted trying to figure it out."

We rode without speaking for a few minutes. Taylor's grip was tight on the "oh shit" handle, and he ground his teeth until he finally spat out the words he had been chewing on. "You never told me what happened to the campus to make it so bleak."

Ah, there it was, I thought. He was drawing connections, probably better than I gave him credit for now that he could calm down and consider what had happened rationally.

"That's true, but I can give you the answer. Have you heard of Skull and Bones?"

Taylor scoffed. "The Yale secret society for all the rich and powerful kids?"

"Got it in one. What do you know about them?"

"Well, I know that it's real. But it's a bunch of stuck-up yuppie brats following in their daddy's footsteps."

I gave a chuckle. "The thing about myth is it's usually grounded in reality."

"So, there's really a secret society making the world dance like a marionette?"

"That's dramatic. No, I'm saying there's a *kernel* of truth. But it's not what you're thinking." We were zipping along the back roads on Paradise Avenue. I took a deep breath, squared my shoulders, and veered the car over the white line and onto the grass beside the street. Coming to a halt with a small jolt, I then unbuckled myself and got out. "Lesson time," I said, not waiting for a response as I closed the door behind me.

Taylor fumbled to release himself, then joined me on the green verge. Other vehicles whipped past us, some even slowing down to make sure we were all right, but I waved them on with a smile. Sometimes humanity gave me a reason to have hope.

I knelt five feet from the road, where the grass transitioned to thicker weeds and small stands of trees. "Watch me." I waited until Taylor's eyes took on a slightly glassy sheen, and I knew he was looking with both sets. I held my hand above a patch of cinquefoil and drew a silver thread up from the serrated leaves. The small yellow flowers connected to them wilted from the loss, bending over like they had fainted. The silver pooled in the palm of my hand as I turned it over for Taylor to see. He nodded in acknowledgement, and I lowered my hand back to the green patch, now grayer. I gently returned the energy through the veins in the leaves like a weird kind of photosynthesis, the tiny buds perking up again on their shafts.

It was over in a minute, but Taylor stared at me like time stood still. Motioning for him to join me, Taylor crouched on the grass.

"Do you see the energy inside the plants?" I asked, gesturing at another patch of greenery.

Taylor nodded and cleared his throat. "Yes."

"Good. I've had a lot of practice, so don't do what I did. Go ahead and touch the plant but *reach* for the threads of life force. You should feel a connection, then draw it out into your hand."

His face screwed up in concentration, Taylor placed his palm on top of the nearest section, which happened to be clover. I watched with my own sight as he sensed the energy under his touch, then slowly brought it up. Where my threads were silver, Taylor's were copper, and they jumped into his palm mixed with the green of the plants.

"Gently!" I said, as he drew out the clover's essence, but it was too late.

The green of the trefoils beneath his hand browned and withered, the tawny energy filling his cupped hand as he turned it over. His smile was triumphant but faltered when he saw my face. "Did I do something wrong?"

He hadn't, on any large scale, but I sighed anyway. It was an important lesson I was trying to teach him, and sometimes those came with a cost. That was part of the teaching as well. "No, you didn't. I was pretty sure that was going to happen."

Taylor stared at the puddle of energy in his hand. "I saw you put yours back. What do I do with this now?"

"You can do a lot. I'd say 'almost anything', but you have to consider the limits. This type of essence is a natural resource. If you treat it carefully, you can take some of it without hurting the source. What do you want to do?"

He nodded. "Can I...throw a fireball?"

I laughed, shaking my head. "Not exactly. The amount of energy you're holding might make a spark or a candle flame at best. It's also harder to do when there's no sympathy." Taylor's confused look was all I needed to continue my explanation. "That's having something relating to what you're doing. If you wanted to start a fire, applying a spark to tinder is easier than generating fire from nowhere. How about this, for our first attempt, why don't you absorb it? One thing you'll need to learn is how to incorporate other energies into your own."

He made to put his hand to his mouth, like he was about to drink, but I put a gentle palm on his wrist. "Not like that. While it would work, you don't need to be so literal. Everything is permeable. Imagine absorbing it through your skin but changing it all to your signature. The copper color that's you, versus the green mix."

He squinted as he stared at his hand, the small amount of essence shifting from orange and green to pure metallic copper. Taylor drew it in slowly through his palm, his eyes widening as he completed the exercise.

"How do you feel?"

He seemed to consider, cocking his head to one side like he was taking stock internally. "Like I just had a cup of coffee. A little jittery."

"Makes sense. You got a bigger boost than you would have if you hadn't killed the grass."

He looked from his hand to the dead patch of grass, and back to me. "Oh–I'm sorry. I didn't mean to–"

I held up my hands in a calming gesture. "It's okay. This is why I chose a patch of weeds instead of something tragic, like a litter of kittens."

He blanched, color draining from his face, clearly contemplating what I had said.

"I would never do that," I said, shaking my head. "But someone might."

I let him chew on those thoughts as we got returned to the car and continued our ride home. We were passing from Hamden into New Haven before either of us spoke again.

"Death is old magic, the oldest there is other than birth. There's power inside everything, and those with the talent for it can bend that energy to their will," I said. "There are people who use this kind of power recklessly. Some of them exist in the upper echelons of society and hide inside the mystique of a secret society. They call themselves The Hand."

Taylor blurted out a laugh. "Now who's being dramatic?"

I shrugged. "You're not wrong, but that doesn't make them any less talented. Now, tell me the difference between your patch of weeds and the bodies we've found."

Taylor didn't answer immediately, taking some time before replying. "The plants weren't all drained like Clyde, or whoever it was we found today."

"Bingo. Regardless of how they died, which I have no way of knowing, they were both entirely devoid of essence."

"What does that have to do with The Hand?" Taylor asked, chewing on a fingernail absentmindedly.

"Elm blight."

"Sorry, come again?"

"New Haven is Elm City, but those trees are far fewer than they used to be. They said Dutch Elm Disease blighted the elms throughout the Northeast in the thirties. But that's not what killed the trees downtown."

"You're shitting me."

"Nope. Magic is limited, in many ways. You can't do more than what your personal reserves can handle, unless you draw it from another source. It's one reason magicians band together. Covens, societies, whatever. So, groups gather for larger workings because they'd never get them done alone. Only rumors exist about what they were doing back then, why they needed so much life force, but in the end, it killed the trees for a square mile around the school."

Glancing over, Taylor's mouth opened and closed, but no words came out.

"Someone, or something, sucked those bodies dry. I can't say whether The Hand is involved, but I think I need to have another conversation with a disagreeable person. This isn't the same as what I expect happened to the elms, but maybe he'll know something about it."

You might think getting an appointment with the head of a double-secret society would be hard. The good news was Doctor Alexander Hughes, professor of History, held office hours posted publicly online. The bad news was, unless I wanted to try to track him down outside of his schedule, I had to wait until Monday. No matter how important this was, it wasn't "get a restraining order for stalking the head of the History College" important.

I bided my time. Sunday was for resting after all, and it had been an unexpectedly "long" week. I was overdue to catch up on some reading and grant writing I had put off. The most unbelievable part of my life wasn't that I could do magic but that I could live on an adjunct professor's salary. I couldn't, actually, and it was why I had the side jobs.

Monday morning was spent in the same fashion, though I did research the Hunter's Rosary, which I hadn't figured out what to do with yet. It still sat like a tiny black hole in my side table drawer.

The hour was approaching for me to ambush Hughes in his office, so I sent off my last query regarding the latest project I was contracted to do. Putting a bookmark in a tome discussing the conversion of native tribes, heavily annotated by the chicken scratch of a former occult researcher, I pulled on my boots and headed downtown.

The offices for the history department were in a tower within Yale's "old campus" but had undergone renovations and construction to renovate the courtyard those buildings surrounded into the "Humanities Quadrangle." Leave it to brilliant people to call something that was arguably a six-sided shape a "quad." I had been there before in a collegiate "checking out the local opportunities" way years ago, when I was considering my academic options. Once I moved back to the area, I had returned in an attempt to "know thine enemy".

The door to his office was open, but it wasn't unoccupied. Alex's expansive "lecture" voice echoed down the hall as I approached. Without waiting for an invitation, I walked into the room to find Amanda sitting across from Hughes, an interested look in profile plastered across her face. She turned her head as I entered, her eyes widening in apparent surprise.

The paint was institutional white, but the rest of the decorations were in dark oak, old brass, and leather. Expansive bookshelves lined the walls, with a set of wingback chairs in front of a massive mahogany desk complete with leather blotter and an inkwell.

Whatever Alexander had been pontificating about died on his lips, which curled into a sneer as he took in my presence. "I wondered when I'd be seeing you next. Are you here to apply for my teaching assistant posting?"

A chuckle escaped my mouth involuntarily. We had a similar sense of humor, if nothing else. "I doubt it pays enough. No, we've got old business to discuss."

"Well, as you can see, I'm quite occupied at the–"

"Have you been killing elms again?" I arched an eyebrow. It was a thinly veiled code that Hughes had no real reason to follow, but the discomfort on his face was worth the shot in the dark.

"Amanda, would you please excuse us? Come back tomorrow during office hours, yes?" He rose and ushered her from the room, closing the door behind her retreating form before rounding on me. "You know *full* well we haven't–"

"Relax, Hughes." I collapsed into the chair Amanda had vacated, propping my boots on the edge of the desk. "I was being dramatic because the *actual* problem is worse, and I doubt you wanted a precious first-year to hear about bodies dropping across city lines."

Alexander walked to his desk with a stiff spine and swatted my feet off the desktop with a grunt of disgust. "What are you playing at, Pierce?"

"Two bodies in the past four days, drained entirely of their essence. One here downtown, and the other in Hamden."

Hughes sat with his elbows propped on the desk, fingers steepled against his lips. "And you're intruding here because...you think they caught a case of Dutch elm disease? I've been clear for decades that we will continue our moratorium on any wholesale siphoning of natural energy. Why do you suspect we'd move from trees to *people,* of all things?"

I sighed and rubbed my temples with one hand. "You're the one 'in charge' of this area, Hughes."

"Well, I haven't heard the slightest thing about it." He puffed his chest up and peered at me studiously. "You would assume I'd be told if there were dead bodies piling up on or near campus."

"They were homeless, both of them."

"Ah, that would explain it. We don't get word about the riffraff unless they're bothering the students or faculty–"

"Don't be an ass, Alexander. They were human beings."

"Well, this is nothing new. The season's moving on. Perhaps they were simply victims of an early cold snap. Weak hearts. Poor health. Who knows with these people?"

I leaned against the nearest bookshelf so I could loom a bit. "Yes, because the cold has been bad enough to *leech every trace of their souls from their bodies.*"

He had the good taste to pause, taken at least slightly aback from my blunt turn of phrase. "You make a point, if a crude one. But I can't help you. I've got a full roster of students to shepherd and a heavy course load to boot. I wasn't joking about needing a TA. If nothing else, I'll warn the others something unusual might be going on, but twice is still in the vicinity of a coincidence." He held up a hand to stop me from interrupting. "Even as strange as this seems."

I stared at him for a solid ten seconds. There was a lack of guile in his eyes, though I was sure he could be lying to my face. He was right, in a way. I didn't have much to go on yet, and it was only the similarities between the incident years ago with The Hand that led me to his door. "I'd appreciate it if you would keep your ears open for anything related to this, as a professional courtesy."

Hughes smiled and stood, reaching out his hand to shake. I rose and grasped it. No oaths were being sworn, so nothing happened more than my feeling of mild regret from the interaction. My feet had nearly crossed the threshold before Hughes's voice stopped me.

"Oh, Corbin. Speaking of professional courtesy, I have something you'll want to know but won't like in the least."

I turned, squinting at him. "I'm listening."

"We've reached the end of an era! The Green is finally being developed. I'm aware it's something you've fought against for years. Good show and all that."

My mouth opened and closed twice before I could get words out. "What?"

"Yes. Think of it as a kind of Chelsea and Borough Market. The early designs are fabulous, I..." He trailed off, and I could only imagine what he saw in my face.

"This is not 'good' news," I finally said.

"Not for you, I suppose." He chuckled. "No, I expect you and your little protests will continue for quite some time. Regardless, someone finally made the board of directors an offer they couldn't pass up. I thought you should hear it from me."

"You could have just told me to go fuck myself. You know that, right?"

"Yes," he said, nodding with a slow grin spreading across his face. "But this was so much better."

Chapter 9

Before I knew it, I had stormed into Bits and Baubles, the bell clattering loudly against the door as I shoved it open.

Harriet looked up from the counter, a jeweler's loupe over one eye. "Who kicked your puppy?"

I stopped in my tracks, caught off guard by the comment. "I don't have a dog. They're not even allowed on my lease."

"Well, the mood you dragged in with you says someone shoved their boot into something."

Harriet was right. I must have carried the weight of Alexander's surprise announcement plain on my face. I took a calming breath and explained the issue to her.

One of the oddest facts about the Green wasn't the whole rapture business but that it was privately managed. A group of five trustees held ownership of the land, dating back to the 1700s, now maintained by their descendants as far as I was aware. There had been multiple attempts over the years to suggest development of the site, but the people in charge allegedly wanted to keep it from becoming commercialized. Those days had clearly come to an end.

By the time I finished, I had worked myself back up again and spoke in clipped sentences. "So, they're going to make it into some gentrified open-air market. Now I've got to dig into that, as if the dead bodies weren't enough already."

"What dead bodies?" Harriet had listened to me rant but kept on the task of appraising whatever piece of antiquity passed over her desk that day. My last statement, however, caused the loupe to fall out of her scrunched eye and drop into a practiced hand.

Had I not told Harriet about the deceased homeless people? I didn't see her every day, so I must not have. "Do you know any of the homeless folk downtown?"

"Not really."

"Well," I said, launching into a second retelling, this time about the two spiritually desiccated bodies Taylor and I had discovered. Harriet's face was impassive as she listened, but she nodded thoughtfully when I finished.

"I wouldn't worry too much about the Green yet. It takes people years to get that kind of bureaucracy moving. You should have a chance to air your grievances. Stay calm."

"This feels like a setup. Hughes had no reason to expect me to drop in at his office, but even though it was a last-minute thing, he seemed to be dying to tell me."

"Because he's excited about a new falafel cart downtown? I bet they'll put a Middle Eastern food stall in that new market."

I shook my head but grinned despite the serious mood I was in. Harriet was trying to distract me, and she was always good for that. "No, because he knew it would hurt me."

"He does sound like that kind of guy, now that you mention it. I'll keep my eyes open, but you're the one with the philanthropy habit. I'm here cataloging and doing online sales most days. The people at the post office recognize my face more than anyone downtown would."

"You're always a help. I'll tell you if I find out anything. Until then, keep me posted if you need any more items looked at."

I took my leave and went up to my apartment. The issues around the essence-drained corpses rattled around in my head like a pair of dice, but everything came up snake-eyes. I made myself a cup of coffee and sat at the kitchen table, glancing around the room until my gaze landed on the side table holding the Hunter's Rosary. It wasn't the same problem as what I had seen with Clyde or the other woman in the woods, but they *were* similar magic.

Any kind of progress would feel good, so I sighed and retrieved the relic from the drawer. The box still radiated a dumb malice. It wasn't inherently evil, but the purpose it was enchanted for tainted it. Opening the case, I examined the necklace in the spirit world. Unlike Taylor, it had been quite a while since I developed headaches from the weird double vision due to long practice, so I used my second sight whenever I needed.

Now that I knew what it was, the fact the beads were made of bone was even more obvious. What little research I found talked more about bone rosaries being used in other cultures, such as Tibetan. But bone was a cheap and plentiful natural material, so many traditions utilized it alongside others. I pushed energy into the palm of my hand, forming it into a protective layer akin to a glove.

Real coverings wouldn't have done me much good, unless I enchanted them too. Not having any gloves of evil-artifact-handling laying around, I settled for a makeshift method to experiment. Lowering my hand within an inch of the rosary, the pull of the enchantment plucked at my thin barrier.

The black tendrils I recalled from the first time I had gotten near the piece rose slowly from the bones, questing toward my hand. The intention of my shield held, and the ebony threads bounced clumsily against my silvered palm, unable to gain purchase.

What if I... As the thought formed, my hand was already in motion, grabbing the black strings. They were an energy in and of themselves, though holding a simple directive or purpose. In this case it was to "absorb." Pinching them between thumb and forefinger, I pulled gently and coiled the inky essence in my protected palm.

There must have been an expectation the energy would be taken out once procured. Like I had shown Taylor, I pushed at the flow, changing it from jet to my own silver. Without thinking too hard about it, I pushed the discrete amount I had removed from the antique back into it. It sucked the bit of spirit in before I could blink, the nearly empty void drawing my offering in like a vortex. The unintelligent hunger of the piece still called out to my senses, but it seemed satiated for the moment.

"Well," I said to no one in particular. "That could come in handy."

Having had enough occult experimentation for one day, I spent the rest of the night working my off-hour contract jobs, getting another proposal roughed out. It was not the first time I mused about getting a lot more done if I didn't have rent to pay. That being said, class was the next day.

Taylor didn't attend my lecture but caught up with me in the cafeteria after my session. I was idly scrolling on my phone and set it face down on the table. He dropped into a seat across the table from me with a "Hey, Corbin." I nodded, a mouthful of my sandwich keeping me from anything more congenial. He unpacked a container from his lunch bag. Clearly the tutoring center paid even less than my faculty job did.

"I wanted to ask you a question," he said, looking side to side as if making sure no one was in eavesdropping range. "Do you ever feel 'pulled' toward something?"

Thinking while I chewed, I eventually settled on a response. "Beside the inevitable march of humanity toward the heat-death of the universe?"

Taylor opened his mouth, then closed it again, shaking his head as if to clear it. "That was bleak, man."

"It's been a rough week so far, and it's only Tuesday. A more serious answer is 'sometimes.' But it depends on a lot of things. Tell me what you're experiencing."

He paused for a minute to take a bite of what looked like a ham and cheese sandwich before continuing. "Sometimes, when I'm not paying attention to anything in particular, I'll feel drawn in a particular direction. Like there's a magnet trying to gently pull me."

I nodded. "That's not uncommon. The sensitive are drawn to sources of energy, whether they've discovered their talents or not. Sometimes that's how it happens, a person gets dragged toward some bigger source of power activating their sight."

Taylor wiped his brow in an exaggerated gesture. "Whew. I was worried there was something wrong with me. It gave me vertigo the first couple of times it happened."

"You're more than fine. Not everyone is as keyed into the space around them, so I'd even call it a good thing–" I broke off as my phone vibrated, echoing through the table. Flipping the phone over, I saw I had a notification from Nour. She rarely texted me outside of protests. "Uh, give me a second, Taylor."

NOUR:

> Get down to the Green, Corbin! There's a short-notice protest going on that you don't want to miss.

CORBIN:

> What happened?

NOUR:

> Didn't you read the paper this morning? I know you're old enough for that.

CORBIN:

> Ouch, right in the generational gap. And no, I canceled my subscription. Stop being a pain in the ass and tell me.

NOUR:

> They're turning the park into some kind of market, and everyone lost their minds. Someone organized a flash mob, and it turned into a big thing. You're missing it!

CORBIN:

> On my way!

I pocketed my phone and turned to Taylor. "Something big is happening downtown. You want to come with me?"

"I don't know, Corbin. I've got a class soon."

"Far be it from me to encourage you to ditch your education, but this might be some of the history-in-the-making we talked about."

Taylor stuffed the last of his sandwich into his mouth and shoved his lunch things into a backpack. "Tell me on the way over?"

I nodded. It was either a five-minute drive or a seven-minute walk, and grabbing my car would waste more than the difference between the two. "Let's hoof it."

Gateway was on Church Street, between George and Crown, so it was only a short couple of blocks of fast-walking until we saw the crowd gathered on the Green near the War Memorial. I rushed my explanation but gave Taylor the gist of the Green's private ownership when he was confused how they could develop a "public park."

Nour must have spotted me before I could find her because a folded-up newspaper slapped against my chest. My hands moved automatically to grab it before I realized Nour had done it.

"Too slow, Corbin," she said. "But I saved this for you. We got a couple into the restaurant. Hey," she said to Taylor, recognizing we were standing together and sticking her hand out. "Nour."

"Taylor," he replied, shaking hers in return.

She turned to me. "What do you make of it, Corbin?"

Her question barely reached me as the front-page article of the New Haven Register absorbed all my attention. The headline read "Private Ownership Rears its Ugly Head in New Haven Green Project." The gist of it was exactly what Hughes had warned me about. Taking their cues from Chelsea Market in New York City or Borough Market in London, a group of private developers were planning to transform the public green space into a covered market. The board of trustees had apparently agreed to an "unspecified amount" of money to make the deal possible. The part that made my eyes bug out was the timeline.

"How the hell do they expect to break ground in two months?" I asked incredulously.

"Your guess is as good as mine," Nour said, turning her back to us to survey the crowd. There was some disorganized chanting, well-meaning locals mixing with the usual homeless folks who this would immediately impact. "But people are *pissed*."

"I'm not surprised," Taylor added. "We grew up with this place. It's been a 'public' park since before I was born."

"Trust me, you're not the first or last person to be surprised it's not owned by the government." I spun slowly, taking in the chaos. Harriet had been so certain there was nothing to worry about for a while, but the universe was conspiring against any silver lining. "The article says there's still an open response period. So, between now and the end of that we'll need to organize. I'm not sure what legs there are to stand on, but we'll find them."

Nour nodded, eyes bright with the energy of the gathering. There was something electric about a protest. The camaraderie, the unified purpose, and the shared outrage filled everyone with the same drumbeat. An injustice was being perpetrated, and something had to be done. It was present in everyone around us, regardless of socioeconomic standing. College kids stood alongside grizzled homeless vets yelling, "Parks over profit!"

My own spirits were rising with the wave of people around me, but as I raised my fist to join in the latest chant, a figure caught my eye. It was there and then gone, the shifting rows of people crossing over my vision and obscuring what I could have sworn was Amanda's face. On top of that, she was staring at me. Like a horror movie, she was gone as soon as someone passed in front of my vision to break eye contact.

The girl from the Owl Shop, Hughes's office, and a burgeoning potential member of The Hand, standing in the middle of a protest. About a project her mentor was clearly elated about. I strode forward, pushing my way through the crowd without waiting to see if Taylor followed me. By the time I reached where she had been, there was no trace. Turning completely around, I scanned for retreating figures and didn't find any matching her profile.

Taylor caught up to me, weaving his own path through the throng. "Hey, why'd you run off?"

"I thought I saw someone, one of the students of The Hand."

His eyes widened, glancing around. "What did they look like?"

"Black dress, middling height, dark hair with bangs. I barely caught a glimpse of her."

"Any idea what she was doing?"

I shrugged. "No, but her being here at all surprised me."

"Uh. Corbin?"

"What is it?" I wasn't paying attention to Taylor, still trying in vain to find Amanda. My frustration over wanting to catch her bled into my interactions with Taylor. An edge lingered in my voice I didn't care for but could only apologize for later.

"I'm feeling one of those 'pulls,' and it's pretty strong."

I spun toward Taylor, and he was staring past my shoulder toward Temple Street. Temple split the Green, with the old Center Church on the other side. Following his gaze, I extended my senses. "What do you see?"

"It...doesn't make any sense. What's a baby bear doing in the middle of downtown? And why can't I see it with my regular eyes?"

It took a minute for me to understand what he was talking about. Sharpening my focus, I noticed the black bear cub wandering near the edge of the road, close to the center of the Green. "That's normal. Some animals only exist on one side of the curtain. But this wild of an animal doesn't usually come this far without reason," I said. Animals could appear in either or both of the worlds. Our fat, masked friend bled over into both. This cub, however, was purely a spirit creature. Which made sense, in a way.

There were few reasons for real bears to wander downtown. They kept to the forests and weren't regular visitors to urban areas unless provoked or ill.

Taylor crept forward with his hand outstretched, like he was offering it to a friendly dog to sniff. "Hey, little guy."

"Taylor..." I tried to get his attention, but he wasn't listening to me. In a way, I couldn't blame him. The bear was adorable. It snuffled in the grass, a bright beacon of energy in this anemic part of town.

Taylor was probably twenty feet ahead of me at that point, maybe five from the bear. I hadn't moved, my brain fighting priority among the protest, looking for Amanda and this new wrinkle which Taylor seemed dead set on petting.

"Taylor!" I repeated, louder this time, and he finally turned back to me.

"What? He's harmless!"

"Yeah, but he won't be the problem."

"What do you–" he started to ask, but a loud growl interrupted him. "Oh."

Rounding the corner of the church on the other side of the street was a much larger version of the species. Black bears were the smallest of their cousins, but that didn't make them any less dangerous. The added complication was these weren't physical animals, and the ones existing solely in the spirit lands would grow bigger than their counterparts. This would be a massive specimen, males being larger than females, but despite that, I suspected this was a mama bear. She crossed the street without bothering to look both ways and advanced on Taylor. Still walking, he had precious little time before she was on him.

"Corbin." Taylor froze with his hand still outstretched but vibrating with a visible tremor. "What do I do?"

"Stay calm and come toward me. Whatever you do, don't turn your back on her."

He followed my instructions, but as soon as he moved a few feet away, he quickened his pace.

"Slowly!" I cried, keeping my voice pitched low. My warning was too late, and mama bear lumbered forward into a charge. "Never mind. Run!"

Taylor turned and bolted toward me. His head start was the only thing keeping him from being within reach of the claws chasing him. The people around us had no idea what was happening, and I didn't have any time to explain. Taylor reached my position, and I grabbed his arm, jumping to the side seconds before the bear could collide with us. Instead, she bowled into the rest of the protesters.

What happened next wouldn't make sense to anyone in the crowd. Bodies were thrown left and right, knocked down as the bear crashed through. She pulled up short, not seeing the mass of humanity, and only had eyes for Taylor and me.

"I thought you said they couldn't affect the real world?" Taylor asked, shock clear in his tone.

"I never said anything like that!" I yelled back, pulling us both to our feet and running in the opposite direction, away from the crowd. "She probably won't really hurt any of them, just bumps and bruises."

There was a weird equation when it came to things in the spirit world affecting the physical one. It was always possible but required its own expenditure of energy. The rage coming off the mother bear was enough to make her impact on our side of the world, but the veil between significantly reduced it.

Instead of a freight train, the shape cutting a swathe through the crowd would have been like a runaway bicycle or big person bumping into everyone and everything. There would be skinned knees and abrasions from falling, but unless she was truly intent on crossing over to do some damage, the bystanders were relatively safe, all things considered.

"What about us?" Taylor panted, running after me.

"That's different. You messed with her cub, and she wants to eat you. She'll make the extra effort, so we're fucked," I said, turning to see whether the bear was following us. I needed to lead her away from the group. Just because it wasn't likely she'd cause grievous injury didn't mean it was impossible.

Thankfully, mother nature had turned to lurch after us. I needed to get her out of downtown, and back toward wherever she had come from. The nearest woods were either East or West Rock Park. If we could get them moving, the pair might take the hint and follow us.

Nearly any animal on four legs could outpace a human easily, so I turned and planted myself instead.

Stretching my arms above my head in a Y, I yelled, "Hey, you!" I followed it with whatever random sounds came to the forefront of my mind when I sent the mental command "be scary" into the depths of my brain.

I augmented my appearance by projecting some essence into a bear-shaped bubble around my body. Unless I wanted to pay the piper in a serious fashion, I could only make myself appear about a foot taller than I was in the "real" world, but I hoped it was enough.

Black bears weren't usually the most dangerous kind, and you could usually scare them away pretty easily. This particular one pulled up short, dropping her loping gait. She reared back on her hind legs, matching my posture instead of being intimidated. We were still standing between her and her cub, so my gamble hadn't paid off how I wanted. The next attack had been delayed, not prevented.

There had to be some way to lure the bears out of the center of town, especially before the mother managed to cause any significant damage. I glanced at the protesters picking themselves off the ground. It appeared Nour's medic instinct had kicked in, and she was checking for injuries.

I had a terrible idea.

"Nour!" I called out. "Where's your car?"

She looked up from the knee she was examining and stared at me with pure confusion on her face. "What the hell is wrong with you? Why are you standing around like that?"

I stalked in a slow circle, the bear keeping in step with me. "It's an emergency! Please, I need to borrow it. It's hard to explain right now."

She pointed toward Chapel Street, which bordered the Green in the direction we had walked over from. "It's over there. Can you tell me later?"

The Fiat she drove was parked two hundred feet from where our standoff was happening. "Probably not. Throw me your keys!"

"Jesus Christ, Corbin, can you not come get–"

"EMERGENCY, NOUR."

She made a loud, disgusted sound, fished in her pocket, and threw the fob in my direction. Luck was finally with me. Nour's throwing arm was good, and I snatched the keychain out of the air before it whipped past.

"Taylor!" I yelled over my shoulder, having done another circle, putting my back to him and the cub. "You have to trust me."

"That sounds like what you say before doing something stupid."

"Yeah...about that." I turned and made a beeline toward the bear cub. Doing about the dumbest thing I could imagine, I used the energy flowing through my arms and picked up the cub. My only option was to sling it over my shoulder like a sack of potatoes. Its claws scrabbled at my clothing, but thankfully the barrier between the worlds kept me from most of the damage it would normally have done.

Whether or not Taylor followed me, I knew the mother would. There was no way I could run and outdistance her, so I made an about face and walked backward, still trying to make my presence as large as possible. "Come on, Mom!"

The bear was...confused. My threat display had kept her at bay, but now I was holding her baby. Primal rage filled her eyes, the muscles under her fur tensing to spring. My impromptu idiotic plan was about to fall apart and turn me into a bear-snack when Taylor yelled behind the mother. I looked past her bulk, and Taylor had done his best to copy what I had done, squeezing his essence into a messy shape around his body to distract the bear. He wasn't as precise, but the effort did what he needed it to do when her attention split, and she slowed. Having to choose which of us to turn into a chew toy first made her switch focus from one to the other.

Still carrying the bear, I pressed the lock button on the key fob until I was close enough to hear the beeps of the car. That was my cue, and I held down the panic button instead. The alarm roared to life, startling both the bears and the passing pedestrians, who were watching some weird mime carry an invisible sack over his shoulder.

The mother reared up again, glaring at the car behind me, but stopped her pursuit. I needed to turn and sprint to the fence surrounding the green. I attempted to hop it sideways and bashed my hips painfully against the hard metal of the railing but managed to swing my legs over and clear it.

I popped the trunk open and set the cub inside. He squirmed, but I laid my hand on his forehead, fingers sinking deeply into the fur between his eyes. I pressed my essence against his face, creating a mask of silver. "Sleep, friend." The young bear fought my compulsion but quickly succumbed. A wave of vertigo hit me as I closed the hatch, making me lean against it to keep myself from falling over. The alarm had stopped shrieking when I unlocked the car, and I glanced back at the park to find the mother bear was advancing again, Taylor still trying to distract her.

My feet found their way to the driver's side door, and I opened it before yelling, "Come on, Taylor!"

He must have heard me because he broke into a loping run, trying to swing wide of the bear. My play must have used up all the luck we had because a swiping paw caught him in the upper arm as he darted past. Taylor gasped in pain, holding his hand where he was struck. A red stain crept across his shirt sleeve as he continued to bolt for the car. I got into the driver's seat and pushed the ignition, the vehicle coming to life. The stereo blared a Lebanese pop song I hadn't heard before, and I pushed the passenger door open toward the sidewalk.

Taylor squeezed between the wide set rails of the fence instead of over. He wasn't carrying the bulk of a wild animal on his shoulder like I was, so he had an easier go of it. Mama bear came up short, stopped by the obstacle, and roared her displeasure. My eyes widened involuntarily as the bear backed up a few paces before charging and launching herself over the barrier.

The door slammed behind Taylor as he jumped into the passenger seat, and I put the car in gear before peeling away from the curb and pulling a U-turn to get onto the other side of Chapel Street. Horns blasted from every direction, despite my best attempt to time our escape correctly. The mother bear ran along the sidewalk and rounded the corner onto Church Street as I executed the same maneuver on the road. She was clearly intent on following us, which meant this part of my plan had worked.

"What the fuck, Corbin!"

Well, mostly worked. Taylor moved his hand away from his wound to examine it, and two bright lines of crimson slashed through his shirt. He was bleeding freely, though not enough that I worried about his immediate survival.

"Check the glove box for napkins," I said, "and try not to bleed on the upholstery."

"I appreciate the concern for my health and well-being, you asshole."

"You'll be fine. We'll get you patched up. You're lucky she wasn't on our side of the veil or you might be down an arm."

A glance into the rearview mirror showed me the mother was following and, more terrifying, matching the pace of the car.

He grunted in agreement. "You don't look so hot yourself."

I was sweating. The vertigo had mostly passed, but the expenditure of energy I made to put our passenger to sleep cost me. "I'll be fine, just running on less than a full tank."

Now that I had the bear following us out of downtown, I had to figure out where to bring her. We were closest to East Rock, but the woods there didn't extend to any large green spaces unless you counted the Quinnipiac River Marsh, which was still surrounded by the city. West Rock would have to be the place. If we could keep mama bear moving westward, the two of them would have the entirety of Woodbridge, which would be teeming with energy. Hopefully, they would never come back downtown again.

We swung left on Grove Street, took it until Goffe and then Crescent Street, which brought us most of the way. The ride that followed was one of the most harrowing of my life. I wasn't aware, but black bears could run up to thirty-five miles per hour. It was a complicated accordion-like dance where I would speed up to get distance from the bear, then slow or stop to follow traffic signals and signs and sweat nervously until I could accelerate again.

The number of red lights I blew through or stop signs that only got the barest acknowledgement before I rolled through them were distinctly non-zero. Cars honked their anger at me, but thankfully no police were on the route we took to get to West Rock Park. By the time we passed through the SCSU campus and hit Wintergreen Street, where the park would be, my knuckles were white and aching from gripping the steering wheel.

Taylor's gashes had responded to the pressure from a wad of napkins, and he was looking to be in better spirits. We had ridden in silence, but he turned to me as I took a left down the lane leading into the park.

"What do we do now?"

"Follow my lead," I said, checking the mirrors again to confirm we still had our hanger-on. I pulled off to the side of the road, past the unmanned gate house. The tires crunched over the stones as we slowed to a stop. As soon as I threw the car into park, I pushed the door open and ran around to the trunk and popped the hatch.

The cub was still asleep, but the mask I had placed on him was almost used up. I hadn't intended it to last forever, so I pulled what remained into myself. The baby bear stretched and groaned, opening his eyes and looking past me at his mom, who I had seen approaching at speed before we made the turn into the drive. I didn't interfere when he hopped from his spot in the trunk. Taylor waited for me in the center of the slim road, so I joined him. Crossing my fingers, I watched to see whether the reunion was going to be enough to get her off our backs.

The mother ran up on her cub, bowling him over lightly in her haste. She snuffled his fur for a few moments, obviously inspecting him for injuries. Once complete, she fixed her gaze on us, her brow heavy with focus. She set her paws firmly in our direction and scraped a back foot against the pavement before charging. Clearly, she held a grudge and was about to take it out on us.

My vertigo was gone. The small amount of essence I had reabsorbed put me closer to normal, but I wasn't at my best. Raising my arms above my head, I bulked out my spiritual appearance again but couldn't reach the same height as before.

"Taylor!" I barked, glancing at the side, and he was copying me again. "Give me your hand!"

He reached out hesitantly, wincing in pain from the cut oozing on his shoulder. "Why?"

"No time! You need to trust me." I grabbed him before he could consider pulling back. "This won't hurt much," I said and combined his essence with mine.

It was a complex concept in the least stressful of times, and a crash course in group work wasn't what I had originally planned for the day, but I didn't have much of a choice. Taylor gasped as copper threads streamed down his arm and up mine, blending our energy into an alloy of rose-gold. My bear-shaped construct grew around us both until we were a towering ursine specimen, glowing brightly in the spirit lands.

I stepped forward and planted one foot in front of me before gathering a roar deep in my chest, letting it out with exhausted fury. Mama stopped in her tracks, ears lowered and eyes wide in surprise. She halted her run and circled back to her cub, nudging him toward the woods and off the road. We stood there, me panting and Taylor looking vaguely ill, until we lost sight of the pair.

The essence I borrowed from Taylor sang in my veins, but I couldn't let it sustain me. Slowly, I flowed his power through our connected hands until we were each whole again. Well, mostly whole since I had been running on less than a full tank since the Green.

I let my grip slacken, and he pulled his hand away. Without speaking, we went to our respective sides of the car and got in.

"So..." I said. "That went well."

Chapter 10

We sat on the outdoor patio behind Mamoun's. Nour was tending to Taylor's wound while I devoured a chicken shawarma sandwich. The food was good all the time, but my earlier efforts turned it into one of the most delicious meals I had ever tasted. It was later in the season, and we were the only people on the patio, but we holed up in the back corner anyway. This was probably a health code violation, so no need to bring attention to ourselves.

"What happened to you two?" Nour asked, pulling another wound closure strip to line up the torn skin of Taylor's upper arm.

Taylor looked at me as if to say, "You tell her."

I stuffed another bite into my mouth to buy time while I came up with a suitable lie and swallowed heavily before replying. "Stray dog."

She stared at me, then moved her gaze to Taylor's arm, and back to me. "That's a tall dog."

"He fell down," I added, nodding sagely, giving Taylor some side-eye until he nodded in agreement. "We needed to get it off the Green before it started biting people."

The skepticism in her eyes didn't fade, but she seemed to accept the explanation. "My car better not have fleas, Corbin."

I raised my hands in surrender. "There isn't a scratch on it." Which was an accurate statement. All the scratches were on Taylor and me. I hadn't suffered any significant injury, but the flannel I had been wearing would need some mending, and small claw marks had perforated various parts of my torso from my rambunctious furry toddler. The mirror in the restaurant's bathroom helped me assess my own minor injuries while I washed up, after we dropped the car off. The restrooms were smaller than New York City efficiency apartments, so there would be more to find the next time I showered.

"What did we miss?" I asked, tucking back into my meal.

Nour blew out a breath and returned to her first-aid task. "Nothing more serious than some abrasions, but the protest broke up pretty soon after that. Rumors were going around. Some people said a wild animal was running around. Others thought some crazy person was going around assaulting people." She gave me a flat look.

"Weird," I said, not offering anything else.

"Anyway," Nour continued, "I think we'll see more protests coming up. I checked the response period. It ends in thirty days, then there's a special session with the city officials to address any issues. Want to bet it's just a bunch of hand-waving?"

I had polished off the sandwich and was sipping a cup of hot tea. "You mean to make everyone feel like they've been heard, but they were going to move forward with it, regardless?"

"Sounds about right to me." She finished wrapping some self-adhesive bandage over a piece of gauze around Taylor's arm. "All right, my friend. You should be all set."

"Thanks," he said.

"Standard disclaimers. I am not a doctor. You should get it looked at by a professional. All that jazz."

"I'll be fine." He rubbed lightly at her handiwork.

"Unless the dog had rabies." I winked. "But he just seemed angry, not 'mad.'"

Nour glared at me before packing her medical kit and walking into the restaurant, leaving Taylor and I alone.

"I need to check something before we head back to campus," I said, getting up from the table and tossing my trash in the bin. Taylor followed me without question as I made my way to the lamppost on the corner. The same one where I had repaired my spiritual invisible fence the other night.

Crouching by the base, I checked for my sigil, and it had been scratched out completely. I swore under my breath, standing with a pop from my knees. It had been a long day, and my body was trying to tell me something. There were going to be miles before I rested, though.

"What are you looking for?" Taylor finally asked, standing with his hands in his pockets.

"There's a kind of barrier I've been maintaining around the campus. It keeps the fauna out of the area and away from the kids who might want to harvest their essence. But someone tampered with this part for a second time. I've got a bad feeling about the rest of it."

We walked the ten blocks back to the garage, where we had originally parked for the day. Taylor's face was pale, clearly wrung out from his effort and injuries. Channeling that much energy for a new practitioner wasn't easy either.

"Did I do well?" Taylor asked, as we were about to part ways and head to our cars.

I managed a short laugh, not having the energy for more than that myself. "You were great. You copied me well. The rest of it will come with practice."

"When you drew that power from me…" He trailed off, rubbing his arm absentmindedly. "I think I understand why people steal from the surrounding environment. That was not a good feeling, being drained like that."

"It's also why some practitioners work together. I didn't have to use it up, but I needed to borrow it to shape our appearance." I put my hand on his shoulder. "Trust me when I say I wouldn't have taken anything from you that you couldn't have spared, if it came down to it."

Taylor nodded. "Thanks. And I do. Trust you, that is."

The smile that crept across my mouth was genuine. "I'm glad. Are you going to make it home okay? I'm going to make a turn around the area to check my other markers, but you should get some rest."

"I'll be fine," he said. "Unless spirit bears really can get rabies."

"Good. And no, they can't. You don't get to skip class tomorrow."

Taylor stared at me with a deadpan expression. I was the one who encouraged him to miss class for the protest, after all.

"Maybe it wasn't the best idea I ever had today," I admitted. "But look on the bright side! We'll probably be in the newspaper tomorrow. Now *that's* history in the making."

Taylor left with a groan, and I made my way back to the street to start my patrol, checking my "tin cans" as Hughes called them. The first problem with using small pieces of magic to ring an area was there was a lot to inspect. The second was that as soon as I started my bad feelings were justified. As I walked around the campus, none of my wards were intact. They were scraped off, defaced, or painted over. The physical act of interference was enough to bleed the energy out of them.

It was dark when I had finished making my circuit, confirming that none of the spiritual signposts had survived. Hopefully, all the spirit life had spent enough time avoiding the area that it would be second nature for them, but I was concerned about a sudden influx of animals that would need redirecting out of downtown.

I returned to my car and drove home, then clomped up the stairs. Standing in the middle of the kitchen, I stared at the fridge. I didn't need to open it to remember I was low on groceries. My shoulders ached and the fresh scabs on my chest and back still stung. Two minutes later, I dropped into the taproom next door for a burger and a beer. My stomach had been growling at me for the past hour, and I had been chased by a bear. I deserved a dinner I didn't have to cook for myself and to soothe my nerves with a drink.

The burger was as delicious as the shawarma sandwich earlier. Needing to replenish my personal stores continued to make everything taste better. I was halfway through it when Harriet sat on the stool next to me at the bar.

"*Saygo*, cousin. Saw you walking by the shop," Harriet said while signaling the bartender.

"Harriet," I replied. "You get the paper today?"

She let out a deep sigh. "Yep. Sure did."

We sat in silence for a minute. I continued mowing through my meal, and she ordered her own beer.

"So much for your theory on how much time we had," I finally said.

Harriet laughed, and it was a rueful sound. "Yeah. I jinxed us, didn't I?"

"No one ever said doing the right thing would be easy."

"True, nobody has. I guess you should get to work then."

I gave a weak chuckle. "Can I at least finish my burger first?"

She plucked a fry off my plate and dipped it in ketchup before popping it into her mouth. "I suppose you'll need to keep your strength up."

I was exhausted from our encounter with the mama bear and spent the next day resting in a contemplative haze. Nothing productive happened, but I tried to use the time to consider my options. I managed to teach my lesson the next day, but it certainly wasn't my best. Taylor didn't come to class, but he wasn't an actual student of mine, so I didn't take offense.

The rest of the week passed in a blur, and I made a short downhill slide to the weekend. The weather did that fall thing in New England where it was balmy in the daytime and the first taste of bitter chill at night. I worried, briefly, about the homeless downtown, but they had their own strategies to survive the real winter. That made me more concerned about the viability of one of their green spaces. Not that the charities couldn't serve the community elsewhere, but the potential change was a shock to morale too. When you had a place that you spent time at regularly, losing it might throw you off significantly.

My weekend was split between the necessities of modern life, those being my paying side jobs, and researching the issues surrounding the development of the Green. The problem with the Green being privately owned for as long as it had been was I couldn't find any significant precedent for preserving the space. Especially since their plans took the historic building into account already.

An attorney friend of mine, Dave, worked on ecological projects for preservation societies in the state, and I made a point to reach out to him. I hoped being friends with the people I went to protests with would continue to pay off. Unfortunately, he didn't have any advice either. The story had crossed his desk, but he said it was likely an open and shut case.

Even if we raised enough money to hire a lawyer to file some paperwork to get the project stalled, that was all it would do. We needed a permanent solution, but unless we found a loophole somewhere, the case was going to end in the developer's favor. He told me to reach out to him if I got any real leads, and he'd do the same, but his docket was full of issues he had a prayer of doing something about.

Monday rolled around, and I was working with Harriet at the shop, going through some new antiques she got in from out of state. It was long bouts of companionable silence broken occasionally by conversation. I had told her about my conversation with Dave, but it took an hour for her to develop her thoughts on the matter.

"So, I used to have this ecology teacher in high school," she said.

"I am desperately curious where this is going," I replied, making notes on what might be some genuine early-Victorian cameo brooches.

She gave me a generous helping of side-eye but went on. "This guy, he was one of those early eco warriors in the eighties. Before he settled down and became a teacher, that is. He used to get into all sorts of trouble, but he told me about something he did one time to stop a bunch of developers." She nodded to herself and settled back into cataloging her own work for a few minutes.

I dropped my pen and gawked at her. "You can't just leave me hanging like that, Harriet."

"Oh?" She looked up from her papers. "Were you interested? I couldn't tell. You know, storytellers prefer a responsive audience."

Turning my body to face hers, I placed my hands studiously in my lap. "Please continue your story, Boss."

Harriet sucked her teeth in obvious displeasure. "I guess I deserved that." She put down her pencil, cracked her knuckles, and cleared her throat. "But there was this developer, see? They were planning to turn a huge chunk of land near the high school into condominiums. It was well past his younger days of chaining himself to trees and that sort of thing, but he still wanted to do something to stop them. Problem was, they had all the right permits. Everything was on the up-and-up. They were set to break ground in three months, but he was determined to get the project canceled."

My passing interest had turned into fully rapt attention. "What did he do?"

"Well, he let his younger spirit free but armed it with the years of knowledge he had gained since becoming an instructor."

"What does that mean?"

"Who's telling this story, hm?" Harriet huffed at me.

I ducked my head a little in apology. "Sorry, please continue."

She grinned. "At least I know I've got your attention now. I told you he taught ecology, right? One surefire way to get your development stopped in this state is to try to build on wetlands. But the surveys they did showed no signs of those types of plants. They had the green light." Harriet paused, clearly for effect.

"But..." I added, motioning for her to continue.

"But they underestimated the persistence of one high school teacher. In the dead of night, for over a week, he transplanted wetlands plants native to the area across their site. Then, for the next two weeks, he checked on them to make sure they had taken root."

"Did they?" I asked excitedly.

Harriet's grin widened, and she had a wicked gleam in her eyes. "When the local inspector got an anonymous tip that the developer had lied on their ecological survey, he threw a fit. The company was required to get another study done, and this time it came back that there were previously undocumented wetland plants throughout the planned development."

"Holy shit, it worked?"

Harriet nodded sagely. "At least for a while. The rest is lost to history."

"Is that just a dramatic way of saying you don't remember?"

She clicked her tongue at me. "Is that how you talk to an elder sharing a story?"

"You're not that old, Harriet."

"I'll take that as a compliment. But no, he never told us what happened next. I think he enjoyed telling us the tale as much as I did stringing you along."

I considered what Harriet had just told me, and unfortunately it wasn't feasible to transplant wetlands onto the Green. It was even less likely anyone would believe they were supposed to be there. "It's a great story, but I don't know how it helps. I doubt I could do anything similar on the Green."

"Yeah, that's true. Shame there isn't anything else that would stop a developer. Something they'd have to do a lot of study on before making any hasty decisions about breaking ground."

I eyed her with a furrowed brow. "Am I being too obtuse to understand what you're trying to tell me right now?"

"You're the archaeologist. You tell me. I just deal in antiques."

Chapter 11

Harriet's wish for an excuse to stop the development, coupled with the story she told me, had my brain spinning. There were too many threads, and I couldn't keep track of them. The two dead bodies still concerned me, but there hadn't been any new activity. I was torn. One part of me wanted Hughes to be right, that there was no pattern and I was being paranoid. The other was sure a growing issue was surrounding the deaths so far.

Jake promised to put his ear to the ground and let me know if anything else weird went down. He also helped circulate a picture of the woman who had died over by Sleeping Giant, but there were no leads on her identity among the locals. The papers didn't even write an obituary or article. My assumption about the track marks on her arm leading to an anonymous death panned out.

I rolled into Tuesday, lost in a fog despite it being a teaching day. The course was progressing through our segment on native settlements and the history of colonization. Their first paper was due, and I was procrastinating on starting my grading with everything going on. The stack stared at me, peeking out of my satchel on the desk, as a spirited discussion moved around the room.

The material spanned North America, not just the Northeast where I had started our discussions the week prior, so the conversation ranged far afield as my mind was stuck inside a square mile.

Watching the dynamics of any given group of students was interesting, as they developed their own opinions about the material and each other.

These kinds of classes would be relatively split. On one side were students who felt colonization was good for the continent. Invariably they have a connection to European heritage or simply grew up with a world view that capitalism and global commerce were the best medicine. Therefore, colonial rule led to the lives we have today. I wasn't there to judge them, despite holding distinctly opposite views.

The other side of the coin was those who understood the impact colonialism had on the native tribes. Puritan culture, being a large part of early settlements, drove the perception of the "heathen" natives and ultimately led to how they were treated. There was also growing anti-capitalist sentiment in a lot of students, driven by the political landscape of the United States. I wasn't there to support them over their counterparts, having to play devil's advocate despite my own beliefs.

At the moment, Beth and John were arguing about the particular merits and flaws of their opposing viewpoints. They were two of my more outspoken students, for entirely different reasons. It was getting heated and somewhat off topic, but the debate had started with the course material. I tried not to stifle those kinds of discussions unless people started being outright rude to each other. They tended to burn themselves out, and the students were able to practice their critical thinking and debate skills without me shutting them down.

"You can't tell me Native Americans didn't benefit from European trade goods, Beth," John said.

"Did they also benefit from the smallpox blankets, *John*?" she asked sarcastically.

I held my hands up. "Time out. While I appreciate the zeal, we don't talk about Manifest Destiny until much later in the course. Western expansion didn't start until the early 1800s, and we're not there yet. Let's at least keep the vitriolic arguments in the right place of the syllabus."

Beth huffed, but John gave a triumphant smile as if my refereeing had awarded a point in his favor.

"If you're going to make that kind of reference," I continued, "it would be better to point to the fact that while trade with the New Englanders benefited many of the natives, they were also sold the tools that would be used to kill and enslave each other more efficiently."

John's smile faded. "That's inevitable when you introduce new technology, though, isn't it?"

I sighed, then hid my face in the cup of cowboy coffee I had brewed myself that morning. There was always at least one John in every class, so committed to the importance of advancing knowledge that the ends always justified the means. "Tell that to the Wampanoag. We talked about the Pequot War, but next class we'll discuss King Philip's war, which began in 1675. Has anyone read ahead enough to tell me what started the conflict?"

Despite my expectation that Beth would raise her hand, John answered. "Plymouth colony executed some people from that tribe, right?"

I raised a surprised eyebrow but gave a few small claps. "Well done, Mr. Fitch. And that was only the beginning."

"All of New England is built on native burial grounds," Beth said with a hint of finality.

"That's a little hyperbolic, Beth…" I trailed off, the fuzziness around the edges of my brain sharpening into focus. "But you're not entirely wrong," I said, almost to myself, then went silent for a minute while the class stared at me.

"Professor Pierce? Is everything okay?" Michael asked.

"Yeah...it might be." I shook my head to clear it, then turned back to the class. "I'll have your papers returned to you by next week with some feedback. Make sure you do the required reading. John is your surprising example for the day. Class dismissed."

Harriet's story about her ecology teacher spun in my head, and it took all my composure to not run down the hall to the computer lab as soon as the room cleared. I cursed myself for leaving my laptop on my desk at home. Yes, I could have done the small amount of research I needed on my phone, but something about having a desktop with as many tabs open as I wanted appealed to me more than punching queries into a tiny screen.

Beth's hyperbole had struck like lightning, and within moments of my ass hitting the seat in front of the computer, I was searching for a news article I remembered from the early aughts. The New Haven Green held many secrets, and one of the least talked about was the number of bodies buried underneath it. Not only had it been used as a legitimate cemetery, but there were rumors of smallpox victims being buried there anonymously.

A large effort in 1821 moved the gravestones to the now-famous Grove Street Cemetery. But I said what I said. The *gravestones* had been moved but not what lay under them. How many? The bones of over four thousand people were interred in those sixteen acres.

My fingers flew over the keys, and I scrolled until I had at least five tabs open with various articles regarding an incident after Hurricane Sandy in October 2012. A famous tree, the "Lincoln Oak", fell during the storm, and its upturned roots unearthed portions of skeletons they had grown around. An archaeological effort to investigate the remains happened, but as they were hundreds of years old, there was little to learn beyond the relative health and age of the deceased.

But I had an idea, and it might be a long shot. Back in 1990, the administration at the time passed the "Native American Grave Protection and Repatriation Act" or NAGPRA. In a nutshell, it provided redress to Native tribes and to have their grave items returned to them.

It also applied to remains found in excavation and other digging projects. The Green wasn't state-owned land, so it wasn't cut-and-dry. If I could prove any of the remains buried under the Green were Native, I could at least stall the project while they conducted a proper investigation to comply with the federal regulation. If my hunch proved true, it might kill the project.

The most important part of all of this was the rumor that the bones recovered as part of the dig after the hurricane hadn't been reburied. There were less than two weeks until the hearing, where the community would respond to the proposed plans to build on the Green. It was doubtful I could get access to them through official channels, and more than likely bringing it to anyone's attention meant a quick trip back into the ground somewhere to wash their hands of the issue entirely.

Imagining a Venn diagram of fraud, trespassing, and theft, I wasn't sure where I expected myself to land yet. But I knew who I had to call. The phone rang as I walked through the halls toward my car.

"Corbin Pierce, as I live and breathe!"

Katie's voice was as cheerful as always. We met years ago at a rally in New York City that drew thousands of people from across the East Coast. Her main base of operations was in West Virginia, and she came complete with an Appalachian accent fit to rival a coal miner. Looks were deceiving because she was a self-professed "old school anti-establishment redneck." The kind with an acoustic guitar sporting "this machine kills fascists" and a backlist of survival skills necessary for any serious protest action.

"Hi, Katie, I need a favor."

"Shoot, don't you still owe me for that little tussle in New Jersey?"

I sighed heavily into the phone. "How long have we been friends? Aren't we past tit-for-tat?"

"No." The word hung heavily in the electrons separating us.

"What about Buffalo?" I asked.

Katie didn't reply immediately, her soft breathing the only thing coming through the speaker. "Damn, I thought you'd forgotten about that. All right, is this your kind of problem or mine?"

She was talking about magic. Katie knew about my talents. Her own grandmother was sensitive and practiced old folk magic, so I never felt the need to hide it from her. It also came in handy that she accepted my abilities at face value, as it made everything easier to explain.

"Probably yours," I offered. "I don't have all the details yet, but it's important and time sensitive."

Katie whistled a sharp, piercing tone. "You need me in person?"

"It'd be hard to get this done otherwise, so yeah."

"Is it a felony?" Her tone made her seem interested, which belied the question.

"Uh, I don't know?"

"Because I don't cross state lines for anything that isn't a felony anymore. Just not worth the time."

I should have mentioned Katie was a bit of an adrenaline junkie. The more dangerous and complicated the situation was, the better for her. It didn't always make for the cleanest execution of a plan, but it was never boring.

"I'm asking for a favor, Katie," I huffed. "Call it an appeal to your good nature and altruism. Make an exception. It might not net you a felony charge, but it'll poke some important people in the eye."

"Hm. All right. Tell me what you're getting us into this time."

It didn't take long to give Katie the rundown on what my thin version of a plan was. Step one: Find out where the bones were. Step two: Gain access to them and gather a sample for genetic testing. Step three: Call in a favor with a friend of mine to get that lab work done on priority. Step four: Owe a different favor to my attorney friend, Dave, to file some paperwork. Step five: Uh...we win, I think.

"Give me a day or two to make some calls and see if I can find out where they stored them after the initial workup," I said, "and we'll know how complicated this is going to be."

"I accept your proposed potential snooze fest."

"Very funny. If it's in the archaeology department, I may not even need your help."

"But..." she said, stretching the word.

"They could have been moved somewhere else, with more security."

"You're getting warmer. All right, stranger, text me when you've got something."

Sometimes the make-or-break part of a plan was whether you could get through the first step. I sat at my desk in the apartment, laptop open and cell phone primed. For all my sudden zeal, I was exhausted. The idea of talking to people and ferreting out the location of the bones made my skin crawl. That was the other problem with plans. I wanted to just "go" instead of slogging through the legwork. But it was unavoidable.

I picked up my cell and scrolled through my contacts until I found Jennifer Santos, the state archaeologist. Yes, states had archaeologists. Who else would deal with the random reports about finding "a human skull in my backyard"? They were also the experts on laws and regulations pertaining to the subject, which was more the bulk of their work than random discoveries. If I ever found a femur buried in the park, Jen was the first person I'd contact.

We weren't exactly friendly but were at least professional acquaintances. I'd never had the occasion to get on her bad side, and every once in a blue moon we met for lunch with other professionals in the state. It wasn't a huge talent pool, and it was worth the effort to network. You never knew what you were going to need. Like right now.

"Jen! Hey, it's Corbin. Just calling to ask you about something if you've got a minute." I checked my watch, and it was midafternoon, so she was probably still in the office. "In at least a semi-professional capacity too."

"Hi, Corbin. Nice to hear from you! I hope they're not working you too hard at GCC." She chuckled lightly, which I didn't take offense to. Jen was a supporter of the community college system in Connecticut, so it was only light ribbing.

"Not yet anyway."

"What've you got? You caught me at a good time."

I didn't expect Jen to be involved in any capacity with what the Hand was doing. She wasn't a Yale alumni or a particular friend of Hughes's, from what I remembered, but I wanted to be circumspect with my question. The good news was my class really had provided suitable cover for bringing it up.

"Do you remember when Hurricane Sandy knocked that tree over in New Haven and exposed some skeletal remains?"

"Oh, yeah, it was a hoot. I wasn't working for the state back then. I was in the Midwest, but everyone heard about it. It wasn't exactly national news, but you news travels about that kind of thing in the community. What about it?"

"I'm teaching a one-hundred level course going through the late 1800s, and one of my students brought it up. They were curious about what happened to the bones after they had been recovered. I said that they were probably reburied, but if they're still kicking around, I'd love to organize something with my class to check them out."

The line was silent for a second longer than made me comfortable, but Jen's tone was casual when she finally replied. "That sounds like a neat idea. Let me make a couple calls—"

"Uh, Jen," I broke in. "Could you do me a favor and not mention my name?"

"Why not?"

I tried to sound contrite. "Well, Yale was involved in the dig, and I'm not exactly a favorite person in their archaeology department."

"Ooohhhh," she said. "Still pissing Hughes off?"

The blush creeping up my neck was real. "How sweet. You remembered."

She laughed loudly enough into her receiver that I had to pull the phone away from my ear. "Hard to forget that dinner. You two were shooting daggers at each other all night. If looks could kill, you'd both be dead."

"Yeah, so you understand why? My students shouldn't suffer from my interpersonal woes."

"I get it, don't worry. I don't have to mention you."

"You're a saint. Thank you."

"Saints are dead, Pierce."

I laughed. "Fine, you can be a miracle worker instead."

"I'll email you if I find anything."

And with that, we ended the call. It was mostly a white lie. It's possible I would tell my students about it, if they were in an accessible place. Jen was a decent person, and I didn't want her to get embroiled in any of my nonsense either.

I went upstairs to make a sandwich and coffee for myself, then headed back to my perch to keep putting out feelers. It was an hour later, and I had authored multiple emails and made some additional phone calls, netting nothing more than positive noises and a few commitments to do the bare minimum and call me if they found anything.

I'd hit the end of my attention span for that particular activity, and the lid of my laptop was half closed before a "ding" alerted me about a new email. I flipped it back open, scanned the recipients, and had a message from Jen waiting for me.

Hey Corbin,

I needed a break, so I looked into what you asked about. Turns out they were transferred to the Yale Peabody Museum to be part of an exhibit about Connecticut. Sounds like your students can go check the display out themselves!

Hitting an unexpected bullseye on a shot in the dark meant step one was complete. Knowing my usual luck, this will have been the easiest part, and the rest would be exponentially more complicated. There was only one way to find out.

Chapter 12

"A museum?" Katie had asked, grinning ear to ear once I told her where we would be going. "This is gonna be fun!"

When I texted her the night before that I knew where the bones were, she said she'd already packed her car and would be on the way to New Haven in the morning. I tried to dissuade her from making the trip on such short notice, but she insisted I'd need her to plan the whole thing.

It was ten o'clock in the morning when the buzzer for my apartment went off, and I ran downstairs to admit a five-foot-two firecracker into the building. Katie cut a solid figure, with a svelte form and muscled arms to rival any casual gym rat. She styled her red hair in a short pixie cut, showing off earrings, which climbed up both her lobes. She wore tomboy chic with ripped jeans and a red flannel that screamed "country".

There was a backpack over one of her shoulders, with what I presumed were some clothes in it. What Katie did for a living never really came up in conversation, and I didn't ask. But she was always down to drop what she was doing for a cause. She had slept on my couch once before, traveling up to New Hampshire for some kind of political action I wasn't involved in, so I knew she traveled light.

I brought us back upstairs and set out coffee as we discussed the situation. "Don't get ahead of yourself. If it's fun, then we're probably doing something wrong."

"Corbin, baby, you're cute when you talk like you've done this kind of thing before."

My flat glare was met with a sweet-as-pie smile.

"And you have?" I asked.

Katie said nothing, but her smile grew wider.

"Fine. It'll be *fun*." I grumped at her.

"That's better," she said, patting my hand as I set a mug of coffee in front of her.

The next phase of Operation Corbin is a Big Dumb Idiot was to access the remains and retrieve a sample, which sounded simpler than it was likely to be.

"I figure we should go check out the museum today." I suggested. "See what we're up against."

"Fine with me, darlin'." She sipped her coffee and winked at me over the rim.

Katie was a notorious flirt, but that was as far as it ever went. I was always happy to trade both barbs and passes but knew where we drew the line. Not that I would have minded if she was actually interested in me, but that type of connection didn't seem to be high on either of our priorities.

We spent the morning catching up on each other's lives. Katie had traveled around the country for most of the summer supporting various nonprofit and anti-fascist organizations as a kind of digital nomad. That explained a bit about how she made rent while still bouncing around like a rubber ball from place to place. Apparently, her grandmother had asked after me when Katie told her she was coming up my way. She re-extended an invitation she'd made previously for me to visit and learn some hill-folk magic. I squirreled that away for consideration when I wasn't neck-deep in other problems.

I told Katie a bit about my current woes and the unexplained deaths I'd encountered. She was sympathetic, always having a soft spot for both the temporarily and permanently displaced. Homelessness was a big problem in coal country, and she wore her heart on her sleeve.

"I would've done this for you as a favor, 'cuz you asked," Katie said. "But if it's spittin' in the eye of a bunch of rich folks, I'm in double now."

"Thanks, Katie. It means a lot. Why don't we go case a museum?"

"Lookit you, gettin' all heisty."

We took my car and headed downtown and onto Whitney Avenue, eventually pulling into the parking lot of the facility proper. I had to give them credit. The Peabody was a beautiful museum, and they had recently undergone a large renovation. Entry was free, which was good for both my wallet and for a lack of paper trail connecting me to the museum I wanted to...borrow something from.

Heavy-looking security doors protected the entrance, complete with serious locks. I glanced at Katie. Her eyes narrowed when she saw what I had already scoped out. She shook her head slightly before we crossed the threshold into the building.

It was fall and getting colder, so wandering the halls in baseball caps and long coats, like Katie and I were doing, wasn't going to call any attention to ourselves. We played the part of good tourists and took in the whole place. We spent a few hours slowly wending our way from the giant dinosaur skeletons to the exhibits on various points in history toward our intended target.

Cameras were all over the place, which was no surprise. I had some ideas of what to do about that, if we could figure out how to gain access after-hours. When we finally came upon the "History of New Haven" exhibit, the diorama was protected by thick glass, looking into a small room with multiple plinths showing off various artifacts.

The only one I had eyes for was a pedestal holding some fragments of bone, likely from a femur or other large limb. A small white card affixed to the surface next to it proclaimed that the remains were as expected, from beneath the Lincoln Oak on the New Haven Green, unearthed during Hurricane Sandy. They were attributed to an unknown family of European origin.

Giving credit where it was due, the Peabody had a public and proven commitment to NAGPRA. Reasonable decisions had been made, otherwise they would have already returned the remains to the relevant tribe. I just had to hope their assumptions were wrong. If I could provide a credible reason to test the bones, they'd probably do it themselves, but I didn't have the time to waste. There was also no reason for them to believe my theory, so I had to give them some proof.

I swore under my breath. The small, enclosed space had a door controlled by keycard access. Katie's furrowed brow told me she was having the same thoughts. This wasn't a movie, and I wasn't a skilled hacker. I didn't know whether hacking worked like it did on TV, anyway. Even if we could get into the building, the room itself was going to be a problem.

A faint mechanical sound caught my attention, and currents of warm air stirred the hem of my long jacket. At the base of the wall, between two exhibits, was a small air duct, about one foot square. My gaze moved back to the exhibit, and I examined the interior.

Set into the floor, near the rear wall, was an identical grate. The wheels turned in my mind, and I spun to face Katie.

"I have an idea," we both said at the same time.

I laughed and gestured for us to head to the exit. "You first."

"Let me work my magic for a bit. Gotta make sure all the details hash out."

"That's my job," I protested.

"Not that kind, my own brand. I'm a people-person. Gotta go see a man about a horse. What about you?"

"Mine is probably stranger than yours. I...need to commune with nature for a little while."

When we got back to the apartment, it was twilight. The conversation on the way home consisted of Katie confidently expressing she could get us into the museum after hours. I was less sure but at least hopeful that I had a plan to break into the exhibit itself to take a sample of the remains.

Katie quickly broke a laptop out of her bag and sat on the couch with that, her phone, and a sense of purpose on her face. I had a different task ahead of me, which sounded much more ridiculous when I thought about it. Pushing the self-doubt aside, I let myself out of the building and walked across the street to the park.

Instead of stopping at the outside edges, I strode down an open path toward the heart of the park, though I kept closer to the tree line. The paper bag I carried in my right hand gave off a light warmth in the cooling evening. Katie had put up with the pit stop on the way back because I bought her a sandwich and introduced her to Nour. The two of them hit it off in the ten minutes we were waiting for our takeout, so it seemed a worthwhile side trip on multiple fronts.

Opening my senses, I breathed in the crisp air. The fading light of day turned into brilliant purples and golds, helping me imagine what the sunset was like when the world was young. I strolled until I came to Iris Pond and left the shelter of the trees to approach the edge. The water was marshy with reeds and spotted with over-grown patches of knotweed. I sat on a convenient rock and took a moment to appreciate the solitude. Parks weren't a popular place to be after dark in the city. Technically, I wasn't supposed to be there either, but unless I made a nuisance of myself, I was unlikely to be noticed.

I closed my eyes and stretched my essence outward in a thin wave, feeling for other living things. The trees and plants all pinged slightly against my mind, but I could ignore them as background noise. Eventually I found what I was looking for, though it might be fairer to say he found me. Just as my outstretched feelers brushed against something bigger than a breadbox, the shining eyes of my once-rescued friend stared at me. I was out in the open, but he was nestled in the anonymity of the tall grass ringing the glen.

I rustled the bag before taking a french fry out of it and tossing it ten feet away from me, in the raccoon's direction. He stepped hes-itantly into the cut grass, creeping to the morsel I offered. Stuffing it into his mouth, he retreated halfway to his former hiding place. His tiny teeth chewed furiously, the small tongue licking salt from his snout.

This was where my scheme got complicated. My less than half-formed plan made some heavy assumptions. The raccoon, who I realized I couldn't just keep calling "Raccoon" if this worked, wasn't only a wild animal. He was a native spirit to the land. In Algonquian, he would be called an *arakun*, "he scratches with his hands".

He existed solidly in both the physical world and the spirit one beside it. Did that make him special? To an extent, yes. Much like the mama bear was a prime specimen of its species, solely in the spirit world, this animal was more than his slightly simpler earthly counterparts. Was he smarter than his brethren? I was about to find out.

I took a small bundle of tobacco out of my bag along with a shell, set the leaf atop the curved dish, and pushed a scrap of energy into the offering. Striking a match might startle my guest, so I lit it gently with a lighter instead. Modern convenience made more sense for earning trust.

Fanning the wisp of smoke in his direction, I tossed another fry into the space between us. His nose twitched, and he slunk closer again, picking up the golden treat and nibbling on it. He sat on his haunches and breathed deeply. The fragment of myself I had placed into the tobacco swirled in a winding path until it disappeared into his black nostrils.

My voice was calm, and I adopted a slow cadence like the one I would use with a child. "I'm going to call you Scratch, okay?"

His pupils flitted from me to the bag in my hands and back again, but he didn't move from his squat. I picked up a small stick, placed another shard of energy into it, and threw it to Scratch's left. He watched it fly but returned his gaze to me and the sack.

Pushing another wave of energy outward in his direction, I concentrated on mental images of Scratch holding the stick and returning it to me. A sense of helpfulness, the warmth of a job well done spreading through his stomach.

"I need your help. Bring me the stick, please? And I'll give you a reward." It wasn't so much the words I used as the tone behind them. I pointed at the stick, then shook the fry bag. Stick. Fries. Stick...

Scratch's eyes narrowed in an oddly human expression, but he sidled over to the stick, not taking his gaze off me. He grabbed it, then crab-walked back to where he had been sitting and placed it in front of himself. I patted the ground in front of me. "Bring it here."

He picked the stick up again and hesitantly approached my perch, dropping it onto the earth where I had indicated but scampering back a few paces. This was the moment of truth. I took another fry out of the bag and held it out gingerly. Scratch stepped forward inch by inch until he was within my reach. I had to show him I wouldn't hurt or grab him, so I stayed stock still.

The thin fingers darted out and snatched the food from my hand before he scrambled backward again, halfway to the trees.

"Thank you, Scratch. Nice to finally meet you. Let's try this again."

Chapter 13

L ife kept moving, whether or not we wanted it to. I finally graded those papers to give back to the class. My grants were in progress, and I continued working with Harriet in the afternoons without additional incident. Taylor's talents were evolving, and he texted me twice about being drawn to innocent creatures in danger, downtown and inside Yale's loose perimeter.

There wasn't enough energy to spare to redraw my warning signs around the campus, so we did the next best thing and opted to be the cavalry. The animals were easy to find, shining like beacons in the muddy energy of downtown, but that didn't make removing them simple.

One was a large rabbit, which took exception to being chased. It was more than two hours before we had managed to herd it to the outskirts of downtown. The other was a coyote, which was as bewildered as we were about its presence there. That situation was more complicated because it caused a public stir. A wild animal going among humans often meant illness, possibly even rabies, but a visual inspection showed nothing wrong with it.

Luckily, that one was less effort than the bunny to corral and move to the woods north of campus. It made the papers, nonetheless, and people were on higher alert than usual for creatures trespassing into civilization.

We also saw Amanda more than once on these escapades. Nothing so obvious to connect her to hunting the animals we were saving, but I couldn't shake the feeling she was there plotting against us. This, plus the sighting during the protest, led me to blame her, at least internally, for my warning signs being destroyed. I didn't know what she had against me, but she could have been trying to score points with Hughes.

It took a solid week of practice with Scratch, in between my usual responsibilities, to give me enough confidence to talk with Katie about my plan. I had purchased a medium-sized cat carrier and worked with Scratch on getting into it as the ultimate test of whether my plans would hold water. It did, though he wasn't happy about it. His time in the sack I had rescued him in had thankfully given him positive memories instead of traumatizing him.

Katie and I were sitting in my living room, sharing a couple of beers, when I let her know about Scratch. She cocked her head to the side but didn't object when I got to the end of my explanation.

"When do I get to meet him?" Her wide smile showed off bright teeth.

"I just told you I've enlisted a raccoon into our little group, and your first question is 'when do I get to meet him?'"

She nodded emphatically. "Uh-huh."

I sighed but said a silent prayer of thanks for friends who trusted me implicitly. There was a lot of trust in what we were attempting to do, so I guess it went both ways. It was Thursday, a week later, and only three were left until the city hearing about the development plans.

"Tonight, if we can make it happen. If I can't get the sample to my friend in the next day or so, we don't stand a chance of having it sequenced in time."

I had called in a favor, and owed another on top of it, to a friend of mine who worked in a high-end, private genetics lab. Several research labs and medical centers did this kind of research, but I counted myself lucky to have an "in" with one of them. He didn't ask too many questions, and I didn't offer any answers beyond assurances that neither his name nor his employer's would end up in whatever headlines this made. If I could get him the sample by the next day, he should have enough of a window for a rush job.

Katie squealed in delight, wrapping her arms around herself. "Ooh, I can't *wait*."

"I'm glad you're being cool about this."

"Mawmaw had a pet raccoon for ages, Corbin. This ain't new to me. They're smart little devils."

I opened my mouth to respond but closed it and shrugged instead. "Yes, they are. Speaking of plans, how are we getting into the museum? I didn't ask how long you needed to put things in motion."

Katie waved her hand dismissively. "Don't you worry. I got my people on standby. We can go in tonight."

"People? *Standby*? I'm impressed you could create a whole criminal organization in a week."

"Pshaw. This ain't no TV show, Corbin. Just a little social engineering and greased palms. Leave it to me."

"It's what you came here for, so I'd be stupid not to. Just tell me where we need to be. I'll have to go get Scratch."

"We're workin' third shift tonight," she said. "So, grab a nap if you have to."

I did not, in fact, nap. It was hard for me to nap when the sun was out, and once it went down, I had other things to handle. Coaxing Scratch into his temporary conveyance took longer than I wanted it to, but I finally succeeded through a combination of offerings and pleading. It was eleven o'clock in the evening, and we stood outside the museum's loading dock next to a custodian's cart.

"Tell me again why we're dressed as janitors?" I plucked at the blue coveralls I had donned over my usual clothing.

Katie quirked an eyebrow at me. "We're not 'dressed as' anything, Corbin. You're about to put in an honest night's work, on top of the dishonest stuff."

She patted the cart, then banged on the smaller access door next to the larger rolling steel one. We waited in silence until it swung outward, and a man I had never met broke into a wide grin on seeing Katie.

"Desmond!" she cried, like she had just seen a long-lost friend.

"Alyssa!" he said, raising his arms to give her a quick hug. Then he thrust his hand toward me. "You must be Carl."

I hoped I didn't hesitate for too long before accepting the handshake. "That's me. I'm Carl." Glancing at Katie, I expected some kind of response, but she winked at me instead.

"Well, you made my night. My crew has been short the last few days, and Alyssa, here, said you needed some extra cash."

We followed Desmond into the building, wheeling the cart in with us. He gave us the rundown on our assignment, which was mostly a laundry list of cleaning activities. "And you'll be on the second floor for your shift—"

Katie interrupted him, a slightly embarrassed look on her face. "Des...could we have the third floor? It's got some of my favorite exhibits."

"I'm not sure, Allie..." He shook his head but seemed to consider the request.

"Pleeeeease," she begged. Her eyes were wide like a child at Christmas. "I might never get to be in a museum after hours again. You know I'm movin' out west." She batted her eyelashes, which apparently put the nail in his coffin.

He sighed heavily, then took out a radio. "Luz, you copy?" When an affirmative noise came through the speaker, he continued, "Work the second floor tonight." Something sounding like "whatever" followed in response. Desmond nodded to us, handed Katie the radio and a clipboard, and pointed to a service elevator. "You need anything you call me on this. Otherwise, we'll see you at break time."

"You got it, Boss." She gave him a casual salute and hit the button for the elevator as he walked away. Neither of us spoke until the elevator door had closed behind us and we were heading upstairs.

"Des? Allie? *Carl*?" I laughed at the brazen ridiculousness of it.

"I figured you wouldn't want real names involved in this, and he's payin' us under the table, anyway."

"We're getting *paid* for this?"

"Shit, man. 'Course we are. We'll be waxin' the floors, too, before we're done. You never asked what I was doin' when I went out on the town those nights. Well, this was it. I made *friends*." Her smile was blinding.

I opened my mouth and closed it again, then tried again to form a coherent thought, but the ding of the elevator hitting the third floor interrupted my attempt.

Katie wheeled the cart out of the lift, and I followed. "Let's give it an hour or two of work, then do whatever needs doin', okay?"

"Fine with me," I replied. "I need some time to put the cameras on the fritz."

The clipboard Desmond had handed us was our bible for the next two hours as we checked off task after task. Katie wasn't joking about the job. It was some of the most detailed physical work I'd done in a while.

It would be worthless if, despite our best efforts in acquiring the bone sample, we got caught because of something as simple as obvious surveillance. Luckily, I had a solution. My style of magic wasn't flashy, even though it was possible to do what no human being would expect to see in their lifetime. It would be problematic if the last image on a recording was some weirdo throwing a lightning bolt into the lens. Things like that would get you a visit from the police and likely a stay in a jail cell, followed by a trip to the psych ward.

One aspect of spirit energy was that it was great at disrupting electronics. It wasn't so bad that every sensitive person blew up their laptop on a daily basis, but unchecked talent would often cause problems with technology. We all had one friend who broke every piece of tech they touched. Did that mean they were sensitive to the spirit world and accidentally channeling their essence into their daily emails? The possibility was there.

Most people wouldn't bleed their energy into their cell phones and computers. But they could if they knew how. I had planned a much subtler approach to our visibility problem, and in between checking off cleaning activities, I began my slow build toward audio-visual invisibility.

A long feather duster on a stick became my wand, and I set bits and spurts of essence into the cameras with a vantage on the target exhibit. I didn't need to touch anything physically to disable them but using the sympathy of the task lessened how much of myself I would have to burn in the process. I visualized the lenses fogging over, the image broken up with static. There and gone, focused, then blurry. The intent was to make the cameras appear to be malfunctioning until we were done with our dirty work.

I had just finished with the final camera when Katie's radio came to life. "Hey, Allie, you copy?"

On the way over in the car, I had explained to Katie what was supposed to happen. She shrugged and nodded at me, picked up the radio, and responded. "Yeah, Des. What's up?"

"Security pinged me. They said a few cameras are acting funny on your floor. You two see anything?"

"Nope, nothin' doin' here. *Carl* was dustin' 'round the cameras, so he might've bumped somethin'. Tell 'em to log a request for maintenance. Everything's looks fine, though."

"Copy that. Remind Carl it's my ass if he breaks anything tonight."

I grimaced and rolled my eyes.

"He knows. Back to work, Des." Katie clipped the radio onto the cart, then nodded to me. "Showtime, Corbin."

I strode over to the janitor's cart and pulled the cloth covering the bottom aside, revealing the cat carrier I had secreted away before rolling up to the entry door earlier. I opened the top of it, liberating our third accomplice. He had laid on his back, a few stray fries strewn across a slightly distended belly.

Scratch hissed when the light hit his eyes, but it was short-lived. He blinked furiously, as if waking from a nap. He had probably fallen asleep after consuming the small tray of fries I had put in to keep him quiet.

"Oh my God, I love him!" Katie squealed in delight, bringing clasped hands to her cheek like a cartoon of a human being.

I turned with widened eyes, shushing her.

"Sorry, Corbin. Hi, little fella'," she crooned.

Scratch climbed out of the carrier—he hadn't deigned to let me pick him up, which was part of what took so long earlier in the evening. He looked up at Katie with his own beady but adorable eyes, and she reached out tentatively until her hand was inches from his head. Scratch closed the distance and rubbed his forehead against her palm, making a soft cooing sound.

"You bitch," I said in a teasing voice. "I've been working with him for a week, and he won't let me get that close."

As if he understood English, he glanced up at me smugly while continuing to accept scratches from Katie.

"Aw, Corbin. Don't take it personally. Us trash pandas recognize each other. Don't we, Scratch."

I watched the tableau with only a slight hint of real envy before redirecting us to the task at hand. "This is adorable and all, but we've got work to do."

Katie relented and stopped petting Scratch, who turned to me with a flat stare.

"Don't look at me like that," I said. "You two can hang out on your own time."

The exhibit was exactly as we had left it, so I knelt beside the air vent and unscrewed the cover. It came off easily, and I set it aside, then stepped back and gestured at it. Scratch glanced at me, then the opening and back but didn't make any moves.

Sighing, I dug another packet of fries out from where I had squirreled them away on the cart. I held it up, then pointed at the vent. Scratch ambled over and sniffed at the currents blowing out of it but waited at the mouth of the duct again. I crossed my fingers and sent a questing thread of silver through the glass and into the largest bone fragment with a small grunt. My expenditure would catch up with me in the morning, but it was for a good cause. Once the bone glowed brightly with my essence, Scratch's ears perked up, and his nose began to twitch.

"That's right, friend," I said in a calm tone. "Time to do your job. Bring me the bone, and all these fries are yours, plus that bit of spirit."

Scratch stuffed his head into the duct, followed by the rest of his bulk. I got concerned when it seemed like his furry ass was stuck, thinking I'd fed him too much food before the gig, but he squeezed himself into the vent like he had crammed his furry butt between the two buildings when we first met.

Katie's eyes were rapt, staring at the vent inside the diorama, waiting for a sign Scratch had figured out a path there. It didn't take long before small fingers reached through the grate and pushed it upward, the large form of Scratch oozing up from the floor and onto the tile.

The fuzzy bandit scampered up the stand holding the remains and snatched the piece I had infused. He knew which side of his bread was buttered, or fried in this case, and was making short work of the challenge. I whistled, impressed, and Katie's grin threatened to split her cheeks.

"He's hired," she whispered.

Scratch stared at me through the window, the bone held lightly in his mouth. It was a six-inch section, so he looked like a small terrier playing fetch. I laughed and pointed at the grate behind him. He either took the hint or had already planned to return the way he came, because he dropped below the floor again, and the sound of scrabbling claws echoed out of the duct.

"Hey, Allie." Desmond's voice crackled on the radio.

Katie dropped an inelegant "fuck" before grabbing the radio to respond. "Yeah, Des?"

"Security didn't like your answer, and they're making it my problem. So, one of their guys is heading to your floor to check the cameras."

"Sure thing, Des," she replied, her voice breaking slightly on the name.

My eyes shot wide as Scratch exited the ductwork again, scurrying over and laying the bone about a foot from my boots. He turned his wide eyes up at me expectantly.

"Katie, you have to handle this. I'll try to finish up, but you need to stall the guard."

Her gaze traveled frantically around the large room until it settled on something on the other side of the hall. She took off at a jog, yelling, "On it."

I crouched to pick up the bone and give Scratch a french fry. He eyed it suspiciously, probably because there was no essence in it, but crammed it into his mouth after only a moment of hesitation.

"We never really got this part right, buddy," I said, pulling out my pocketknife and carving a two-inch section from the larger piece of bone. "But I need you to put this back where you found it."

Scratch stared at me, head cocked to the side. He didn't actually understand English, no matter how clever he was. Our communication over the past week had been an exercise in tone, signals, and repetition. What I hadn't told Katie was while I managed to get Scratch to fetch objects for me, he had a much harder time with the more abstract concept of returning them.

I held the piece of bone in one hand, the bag of fries in the other, showing them to Scratch in turn. Pointing to the window and subsequently the pedestal, I motioned with the bone and placed it on the floor between us.

He didn't do more than twitch his nose. There was the sudden whirr of a floor polisher and an upraised voice I didn't recognize, followed by a similarly loud reply from Katie. I couldn't make out the words, but I knew she was buying me the delay I asked for.

I let out a sharp breath, then shot a silver thread to the empty spot on the pedestal, leaving a small pool of spirit there. Scratch's ears perked up, and his eyes darted to the duct again.

"Yeah, you can have that too, if you bring the bone back." I pushed energy toward Scratch in a gentle wave, concentrating on those positive feelings of doing a good job and the treats that came with it.

He finally took the hint and made his way through the vent and popped up in the locked room again. He quickly climbed the plinth, but there was a tense moment where he seemed to consider not returning the bone. He looked from the puddle of silver to me through the window and I held my breath. Finally, he dropped the bone where he had gotten it, and I let out an explosive sigh.

Scratch greedily sucked up the small pool of energy before scurrying down into the hole.

"No! Scratch! The grate!" *Shit. Shit, shit, shit.* There was no reason for me to be surprised. We hadn't practiced "reset the grate" in the park for obvious reasons. Scratch was a talented mammal, but this would have been too much for him under any circumstances. The bone was a little smaller than before and not in the perfect orientation, but that would easily get chalked up to circumstance. The air duct grate being entirely displaced would cause a whole different level of suspicion.

The sounds coming down the hallway intensified, and the raised voices were getting closer. In Taylor's lessons, I was doing my best to teach him restraint because using up your personal reserves was a dangerous proposition. If you drained yourself too much, you might not be able to recover. I'd probably pass out before I ended up like the black-and-white husks popping up in the city, but I eyed the grate in the exhibit with a dubious expression.

It all happened in a matter of moments. Scratch ducked below the surface of the floor, and I reached out with an invisible hand, pushing through the barrier between the spirit world and our own and shoved at the metal covering. Sweat broke out across my brow, and my breathing grew heavy. It couldn't have weighed more than a pound, but the effort equated to lifting a twenty-pound dumbbell with my pinky. With a grunt of effort that drove me to my knees, the black metal rested in its place on the floor again.

Katie's voice came sharply into focus. The good news was she was laughing, so she must have made friends with the security guard already. The bad news was Scratch hadn't emerged from the ductwork, and the two of them were about to come around the corner. I dove for the vent cover, shoved it into place, and sat with my back to the wall, covering it.

The amount of my own spirit I had burned to move a physical object was intense. I must have looked terrible because when Katie rounded into the room with a six-foot tall brick shithouse of a security guard, she ran over to me.

"Cor—Carl!" she yelled.

The man was quick to follow, and he towered over us both as Katie knelt next to me. "Hey, what's wrong with your friend?"

Improvisation was the name of the game, and I held up the bag of fries in a trembling hand. "Low blood sugar. Forgot to eat before coming to work tonight."

The guard frowned slightly but not in a disapproving way. It was more like commiseration. I popped a fry into my mouth and leaned my head against the cool stone wall, closing my eyes for a moment. They were still delicious, even cold. My body was desperately trying to find some energy, so I expected any carbohydrate would be a meal fit for a king at this point.

"My husband's diabetic," the man said, shaking his head ruefully. "That man would pass out at work every morning if I didn't remind him to have breakfast. I need to check these cameras. You going to be okay? I can call someone if you need medical assistance, but then there'll be a bunch of paperwork for both of us."

I nodded, sagely, and ate another fry. "We're going on lunch soon. I'll be good until then."

He leaned over and clapped me on the shoulder, then took off to make his circuit of the surveillance equipment. Scratch took that moment to live up to his namesake and scraped his claws against the inside of the vent cover. The noise was sharp, though muffled by my back covering the opening. The guard turned around and eyed us both. I rubbed my shoulders against the wall, doing my best to reproduce a sound even remotely similar.

"Sorry, that was me," I said, quirking my mouth in a chagrined expression. He must have bought it because he went back toward his intended path. I glanced at Katie, and we wore identical relieved expressions.

We waited until he was out of sight before I moved away from the vent and let Scratch out. He didn't hiss as much as make indignant growling noises but followed me willingly enough to the cart. I took another sliver of spirit and infused the bag of fries with it, even though the effort made me list to the side with vertigo. I also added a small dose of "victorious rest" to my intention.

Scratch climbed into the carrier, and I closed the cloth cover again to the sounds of happy munching. I drew whatever residual essence remained from my mucking around with the cameras into my body, but it wasn't more than a thimbleful. It wore the edge off my dizziness but not much else.

Katie offered a hand to help me, but once I was standing, she punched me in the arm.

"Ow! What was that for?" I asked.

"You had me worried there for a second." She was all business for a moment but then laughed. "That was a good idea with the blood sugar thing. I'll have to remember that one."

"It's yours, on the house. Seems like you made out okay with the guard."

"Maurice? Yeah, he's a nice guy. Took me a while to get introduced, what with the buffer runnin' so loud and me gettin' in his way and all." She winked at me, then pushed the cart into the next section of the floor we had to clean.

"Allie, you two are all good," Desmond said, the radio echoing loudly in the empty room. "Whatever the security guys did must have fixed it. They say everything's working now."

"Good to hear, Des," Katie replied and glanced at me, flashing a brilliant smile. "Wouldn't want to get you in trouble dustin' these cameras too hard. We'll see you at break time."

Lunch was a lackluster affair, by all accounts, though I wouldn't remember much about it later. Putting in more physical effort on top of my spiritual drain threw me over the edge into exhaustion. I barely made it through the rest of the night, Katie handling the lion's share of work and keeping me on task. False dawn warmed the sky with the barest hint of light when we finally returned to the apartment.

We released Scratch into the park first. He blinked furiously after we let him out of the carrier and wandered off to wherever he planned to sleep the day away. As soon as we got up the stairs to my place, Katie and I collapsed onto the couch, though she had grabbed two celebratory bottles of beer out of the fridge on her way.

I set an alarm to wake me in time to get the sample to my friend, but Katie looked at me like I was a special kind of stupid. "I'll be the courier, you big idiot. You looked like death warmed over. Crash your car and you're no good to anyone."

Texting her the address was the last thing my wrung-out brain could force my body to do before I drifted into unconsciousness.

Chapter 14

I'd better start with the good news. My lab friend got back to me within a day of receiving the sample and let me know he had extracted enough DNA to sequence. This was a relief because the idea of somehow getting another larger sample was simply ridiculous. My efforts laid me up for a weekend with a clear case of the flu. And by that, I meant magically-induced exhaustion similar in every way to the flu. The body aches, chills, and fever kept me useless for days. Katie was kind enough to stick around and see me past the worst of it before heading south.

I promised her I'd visit her and her grandmother sometime, and I owed her about ten different flavors of favors. She just gave me that lopsided grin of hers, a hug since I wasn't contagious, and skipped out of my life again for a while.

Now, the bad news wasn't entirely bad. There were no guarantees I'd get a lab report with the sequenced DNA in time for the paperwork I needed to file. Well, that Dave needed to file on my behalf. I kept him in the loop, being cagey enough that he groused at me over the phone. He relented a bit when I claimed illness and agreed to be ready to file for an injunction against the building development.

By Monday of the following week, I was on the mend. On Tuesday, I even dragged my ass into class to teach. Taylor noticed but didn't comment about my rough appearance. I barely kept it together for another week as I continued restoring my reserves and recovered from overtaxing myself.

In the meantime, a grassroots effort to preserve the Green had sprung up while I was playing secret agent. Nour was a loud voice in the movement, but it had support from a wide variety of nonprofits and environmental groups around the state. They held sit-ins and protests over the intervening weeks, and the "Save the Green Alliance" was organizing a list of speakers for the city meeting.

It was an open forum, but those often devolved into chaos with people fighting for the limited time available for comment. Planning together, the new organization stood a better chance of crafting a cohesive message they could all rally around.

Taylor and I had lunch together regularly, as was becoming our custom, and it was the last week of the comment period when Nour texted me.

NOUR:

You're going to speak, right?

CORBIN:

About what?

If everything went the way I hoped it would, there would be a good reason for me to be a speaker at the event. Nour didn't know that, and I couldn't help but give her a hard time.

NOUR:

Funny. You're our star expert, Corbin. Talk about how important the place is, crack a whip, or whatever archaeologists do. Figure it out!

CORBIN:

I'll come up with something. Promise.

"You nervous about the council meeting?" Taylor asked, taking a bite of his ubiquitous ham and cheese.

I hadn't told Taylor about my escapades; plausible deniability was alive and well. There was no reason to drag him into the seedier side of my recent activities. Not that I expected a repeat performance, but it never hurt to keep your friends clean when it came to illegal extracurriculars. It would have been nice to give him my most recent cautionary tale about overextending myself, but I'd have to find an excuse for more bad decisions.

"Not really. Either we make the right impression, and the city considers its options, or they've already decided, and this is going to be for show. In any case, we did our best."

And just like that, it was Thursday. They said a watched pot didn't boil, but I swear if you didn't want the water to get hot, it would be bubbling in seconds. Time moved quickest when we wanted it to stand still.

My nerves were on a hair trigger all day, and let's say I didn't give my best lecture ever. The students were well aware of my concerns. Some of my worry had seeped into our conversations, and they had noticed. A few of them even planned to attend the council meeting that night.

Mid-October was usually one of my favorite times of year. The days were still reasonably comfortable, and the nights were brisk, heading toward a wintry cold. There was no way I could actually enjoy it because I hadn't received any results from my lab tech friend. The last I had heard from him was the day before, promising to do his best, but there was no guarantee he'd have the report to me before the hearing. I told Dave to stand down, and we'd have to play catch-up if things suddenly went in our favor. Nour would have to settle for a heartfelt speech I prepared, calling on the history of the space.

I leaned on the window outside of Bits and Baubles, having offered to drive Harriet downtown with me. She wasn't going to pass up an opportunity to listen to a "bunch of white folk fighting for the right cause, for once." She'd said it with a grin, but she wasn't wrong. It was hard to engage people who weren't affected by the world around them. There was a lot of privilege in a college town, and it took something special to break through the casual blinders everyone wore every day.

It was why I saw so many returning faces at local protests. We tended to know the core groups who were regularly engaging in political and environmental action. The rest were random faces walking through a revolving door of temporary assistance. When the spirit moved them, they'd be there, but otherwise, they stayed home.

Parking was a nightmare, but we eventually made our way to City Hall. Ironically, the building was situated across from the part of the Green where Taylor and I had been spiritual animal control. It was a beautiful, old building. The age of the city itself held weight and volumes, though it stood on the bones of history before it.

People packed the meeting hall, and the attendees who wanted to speak stood shoulder-to-shoulder in the back of the room, crammed in behind the rows of seats for council members or other officials. Once everything started, it was reasonably order-ly. Thankfully, no one wasted time hearing from the developers, and the meat of the event was listening to public comments. The organizers from the Alliance held clipboards and spoke quietly, getting their ducks in a row and sending speakers one-by-one to the podium.

Each person only received two minutes, given the expected volume of interested parties, and I didn't blame them. I wasn't scheduled to go last, but I was toward the end of the list. I agreed with their approach, starting with the impassioned laypeople and layering expertise on top of that.

Much like the energy of the protest, a vibration hummed through the crowd. As each person burned through their time, they hammered on the importance of green spaces in a city. One advocate for the homeless spoke about the loss of the area as a safe gathering place for the indigent and the impact it would have. Others talked about their personal experiences growing up with the fixture that was the Green. It was moving and emotional, every sentence building on the last.

Harriet nodded along with most of the speeches, giving me appraising looks whenever someone said something she seemed to find insightful or powerful. Finally, it was my turn. I strode to the podium through the din of a crowd clamoring for more support to be laid, like a mason building a retaining wall stone by stone. Three steps were between me and the microphone when my phone buzzed. I broke into a cold sweat and hastily brought it out to check my messages. My eyes flitted back and forth, reading the note before I shoved my cell into my pocket with a shaky hand. I closed the small final distance, breathing heavily while the council called for order.

Clearing my throat as the muttering died away, I launched into my prepared notes. As a local archaeologist and anthropologist, I tried to connect the two subjects. The history of the city with the evolution of the Green as a meeting place. Yes, the development intended to honor the intention of the creators in having a marketplace, but the value of the park as a cultural touchstone couldn't be overstated.

I could see people on either side of me, agreement plain on their faces, and it bolstered my resolve. Whether or not we could stop the development through legal means, there was a clear call to action in preventing the destruction of yet another historical landmark in favor of the almighty dollar.

That being said...

"Perhaps more important than any of my prior comments is to elaborate on the true history of the Green. In fact, it is a graveyard. No stones indicate the poor souls still buried there today, but thousands of skeletons are beneath our very feet."

Gasps from the crowd rose in waves, and the council members looked at each other with what appeared to be sudden and growing discomfort. I pushed on, knowing I had less than thirty seconds to make my point.

"The early colonies traded and intermingled with the natives of New Haven, primarily the Quinnipiac. It is impossible to assume there are no Indigenous bones interred less than two hundred feet from where we stand today. I have it on good authority the bones recovered from the Green in a previous archaeological dig contain tribal remains—"

A dissonant chorus rose around me, drowning out my attempts to continue. I waited, hoping they wouldn't count the pause against my time.

"I would be happy to consult with the state archaeologist and any other relevant professionals in the community about my concerns. Until then, I am recommending the project be placed on hold until a proper investigation can be made to comply with NAGPRA guidelines, otherwise legal action may be the only remedy."

Stepping back, I immediately encountered the hands of other attendees, patting my shoulders and helping to usher me to the rear of the room. I made it to where Harriet stood, and she gave me a considerate look. "Well, that was something."

I leaned in close enough to whisper in her ear. "Wetland plants, only they were already there."

She nodded, and we both stood smugly while the city council wrangled the room into some semblance of decorum. It took a while.

What didn't take long was the city council's decision to suspend the permits, effectively stopping the development company from breaking ground on their proposed schedule. Something about wanting to ensure the cultural and historical integrity of a city landmark. There was obviously no promise they wouldn't approve it again later, but for now, all our hard work had paid off. The protesters and organizers had rallied the city around their message and sentiment, and I was happy enough to tie the argument up with a bow of my own design.

Harriet and I made our way over to the Green after the meeting, where an impromptu block party had broken out. Bottles in brown paper bags were being passed around with a joyful spirit I hadn't seen in some time. The Save the Green Alliance members were shoulder to shoulder with the homeless, celebrating the win.

Boom boxes and portable speakers pushed out energetic dance music, and perfect strangers danced salsa together in abandon. We sat on the smooth stone ringing the war memorial, breathing in the cool night air. The report had come in with seconds to spare, and thankfully I had felt the alert. The results were as I had hoped. Over fifty percent of the DNA was of native descent. We could have made arguments with less, but hopefully they wouldn't be needed.

I removed a small pipe from my leg bag, along with my tobacco pouch. Harriet raised an eyebrow at me but only watched as I prepared the bowl. I sprinkled loose leaf to the top, tamped it down until it was springy, then repeated the process. Once it was ready, I held it up.

"I think it's appropriate to give some thanks and make an offering. If you'll join me?" I asked.

"*Aho.* You did well today, but good idea, especially if the Creator guided your hand in any of this."

I nodded and brought out a matchbox. "Do you want to do the honors?"

Harriet took the matches and pipe from me, then stared down at the stone for a minute before looking up again. "Thank you, Creator, for guiding our steps on the Red Road. Today we sit in victory against people who would take more of Father Sky from us." She struck the match against the sandpaper on the box and lit the packed pipe with a few puffs. "We smoke this *kinnickinnick* to honor you and the spirits who stood with us. *Aho.*"

"*Aho,*" I echoed, hesitantly, but Harriet clapped me on the shoulder.

The tobacco tasted of leather and metal, heavy and thick. After only a draw or two, we set the bowl between us and let it burn slowly. The tendrils of smoke danced upward until a current of air drew them away.

"What now, little cousin?" Harriet's eyes gleamed in the light from the lampposts.

"Well—"

"Corbin!" Jake's voice came from behind me, and I whipped around.

"What's going on, Jake?"

"I've been trying to find you, man. Something bad's happening."

My stomach dropped, and it wasn't from the brief hit of nicotine. "Tell me what happened."

Tension radiated from his posture, his body coiled like a spring. "It's like Clyde. Well, I don't know if it's like him. There's more, and I—"

I reached out and placed a hand on Jake's shoulder, trying to calm him. "Take a breath and start at the beginning."

Fear reflected in Jake's eyes as he inhaled shakily, letting it out in a rush. "There are two people missing this time, Corbin."

"Okay, are you sure they haven't moved somewhere else for the winter? It could be a simple explanation."

Jake sighed. "You might be right. Except I saw one of 'em go off with someone. And then they never came back."

Chapter 15

Jake filled me in on the rest of his story as the revelers danced and drank the evening away around us. While I had been convalescing, two more locals disappeared. Sasha and Erik were relatively new to the community downtown, each arriving independently some months prior.

Sasha was the first to disappear. Jake was on high alert for gaps in the chow line, as he called it, and had noted her absence more than a week ago. Erik was next, several days later, missing from the lunch handouts.

"Haven't seen Sasha for a while, so I was getting jumpy. Erik's a big guy and has an appetite. No way I was going to overlook the fact that he wasn't there to ask me 'if I was gonna eat that'." Jake had told me with a smile, though it faltered as he continued.

The big difference this time was that Jake saw him the night before, talking with some guy near his squat. The stranger wore a clean beige trench coat over office clothes, button-up shirt and slacks, something along those lines, but the jacket had stuck in Jake's memory.

"Someone who keeps a jacket like that spotless isn't the kind I'd expect to find slumming around here. I watched from a block away, like I was minding my own business. The fella gave Erik a business card before he left."

"Did you get a look at it?" I asked.

Jake shook his head. "No. Erik's not too friendly a guy, even if he'll buddy up to you for your leftovers. I didn't bother him, but I noticed when he wasn't around the next day. It's been about a week now since I've seen him."

I eyed Harriet, who shrugged as if to say she had nothing helpful to add to the conversation. The wheels turned in my mind as I considered Jake's information. Hughes was right. Twice was still potentially a coincidence. But if I assumed all the missing people were dead, we'd already passed three, and now there was a pattern. "Have you seen that person around lately? The one with the coat?"

"Nah, not since Erik anyway."

"Tell me if you run across him again, okay? Do you have a phone?"

Jake flashed a small smartphone at me, and we traded numbers.

"I can't be everywhere at once, Corbin," Jake said, a rueful expression on his face. "But I don't want anyone else ending up like Clyde."

Jake was still strongly under the impression that Clyde's death was foul play, and I didn't dissuade him of the notion. I couldn't confirm it without causing a lot of other complicated conversations to take place, but I wasn't going to gaslight him either.

"I need to know the next time someone gets approached by the man you saw. Can you put out the word? Have them get in touch with you, and you text me. Fifty bucks to whoever puts one of those cards in my hand too."

Jake's dour expression brightened, and he gave a broad smile. "You really care about people, don't you?"

"Hey, I believe something weird is going on and we can try to help stop it. We just need to figure out what it is."

"I'll put the word out." Jake extended his hand, but as soon as I grasped it, he pulled me in for a quick hug, slapping me on the back. "You're a good man, Corbin."

The darkness probably kept my blush from being visible, but the heat of it radiated from my cheeks. "I'd like to think it's what people do for each other, but that's a little too idealistic. Especially from me."

Jake nodded and set off, clearly intent on spreading my message as quickly as possible because he made a beeline for one of the other regular downtown denizens.

"See, there's your problem," Harriet said from her perch. She hadn't moved during my conversation with Jake.

"That being..."

"You did your job too well, so now you get another."

I spared her a flat stare, but she returned it with a guileless one of her own. The reality was, she wasn't wrong. The reward for a job well done *was* usually more work.

We drove back to the shop, and Harriet headed home after giving me another congratulatory slap on the back. This left me alone to contemplate the evolving roster of missing people.

Taking a page from Katie's book, I cracked a celebratory beer and drank to the successful roadblock I had thrown in the face of "progress." I was a villain in someone's story tonight, and it was a role I relished.

But the last month had been a mess. The whole situation was a few different shades of ridiculous, looking back on it. When I was waiting for something, like a text from Jake, my mind tended to dwell on possibilities.

Morals and ethics were weird when you considered the intertwining of society and culture. Society established laws, and following them made you a fine and upstanding member. Ethics existed independently from but related to morals and could clash with them at the best of times.

In hindsight, I could have lied from the start and said Native bones were buried under the Green. The paperwork, if I scrounged enough money to cover the legal fees, would have likely tied the project up for at least a few weeks. But it wouldn't have been an actual solution. In an alternate reality, a different version of me without a shred of ethics buried known remains and called in a hot tip.

Instead, I broke into a museum exhibit to steal a piece of bone to run tests on, which might have ultimately failed: morals. The purpose of which was to establish the truth of the Green being a resting place for members of Native tribes and to stop a business development from destroying it: ethics.

I thought about it more, but by the time I had finished my first beer, I was pretty sure I'd drive myself insane trying to decide what kind of man I was. Complicated was my middle name. *Gods, I hated waiting.*

My phone buzzed as I was popping the top off my second beer. It was Jake, which was surprisingly quick given I had seen him only a few hours prior.

JAKE:

> You owe Ronnie fifty bucks.

CORBIN:

> No shit, really? That was fast. Is he pulling your leg?

JAKE:

It's legit. You're gonna want to talk to him too. Trust me. Get down to the corner of College and Chapel, next to the bus stop. He'll meet you there in twenty minutes.

You're the best, Jake.

Damn right. You owe me a coffee, at least.

I'm good for it. Thanks for the help.

I threw a light jacket over my flannel before grabbing my keys off the kitchen counter where I had tossed them, my eyes passing over the side table where I had stashed the Hunter's Rosary. Something scratched around in the recesses of my mind, but I ignored the itch and headed downtown.

Ronnie wasn't the most trustworthy person. But if Jake believed him, I would too. The chilly night air had pricked at the back of my neck while I was getting in the car, so I stopped on the way to grab two cups of coffee. Part in thanks but also acknowledgement of and a little armor against the coming cold.

It was late, so parking was easy, and Ronnie was waiting on the bench next to the bus stop as expected.

This wasn't a spy movie, and we didn't have pass phrases, so I sat next to him with a grunt. I handed him one of the polystyrene cups, holding a small billfold against the side with my thumb. "Cheers, Ronnie."

He smiled and accepted the cup, pocketing the cash in a smooth motion before holding the coffee up in salute. Ronnie sipped at his, savoring the brew with a "ah" of enjoyment. It wasn't great coffee, but I imagined the fifty bucks added some extra sweetness.

He held a business card out and waited until I took it. Turning it over to examine the glossy details, I found it was only printed on one side. The company name in bold lettering was "Many Hands Support Network of New England," and the text below gave me the name of the representative who had apparently approached Ronnie. Theodore Stanclift.

"Who was this guy?" I asked.

"Dunno," Ronnie said. "Never seen him before. Tall guy. Skinny. Definitely one of those do-gooders from the charities. He said there was a new program, and he wanted to get me into it."

I flipped the card repeatedly, staring with my eyes only half focused, taking in the details. "Did he tell you what it was about?"

"Yeah, it was residential. Something about getting me back on my feet. What, are mine broken?" We both laughed and drank more coffee before he continued. "He caught me over on Park near Crown. I was trying to get a few bucks, maybe something to eat. Teddy had this trench coat. Clean like a surgeon, really stuck out. Anyway, I told him I'd think about it and he should come see me again tomorrow. Same place, same time, around ten o'clock."

"Sounds like an interesting deal. Did you want to take it?"

"Fuck no, man. Jake told the guys you had a fifty for anyone who could put that card in your hand," he said, gesturing at the object I still held in front of me. "With people going missing, the fact that the shelter's full, and since I'd never heard of this 'Many Hands' before? Usually means it's some well-intentioned people who can't tell their ass from their elbow. Those fail as quick as they start, and I'd take a sure fifty over that any day."

"Makes sense to me. Thanks, Ronnie."

"Don't mention it." Ronnie stood and walked to the crosswalk, away from the Green.

"Hey, Ronnie?"

He turned back, his eyes cast into shadow by the streetlight above him. "Yeah, Corbin?"

"Stay away from Park Street tomorrow night, okay?"

"You're the real deal, Corbin. I know why Jake likes you." He flashed a peace sign, then turned and sauntered across the street.

Less than twenty-four hours later, my watch told me it was nine-thirty. The streets were busy but not packed. Friday nights were busy downtown. It was past rush week, so there weren't any parades of almost twenty-somethings meandering in untidy groups down Crown Street from bar to bar.

I was wearing shabby chic in as close to an approximation of Ronnie's outfit as I could get from the day before. Ripped jeans, a battered Henley I should have donated or trashed years ago, and a medium-weight jacket, which had seen better days. I had left my leg bag at home; it was too much of an identifiable piece of kit.

A late addition to my equipment was the Hunter's Rosary. I had walked by the side table multiple times, the artifact still scratching at an itch at the back of my mind, until I had given in to whatever intuition was rubbing my brain cells together and had taken it with me.

Not without precautions, of course. I wrapped the necklace in a thin layer of silvery energy, insulating it from contact with my essence beyond that barrier. The rosary sitting in my pocket wasn't likely to endanger me, and something told me it was going to come in handy. Things were getting weird, and having a tool that could absorb energy might be useful.

So, I sat there on Park Street, around the corner from one of the local gay bars, leaning against the painted brick wall near the edge of an alleyway. Every passerby pinged my senses, and I was jittery an hour later when my target came into sight. Ronnie was right. The trench coat almost glowed in the streetlight like a beacon. Waiting for him to approach, I took his measure.

He was tall, as Ronnie mentioned, but gaunt to the point of being skeletal. It was in the way of people genetically predisposed to the body type. His bald head reflected the same light illuminating his coat, shining like it was freshly shaved. The pants and shirt were the same generic business-casual style Ronnie described, but he wore an affable smile as well. He was about to pass me when I held my palm out.

"Got any change, buddy?" I asked, putting more than a hint of gruffness into my voice.

He stopped, realizing I was speaking to him, and fished in his pocket. His hand came out holding a dollar and a small white business card. The man I assumed was Theodore pressed the bill into my hand with the paper on top of it.

"Hope it helps, friend," he said, with what seemed to be a sincere tone.

"Thanks." Flipping the card, I made a show of examining it. "Theodore. Any little bit counts, I'm trying to get enough for a couple nights off the street. It's getting cold." I didn't know if he was going to pitch me the same way he did Ronnie, but putting some bait out couldn't hurt. He had probably come here expecting a different guy, but I needed him to believe I was an equally appealing fish to reel in. Given he included his card with the gift, I was on a reasonable track.

"Call me Teddy." He nodded affably, stroking his chin. "My charity helps gentlemen like you get back on your feet, if you're interested."

"Is that right? Mind telling me more about it?"

His grin didn't dissuade me from thinking of him as a walking skeleton. "Sure! We have a residential program. You get room and board, career training, and an opportunity to rest for a bit before tackling the tough problems."

"Sounds too good to be true," I said with a healthy dose of skepticism.

He held his hands up. "Sometimes things are exactly what they seem, but I understand the hesitancy. It's state-funded, nothing out of pocket from you, so no worries about coming home with a bill or any of that nonsense. We can even help get you clean if you deal with any substance abuse problems or need mental health support. We've got trained professionals for any situation."

"Say, are you the folks who helped Sasha? I haven't seen her around lately, and someone told me she got accepted into a program."

Teddy nodded vigorously. "Yeah, and she's doing great. It's so nice to hear word is spreading about what we do."

I rubbed the back of my head, considering. "What kind of a waitlist do you have? If it's not too good to be true, you've got to have a line of people around the block."

"Not true. We have plenty of room."

I whistled a low, surprised note. "All right. What would you need from me?"

Teddy's smile widened. "Why don't you come with me, and we'll get you set up. I've got a vehicle nearby and can give you a ride."

I surveyed the street. We were alone for the moment. Holding my hand out, I waited until he grasped it and pulled me to my feet. Once I was upright, I kept my grip on him and leaned in to whisper in his ear. "Is that what you said to Clyde?" He jerked backward, but I kept my grip. His eyes were wide with sudden recognition, and it was all the admission I needed.

His pull against my arm was strong enough that when I stopped fighting against it he knocked himself off-balance. I used the momentum to swing him around and throw him into the alley behind me. Teddy might have been tall, but he was all bird bones with little mass. He tumbled to the ground as I stalked into the dark passage after him.

"Please!" he cried as I rushed toward him.

I slapped him across the cheek with an open palm, and his voice cut off. It wasn't enough to do more than break some blood vessels, but it shocked him like I hoped it would. He backed himself against a chain-link fence, covered with privacy strips, halfway down the alley.

"You and I need to have a talk, Teddy," I said, looming over him. "Do you know who I am?"

"Yes," he replied but didn't elaborate. His gaze flicked from side to side, reflecting in the dim light from the street, since he was clearly looking for an escape route.

"What are you doing with the people you've taken?"

Teddy must have gotten some of his equilibrium back, the surprise from my slap wearing off, because he laughed. "Why do you care?"

I knelt and grabbed the front of his shirt in one fist, shaking him. "Why don't you? Who's putting you up to this?"

He pushed my arm to the side but didn't seem to be trying to get away so I didn't protest. "I'm doing my job, like everyone else.

I know who you are, Pierce, and you've got a reputation to uphold if you want to keep your position."

He was on the ropes initially, but I hadn't kept him off-kilter enough to press the advantage. I didn't like the turn this was taking. Teddy was rebounding and apparently remembered we lived in a semi-polite society. He finally stood but wasn't an intimidating figure, despite his height.

"Tell me who you're working for and why they want these bodies. You're a front for something. No charity I've ever met churns out dead and missing people like you do."

"Or what? You think you can rough me up without consequences? You'll be fired first thing Monday morning, all for the sake of what? Your conscience?" Teddy moved to push past me, but I wasn't having any of it and kept blocking his path.

"How much is the Hand paying you?"

I figured a shot in the dark was worth it to see if I could strike home. Teddy didn't have much of a poker face, and his lips twitched when I mentioned the Hand.

"You know they're killing them, right? You're sourcing *people* to feed to the meat grinder." I advanced a step, and he retreated the same, maintaining his distance.

"Come on, Pierce," Teddy said, with a growing bravado. "You can't do anything to me. If I work for who you think I do, they've got deep pockets and friends in high places. You lay another finger on me, and it'll be the end for you."

He wasn't confirming much, but I wasn't looking for statements that would hold up in court. It was more important to stop whatever was happening than to worry about whether I could put this guy away. I wasn't a detective or a cop. I only cared about stopping the murders and disappearances. Anger stoked in my belly from this whole interaction.

"You're not getting it, Teddy. I don't need you to go to jail to keep people safe. Just like I don't have to lay a finger on you to make you wish I had."

"What—" was all that came out of Teddy's mouth before an avalanche of bad things happened.

I whipped the Hunter's Rosary out of my pocket and lunged at the tall man. It was a split second from thought to action, drawing the silvery layer back from the artifact and shoving it toward him. Like *rondori* with my old *sensei*, I went for the throat. Focusing my energy, I sent a single intention to the small magical black hole I held against his neck. *Absorb.*

That was when everything went wrong.

Teddy gasped, his eyes panic-stricken, and he struggled to get away. But he didn't stand a chance. The rosary was suddenly something more than I had seen when I examined and even experimented with it before. Where it had been hungry, now it was ravenous. Not sentient but an unconscious and implacable force.

My partial barrier kept the artifact's focus on Teddy, otherwise it would likely have consumed me too. I tried to pull it back, but the necklace had an iron grip on his neck like a magnet. I couldn't get it more than an inch away before it snapped back, insatiable in its mindless pursuit. I extended my senses, showing a maelstrom of essence being pulled from Teddy, his body growing limp and slumping to the ground.

An eternity packed into a handful of heartbeats later and an almost audible sigh of contentment came from the rosary. A deep, animalistic sound no one but me would have been able to hear. The bone beads glowed with stolen essence; brighter than any natural source I'd seen in a long time. I knelt by the tall, still form and tried to find a pulse despite my sight showing me what I already knew to be true.

The Hunter's Rosary was full, and Teddy was dead.

Chapter 16

It was hours later, the sun threatening to rise over the city skyline, before the police let me go. Other than a slight abrasion on his cheek, Teddy didn't have a bruise on him. When I had called 911 to report a dead body, he lay on the ground in the alley, horror twisting his face. The report was simple—I had been talking to the charity worker, and he dropped dead from a stroke or a heart attack.

No, I hadn't attempted CPR because I wasn't certified. Yes, I had rolled him over from where he fell down to check for a pulse. When the EMS and police arrived, I gave them my statement and they canvased the area, looking for other witnesses. They didn't seem particularly suspicious of me. Apparently no one around had offered a different story than the one I gave. The guy in charge took my information in case they had further questions. I complied, numb to my core, without a shred of pretense.

I was pretty sure what they would find, though I couldn't be certain. Sudden cardiac arrest, no apparent cause. Except I was the cause. But what would giving myself over to the police do, other than take the one person trying to stop the murders off the playing field? Teddy as much as admitted the Hand was involved, and the missing people were likely as dead as Clyde. The spiral I walked toward the truth was going deeper.

What would I have told the cops, anyway? "Yes, officers, I killed him. How? I touched him with this magical relic and sucked his life force away. No, sir or madame, I wasn't on any antipsychotic medication." It would have been more complicated confessing to a crime I couldn't prove I committed than to explain it away.

I wasn't a monster, or at least that was what I told myself as I drove home. My bed called, but my mind raced, and instead of seeking the comfort of unconsciousness, I walked into Edgewood Park to watch the sunrise. Shock was my self-diagnosis. I still didn't feel anything more than surprise and horror at the mistake. Because it *was* a mistake. Teddy should have been alive, spilling his guts to me about his part in the Hand's plot.

Sitting by the pond where I had trained Scratch, I opened my senses, desperate to break open the shell of calm my brain had constructed around itself. Golden rays peeked over and through the treetops, landing on my face and chest, driving some small warmth into me.

I stayed that way for an hour or more until the heat had melted my icy calm away, and I finally broke. It wasn't a raging torrent, more like a trickle escaping the dam, but remorse and self-doubt ran through my veins. I had always been a person willing to side-step legality in pursuit of justice, but I never expected to kill another human being in the process.

Rationalization was also hard at work, reminding me that Teddy was at least kidnapping if not straight-up murdering people. Didn't he deserve to pay for what he had done? But using the Hunter's Rosary had been an unnecessary risk. The artifact glowed brightly through my pocket, still satisfied. I hadn't done enough research or experimentation to know its limits, which were apparently well beyond where I expected them to be. My carelessness had cost Teddy his life, and me, some of the last drops of innocence I possessed.

But I had a job to do and was armed with new information. The question was, how to get my mind right to pursue it now? Walking back to my building, the shop below was open, and I stumbled through the entryway to find Harriet sitting behind the counter.

"What happened to you? You're paid up on your rent. You don't need to sleep rough," she said, chuckling, but stopped short. My face must have telegraphed my mood because she cocked her head to one side. "You want to talk?"

"I need *something*, Harriet," I said, coming to rest my elbows on the counter and lay my head in my hands. I laughed, but it held no mirth. "If the Creator is guiding my hand, they've got a weird sense of humor. But I'm pretty sure this was all me. I messed up bad."

"Sounds like you've got some demons fighting inside you, Corbin."

"Got any demon cures lying around?"

"Actually—" she started to say, but I interrupted her.

"Cut the shit, Harriet. It's been a hell of a night." I didn't want to be unkind, especially if she was trying to lighten the mood, but even after I had initiated the joke about cures, I regretted it.

"Oh, look at you all high and mighty. Fine, I'll keep it to myself. Go play Tetris or whatever it is they say you should do after something traumatic."

I eyed her sideways. "Sorry, I'm not good company this morning."

"You're telling me."

"I...someone's dead, Harriet. And it's my fault."

She gave me an appraising look. It wasn't judgment, though I feared it, more like consideration. "Does this have to do with all the weird things going on with the homeless downtown?"

I nodded, though I didn't want to elaborate. Harriet didn't deserve to get roped into my problems if the cops decided I was a suspect after all.

"Did you mean to do it?" she asked. "Was there hate in your heart?"

"No. I was trying to help people, and the situation—it ...got away from me."

She nodded. "You're a special kind of stupid sometimes, Corbin, but you're a good man. You may hate yourself right now, but that fire inside is telling you something. Maybe I can help get it out."

That piqued my curiosity, and I was desperate for some answers. "Please, give me your demon cure."

Harriet puffed herself up the way she did before she told a story, but none were forthcoming. Instead, she said simply, "I know a guy. Bring shorts."

Apparently, when Harriet said she knew a guy, she was serious. We had driven east of New Haven, out to Branford, where a friend of hers had a farm. Tom's produce wasn't the important part. He also hosted regular sweats at his own sweat lodge. They were invitation-only, and Harriet was my entry pass. My luck had ridden a sawtooth lately, but it must have been on an upward path again because Tom had one planned for that night.

Harriet introduced me, and Tom was kind enough, but there was a lot of sitting around and waiting for things to happen initially. More than a handful of people were taking part, and many of them seemed to run on pagan-standard-time, which was a loose approximation of meeting any particular schedule.

It had the surreal quality of *Waiting for Godot*, existing in a perpetual state of expecting something to happen but nothing breaking it. Since I was stuck between brief bouts of self-loathing and righteous indignation, the silence made me a palatable person to be around. Tom, aided by another friend of his, tended a fire outside the tent where they heated rocks to prepare for the lodge.

Eventually, all the attendees arrived, or Tom decided to move on without them, and we began. Despite the cool fall weather, we stripped down to the essentials, shorts in Harriet and my case, and he ushered us inside a small domed structure covered with hides and other natural material.

Some participants, more the women than the men, wore long thin dresses instead of the shorts we had on. Inside it was nearly pitch-black, the only illumination being pinpricks of light filtering through from outside. We arranged ourselves in a semi-circle, leaving a path to the opening, with men on one side and women on the other. Harriet sat with me, a sports bra covering her chest.

Tom made trips in and out with rocks, which radiated heat, held in iron tongs. Everyone remained silent and respectful, most of us seemingly unsure of what would happen next but not screwing with the clear solemnity. My back was already slick with sweat, the press of bodies raising the temperature even as the dim red glow of the stones brought it higher. Tom lit a small brazier holding sweet-smelling herbs and tobacco. The smoke filled the small space until tiny beams of light crisscrossed the hut through the haze.

"What—" I started to ask.

Harriet laid a hand on my knee, squeezing lightly. We hadn't discussed proper etiquette, and I must have already made a misstep. I mouthed a silent "Oh" she likely couldn't see but shut up regardless. On our way to the farm, she hadn't said much, but I trusted her to know whether this was something that could help me.

I opened my senses to the energy around us. The hide walls blocked out the farm, but each person had their own dose of spirit. The essence rising from the brazier wove patterns in the air that couldn't be seen by the naked eye, flowing around everyone. It had the taste of luck or a blessing. An offering to the spirits and to those present.

Most times, the average person wouldn't feel the energy around them. There were, however, tools to bring someone without sensitivity closer to the spiritual world. Practices varied on how to open your senses to the hidden worlds, but most involved an intentional change of perception. A shift in focus, meant to distance yourself from the "normal" and touch the supernatural.

European witchcraft had a historical reputation for potions and ointments, often containing psychedelic or poisonous substances. Despite the debatable validity of the accounts or recipes, many cultures had deep religious and spiritual practices, including the use of psychoactive substances. Tribes in South America utilized ayahuasca. Many of the native Americans in the southwestern United States held peyote ceremonies. Modern medicine has even made the use of psychedelics like MDMA or ketamine more common in treating mental illness.

All of that to say, humanity had a long history of loosening its tether to the physical world. Challenging the body, in ceremonies like fasts and sweats, was another way to achieve similar heightened states of mind. The herbs Tom used wouldn't launch us into outer space but served to set the tone, make spiritual offerings, and start binding us together in a shared experience. My eyes showed me what others wouldn't see, and the threads of spirit wove the beginning of a tapestry around us as we were getting ready.

Apparently satisfied with his preparations, Tom joined us. He had geared down to his own pair of trunks, a towel wrapped around his shoulders. The silence in the hut was palpable, and Tom didn't waste time with any preamble. This was clearly a ceremony he had long experience with, and he launched ahead. As he spoke, the wisps of smoke swirled through the beams of light.

"We pray. To the Creator, to the universe, to our ancestors. The connections that bind everything together hold us to the Earth. Our breath gives wings to our words to fly them through the air to Father Sky. We make offerings through the fire, the breath of our spirit. The water of our bodies cleanses us in this ceremony. May you find the answers you seek or the comfort you need."

Taking a ladle from a small bucket, he sprinkled water in the center, and a loud hiss echoed in the small space. The heat rose exponentially with the added humidity. Harriet hadn't said how long this was going to last. I hadn't even known it was a sweat lodge until we arrived, but I assumed the experience was going to be at least several hours. I settled in as we sat in a communal quiet.

As people's breathing slowed into a pattern, we synchronized more often than not. Unconsciously, the participants' own essence saturated their breath, and the room was a riot of colors. My silver blended with other metallics, pastels, and primaries. No one took from the pool; this was a mingling not a sharing, and everyone remained whole.

I held magic but wasn't psychic. There was no way for me to know why the other people were there, but in a sense, I tasted the air like a cat scenting the world around it. It took me more than a few minutes to realize my focus was on curiosities that had nothing to do with my own search for answers.

Get with the program, I told myself. The effort to return my gaze inward was significant, but the others here wouldn't solve my problems.

Time passed in a literal haze. The fire tender and helper worked to swap out the rocks in the center, replacing them with ones freshly radiating a blazing heat. I had no idea how long it had been when Tom poured a second ladle of water onto the hot stones, but the sound startled me out of a lazy contemplation. I had sat for various meditation styles before, but this was my first sweat.

Where did I go? I wondered. The whole idea was to pray, connect, or whatever you had to do. *What did I need?* This was introspection on steroids, but the concept wasn't new.

The Japanese held a practice called *zazen,* a form of Zen meditation where the practitioners sat in a kneeling posture cultivating a sense of "no mind." More specifically, for the ones that held multiple daylong practices, it was said to be a way to experience dying.

Teddy hadn't been looking to face death when it came for him. The admonition came unbidden to my mind as my consciousness drifted.

I jerked upright, suddenly aware of the relaxed posture of those around me, like I had been the only one in the group to receive an electric shock. I attuned my senses again, and my connection to the room was gone. The breath, smoke, and light wove a beautiful picture in front of my eyes, but I was the kid in the corner of the classroom with my nose to the wall. Disconnected.

Just like Teddy.

The realization dropped me through the pit of my stomach and out into the universe. If I had been wearing a shirt, it would have been soaked through with the sweat I produced. Instead, it traced rivulets down my chest and back, settling into the waistband of my shorts.

I didn't want it to happen. This doesn't make me a monster. I was rationalizing again. My train of thought whipped around a small track, gaining speed until vertigo threatened to toss me to the ground.

The crackle of a third dipper of water onto the hot stones brought me back. I had lost time, a novel experience for me. It was not a welcome one. A deep sadness welled from where I had crawled up and out of my center. Maybe dehydration was getting to me. My threads were still missing from the air around me. Some of the other participants were closely enmeshed, likely people who had come together, but everyone's spirits touched, at least lightly.

Except for me, I thought. *Which is ironic because I'm the only one who can see how disconnected I am right now.*

My essence coiled tightly around me, almost suffocatingly so. Had I done that to myself? Harriet's spirit, a soft lavender, quested around me. I was clearly on her mind, but my own recoiled from the connection.

You're self-isolating, taking yourself out of the world. No one's punishing you for killing that guy, I thought. *Why are you doing it?*

Was I following a script, even unconsciously? Society had rules for a reason, regardless of laws. Not murdering people was pretty high on the list, in both ethical and moral frameworks. Those who broke the rules were the "others", outcasts and rejects. No one here knew what I had done, and even Harriet was only aware of my involvement, not that I had pulled the metaphorical trigger. Without anyone asking, no prosecution necessary, I had begun taking myself out of the comfort of the community.

You don't think you belong there anymore because you broke the contract. Self-loathing isn't a good look for you, Pierce.

A fourth dipper and another hiss. The most intense heat of the night radiated in waves out from the center. I didn't have any sweat left, and my shoulders were dry, which was why the tears streaming down my cheeks were a surprise. I had killed a man, intentionally or not, and worried more about being ostracized for trying to help than any legal ramifications.

But a kernel of truth burned like a bright seed in my mind, and possibilities blossomed as slivers of my silver reached tentatively for the people around me in an effort to feel like a part of the ceremony.

What kind of debt do I owe for something like that? I couldn't get the thought out of my head. *Blood money?* I laughed aloud, and the sound echoed in the hut, multiple sets of eyes turning to me in surprise. *You're losing it, Pierce.* I probably was.

You've always been a little vigilante. You did your best with what you had at the time. It seemed all I could provide myself was cold comfort. But I wasn't entirely off base.

By all accounts, Teddy was probably not a good man. Though if he had a wife, partner, or kids they likely thought he was. We fought so hard against the injustice the legal system stacked against us, the imbalance where the wealthy could choose to commit crimes because they could afford the associated fines. "Innocent until proven bankrupt" as the saying went. When the breaking of laws was compensated with money, they became guidelines to the rich and powerful. In my own efforts to push back at a system failing the people below its radar, I had blown past reasonable action. But how far would I go to set things right?

How far? You've still got blood in your veins and a job to do. Keep going. It has to count for something. Teddy died because he was getting other people killed, even if he didn't hold the knife. It doesn't square what you did, but you can repay the debt.

"I'm sorry," I whispered. "I'll try to make it right." Bright motes of silver left my mouth, joined the smoke dancing about the hut, and escaped through the same cracks. I hoped they would find Teddy's spirit, wherever it might have been.

Tom clapped his hands together four times, breaking our reveries with a start. We all blinked heavily at one another as the fire tender opened the flaps from outside. No light streamed in, and the burst of cold blowing in was a welcome respite from the heat, despite the enormous temperature difference.

We crawled, one by one, out of the hut, until everyone stood staring at the empty sky. It was pitch-black, a partial moon high above. The stars twinkled back at us, impossibly distant, but for the moment I felt close to them somehow. Fellow outcasts, drifting through space. A heavy hand rested on my shoulders, Harriet standing next to me.

"Feel any better?" she asked.

"How—" My voice cracked and broke, and I had to wet my lips with what little moisture I had left to try again. "How long were we in there?"

"Oh, about eight hours. Give or take."

It should have surprised me, but the journey my mind had gone on drained my body. I breathed in the cool night air, and the warmth of Harriet's palm seeped into my skin. I turned and threw my arms around her, eliciting a squawk of surprise, but she returned the embrace and held me closely. For a moment, my silver threads meshed with her lavender ones.

"Thank you," I said, quietly, muffled by her hair.

"Sounded like you needed it. Hope it helped."

I pulled back, wiping my eyes and clearing my throat. "I'll try my best to make it right, but I've got a lot more work to do."

Harriet gave a short laugh. "You and me, both, little cousin."

Chapter 17

I drank a gallon of water after we got home, then passed out for the rest of the night and half the next day. When I woke, my head was the clearest it had been in a long time. According to Harriet, sweats were supposed to do that, but I hadn't known what to expect. I half-thought the experience would leave me hungover. Instead a clarity of purpose buzzed in my head.

There was a job to do, and I was the only one to do it. Grief wasn't linear, but making Teddy's death mean something helped me put it away for now. My brief existential crisis almost pushed me off track of what I discovered in confronting Mr. Stanclift. The Hand was almost certainly involved.

But why? What would Hughes and his cronies stand to gain from a pile of dead bodies? *No, not dead. Drained.*

"Fuck me, I was right." I didn't even have a cat to talk to, so my words bounced around my empty apartment before the realization slapped me in the face. When I confronted Hughes about the elms, he couldn't even talk about the homeless like they were real people. I assumed he was being an elitist bastard, not casually tipping his hand.

Rushing to his office again wouldn't net me much, especially being a Sunday. Even if he was there, what was I going to do? Call him a murderer in front of the rest of the faculty? Chasing him around town would be even less effective. The irony would have been getting thrown in jail for harassment when killing a man hadn't put me there.

No, I needed to know what he was up to. What were they planning with the essence taken from four people, assuming the latest two were dead? What was it for?

I grabbed my flannel and sped down the stairs, only pausing long enough to pocket the rosary. Teddy was coming with me. When I hit the street, my steps faltered, vertigo almost pitching me headfirst into the road. An oncoming car blared its horn as I pulled myself back from the pavement and squatted on the concrete.

A few breaths later and the dizziness subsided enough for me to stand. My heart raced, and a wave of energy blew past me, southward, on the winds across the veil. I raised my eyes toward the source, and a glow like sunrise teased at the horizon to the northeast and downtown.

But it was midday.

My phone buzzed, and a text from Taylor was waiting for me.

TAYLOR:

I'm in trouble, Corbin.

CORBIN:

Did you feel that, too? What happened?

TAYLOR:

Mama bear is back. I sensed her nearby, and I thought I could take care of it myself. But I need your help.

CORBIN:

Where are you?

TAYLOR:

Over by East Rock, by the Giant's Steps Trail-head on English Drive. Hurry!

I ran to my car and whipped through the SCSU campus, taking Fitch Street and its subsequent turns, wending my way to East Rock Park. The farther I got from home, the faster the lingering fuzziness in my head faded. There wasn't any more glowing on the horizon. I'd have to investigate that once I got Taylor out of his bind.

Thankfully, the fastest route avoided downtown, and I broke every speed limit getting there. I could also drive all the way to the trailhead and park, instead of having to hoof it for any significant period.

I passed Taylor's nervous face as I pulled over to the side of the road where a large metal gate blocked a service road. About a hundred feet behind me was the trailhead, where my anxious apprentice waited.

"Corbin!" Taylor cried, waving for me to hurry.

I broke into a trot and made my way to where he stood. "Where is she?"

Taylor gestured to the trail, which snaked quickly uphill and into the woods. I let him lead, and we gained altitude swiftly, talking in hushed tones.

"I hoped she would stay away," I said, brushing aside an overgrown branch.

Taylor gave a sarcastic laugh. "Well, tell her when you see her."

She was a spirit bear, so there wouldn't be any prints to track in the dirt, but I opened my senses to check for other signs. We walked at a brisk pace for about ten minutes, winding through the trees, before taking a break and getting our bearings. I didn't detect a specific presence, though in a lush area like the park, there was plenty of life.

I panted, sweating. "Are you sure you saw her?"

Taylor glanced nervously around. "Yeah, one hundred percent."

"Well, I—" The words didn't make it out of my mouth before turning into a jumbled mess, my equilibrium evaporating. Another wave of energy, this one stronger than before, washed over us both. My head swam, and I sat directly on my ass in the middle of the trail to keep from falling over.

Taylor's talents were still growing, but it wasn't possible I was the only person having this experience. He looked a little green around the gills, maybe a little off-balance. "Did you feel that this time?"

Taylor nodded, an embarrassed look on his face. "I felt it before, too, but I didn't want to get distracted."

The glow I saw earlier, at my apartment, was present again to the north of where we stood.

"Mama bear is going to have to wait—" I didn't finish my sentence before Taylor broke into a run, heading up the trail.

"I see her!" he yelled, not waiting for any acknowledgement before disappearing around the corner.

"Goddamn it, Taylor!" I cried, my voice was thick with frustration. I took off after him. Despite my endurance being better than his the last time we hiked at a state park, I was still recovering from the night before. Whenever I thought I would catch up with him, he turned down another path and kept out of reach. It was a solid ten minutes before Taylor stopped for a break, sitting on a rock beside the trail.

"What the hell was that about?" I demanded, leaning over and resting my hands on my knees as I sucked lungfuls of air.

"I swear it was her," Taylor gasped, also out of breath.

Before he could say anything else, the ground shook. A deep rumbling passed through the earth underneath us, and my sense of vertigo returned with a vengeance, toppling me to the ground. Taylor must have been similarly affected because when my vision righted itself, he lay an arm's length away from me.

My head ached with the effort of opening my senses, peering into the spirit world. An explosion of color greeted my eyes, fountaining from the north above the tree line. An aftershock of what seemed to be a legitimate earthquake vibrated through my legs.

I stood and rounded on Taylor as he regained his feet. "Something isn't right, and this is starting to smell like bullshit, Taylor."

"Corbin..."

The tone of my name coming out of his mouth was the only thing I needed to know he had played me. It was my turn to take off at speed, but not down the trail. Running as fast as I could, I went straight through the trees to the northwest, heading for the Giant's Steps. I broke through the brush and across the access road, loping up the crude stairs two at a time.

Breaking twigs signaled Taylor's pursuit, with a muffled cry of "wait!" barely reaching my ears. I didn't care. The summit wasn't far, and I passed over the top of East Rock and down the backside to the north into the parking lot and observation area where a clear view of whatever the hell was going on awaited.

My sides ached, unaccustomed to this much cardio at once. I swore to my future self I'd start going to a gym and gulped air until I caught my breath. Other people sat and stood around the fence where I'd ended up, but they gave me a wide berth. A strange man running through the parking lot wearing normal clothes didn't give me the look of someone who was exercising for fun.

At first, nothing on the horizon clued me into the source of the earlier fireworks. The prior light show had dissipated while I made my way to the top. Waiting wasn't my strong suit, but the sprint wore me out, so I leaned against the railing and scanned the land below.

From this vantage West Rock, the other trails, parts of New Haven and Hamden and Sleeping Giant were all visible. Nothing was on fire, no smoke billowed on either side of the veil. There wasn't anything out of the ordinary—except for the restless shifting of a giant.

"Jesus, fuck," I breathed out quietly, taking in a slow rolling motion along the hills of the Sleeping Giant. Trees trembled in the distance like nothing more than quaking aspen. The head of Hobbomock, stone spirit of the Quinnipiac, rose with his chest. As if he woke from a dream, arms made from the mountain lifted the enormous torso until he leaned back on his elbows.

The double vision was nauseating. While the physical mounds didn't move, though you could hear tree trunks cracking and stone grinding from where I stood, the giant had risen in the spirit world. He was bigger than any *kaiju* I'd ever heard of, and in the spirit lands, the laws of physics didn't apply. Tendrils of spirit as thick as bridge cables tethered his spirit form to the earth. My mouth hung open, witnessing his motion translating into smaller shifts in the world itself. All the while, the ground trembled and shook.

At some point Taylor had caught up to me and was apparently trying to get my attention. I finally turned to him and attempted to make sense of what he was saying.

"I'm sorry. I didn't have a choice," he said, close to tears.

I didn't have the time or energy to care about whatever he was apologizing for. Grabbing his shirt by the shoulder I then spun him to face the waking giant. "What do you see, *apprentice*?"

"I don't—" he started to say but stopped as he recognized what I pointed him toward. "Oh. Oh my god."

"What have you done?" I asked. He couldn't answer before my fist hit him square in the jaw. He collapsed to the ground, and I followed him. "What have you *done*?" I repeated, standing over his prone form.

Taylor held his hands in front of his face, guarding against another assault. "It was Hughes!" he cried, spitting blood into the dirt to clear his mouth.

"What do you—Hughes?! Explain, fast, before I throw you off this god damn ridge." We would have been causing a scene, except the earthquake drove everyone to their cars seeking shelter and leaving the park.

"The Hand, they're doing something big. I don't know what, but I had to keep you away from the Green."

My eyes flew wide open, and I grabbed Taylor's jacket, hauling him to his feet and shoving him ahead of me toward the trail where we'd come from. We were over the hill and back down the steps before I spoke again. "Talk while you walk. What the fuck is going on?"

"I was on a waitlist for Yale," Taylor said, huffing and puffing his way along the track. "Hughes recognized my talent and said he'd get me in, next semester, if I did him a favor."

"So, you hung with the plebs at GCC for what? To get into bed with me?"

"Hughes said you were a thorn in his side, and if I distracted you he'd teach me magic on top of getting me off the waitlist."

I would have stopped to have this argument out properly, but we didn't have time. Hobbomock didn't seem fully awake yet, and there was still magic brewing in the air. The universe backed me up by knocking us off our feet with another burst of energy pulsing out from the giant. We recovered enough to continue stumbling down the trail, but aftershocks kept us unsteady as we made our way down the slope.

"Where are they, and what are they doing?"

Taylor glanced back at me, but I pushed him forward again, forcing him into the lead. "I don't know where, specifically, somewhere on the Green. He didn't tell me what they were doing, but they couldn't be interrupted, and he said to keep you out of their hair."

When we were close enough to the road, I veered us off the path and through the trees, breaking through a small thicket and trotting the remaining distance to my car. I jumped into the driver's seat, then shoved the passenger door open. "Get in."

He gave me a reluctant look. "You want my help?"

"At this very moment I *want* you to die in a fire." Taylor flinched at that. "But you're not done explaining, and if I have to throw you in front of Hobbomock to slow him down, I will. So, get in the fucking car."

Chapter 18

The ride downtown was short, but I had enough time to get a bit more out of Taylor. I was as calm as a cucumber on the outside, despite reeling from the shock of Taylor's betrayal. Crisis mode did that to a person. An endocrine cocktail sang through my veins as I gripped the wheel.

"Talk," I demanded, jerking the car around and speeding back the way I had come.

"I hadn't met you, Corbin. It was the best decision I could make for myself."

"I'm glad you're comfortable justifying it to yourself," I retorted.

"Yeah, but you started teaching me, and I realized Hughes was using me because he could. I wasn't anything more than a pawn to him."

"You think?" There wasn't a charitable bone in my body at the moment. I swerved around a bicyclist, then sped through a yellow light about to turn red.

"There's no reason for you to believe me, but I tried to get out. I told him I wasn't going to help him anymore, but Hughes, he...threatened me. Said he'd blacklist me, and I'd never attend a university again. But he also promised no one would get hurt."

"Well, he lied. Did you know the Hand was responsible for Clyde's death?" I glanced over to see what appeared to be genuine horror on his face.

"No," he said glumly. "I had no idea they were involved at all."

"So, you finding the body was a coincidence?" Now every random happenstance stank like a conspiracy as I went over the last month in my mind. "And those spirits we chased around downtown, did you lure those in just to set me up for today?"

"Jesus, Corbin. I'm not good at any of this. You think I'm rounding up jackrabbits? No. Those weren't my fault, though Hughes's people did tell me they were there and to ask for your help in getting rid of them…" He trailed off, likely realizing he was describing a literal setup. "I lied about being able to detect them. There wasn't any other way to explain how I knew. I didn't expect Clyde would be there when I went looking, I swear."

"Trust isn't my strong suit right now."

He winced but didn't say anything else. I let the silence stretch on, instead concentrating on combat driving as we made our way to the Green. The closer we got, the more my head ached. It was pressure, like the worst sinus headache I'd ever had. That alone could have guided me to the right place like a terrible magnet, but a surprise waited that clued me in faster than following the pain growing behind my eyes.

Amanda. Alexander Hughes's student. The girl who kept showing up when I least expected her stood outside of the Center Church on the Green. Taylor seemed as confused as I was, and after I parked on Elm Street, we both ran to the steps. Whatever guard duty she was serving, I wasn't going to let her stop me. "Let me by—"

She stepped to the side without hesitation before I finished my demand. "You'd have found this place sooner," she said, her airy voice rich with derision, "if *someone* hadn't scared away all the bait I attracted to bring you here." She eyed Taylor with disdain for a moment but turned her gaze back to me.

I paused, shaking my head. "Wait—you—you're helping me? I thought you were one of Hughes's disciples."

She sighed, rolled her eyes, and clicked her tongue. "Hughes likes the sounds of his own voice. When I found out what was going on, I didn't want to play any part in it. I couldn't do much, since I *literally* can't *talk* about it." Amanda widened her eyes purposefully, and I got the hint.

"He had you swear an oath. Figures." She also could have been playing both sides, but I wasn't going to look this particular gift horse in the mouth.

"So now you understand why I had to let the petting zoo loose. You're nothing if not predictable. Anyway." She jerked her head toward the building. "If your head hurts as much as mine does, you should hurry."

"I'm guessing there isn't anything else you can..." Without knowing the restrictions placed on her, I had to assume Amanda couldn't do more than talk in vague terms and wouldn't be able to help me in any material way. I motioned at the door, but she shrugged at me. "Got it." I nodded and rushed past her into the building.

The Center Church was constructed in the early 1800s and held over a hundred gravestones from the original settlement. Where the rest of the stones had been moved, these stayed. Many unidentified remains were also interred there.

If you were wondering why I didn't steal bones from the Church instead of training a raccoon, well, it was complicated. Most of those would have been the latest of the colony and also less likely to have been of native or mixed heritage as they were named colonists.

I stood by my gamble, and while I wasn't Christian, my original plan didn't involve desecrating graves. I tried to have some principles, even if they were a moving target.

The crypt was below the church, so I ran through the building to the stairs downward. I attended a tour when I moved back to the city. They'd have taken my degree away if I hadn't at least seen this particular local landmark, so I remembered roughly how to get there.

I fell against the wall of the stairwell, an icepick of agony slamming directly into the center of my skull, and I nearly tumbled the rest of the way down. A painted metal gate that normally barred entrance was conspicuously open. Stumbling through it, onto the floor of the crypt itself, I righted myself and scanned the brightly lit space.

I wasn't sure if I expected a torchlit tableau, complete with pentagram and candles, but the reality didn't disappoint. Five figures stood in a circle around a central stone table, each where a point of an invisible star would lay. They wore ceremonial garb, a combination of robes and cloaks, with Mr. Hughes himself at the apex. His was the most ornate robe with a pattern picked out in silver along the arms. Alexander's bearing was much less professorial than usual, leaning heavily toward an overblown cult leader, eyes wide and voice booming.

His words couldn't reach me clearly but echoed dissonantly in the short ceiling of the basement. This style of magic had never been my forte. European magic, especially Western, tended to the ornate and highly prescriptive. Amanda was right though, and whatever they were doing was on its way to a crescendo.

I approached the group, though none of them had eyes for me, and was about twenty feet away when the figure lying on the stone in the middle of the group came into focus. It was Sonia, one of the people missing from the downtown crew. She wasn't tied down but also didn't move. I had to assume she was unconscious, rather than dead. Whatever Hughes and his cronies were doing likely required a living sacrifice.

Next to the table was a hole of about the same size, excavated from the brick floor.

A dim white light pulsed below the surface, like a heartbeat. I took all this in as I ran toward the cabal, but I wasn't going to make it.

Hughes raised a large syringe, like the kind you saw in movies that seemed comically large but ended up being real. He held it in his hand like a dagger, poised over Sonia's still form. I opened my mouth to yell, but time nearly stood still as his hand dropped inch by inch until the needle plunged into Sonia's chest. Hughes drove the plunger downward as I finally screamed.

"No!"

All eyes were on me in an instant, but most flicked back to their task. Hughes motioned with his head, and the Finger of the Hand closest to me turned in my direction. He was of middling height and build, mostly concealed within layers of flowing cloth, but a square chin jutted out from the hood.

Chanting rose from the remaining participants as Square-Chin took a few steps forward and placed himself between me and the ritual. I pulled the Hunter's Rosary free of my pocket and in a smooth motion coiled it around my fist like a righteous brass knuckle. It blazed with stolen essence, and Square-Chin's eyes widened briefly.

Magic wasn't great for fighting, in a literal sense. It was usually a scorched earth policy. To impact the physical world strongly enough, you have to take resources from somewhere, and in combat situations, draining your personal reserves is usually a bad choice. Most practitioners didn't think it was fair. They wanted to do everything they dreamed of since they were children. But the desired outcome required more essence than they could generate themselves, pool together on a regular basis, or steal from the environment without drastic consequences.

But I wasn't playing fair.

I strode to meet him and ducked his attempt to grapple with me. I dropped to one knee and drove up into his stomach with my improvised weapon. *Stay down*, I thought, driving the intention through the rosary and spending Teddy's life force with abandon.

My would-be assailant lifted off his feet and fell heavily onto the floor, the unexpected ferocity of my assault catching him off guard. He landed with a thump and an involuntary grunt before lying still.

I glanced at the necklace. It still shone with energy. Whatever I had done either took less effort than I expected or there was more juice than I had anticipated stored in those discs of bone. More proof that sacrifices, even unwilling ones, harnessed great power. Which, perhaps ironically, was what I had come here to stop.

Looking past the prone form on the floor, Hughes and his cronies reached a fever pitch in their chant. Sonia's essence flowed in a verdigris stream into space next to the table where she lay, merging with the white light below the surface. Instantly the glow brightened until it was nearly incandescent, and tears blurred my vision.

Wiping my eyes, the scene before me changed again. There was no more chanting, no more light flowing from poor Sonia, whose lifeless body lay drained and empty on the stone. Only Hughes, standing triumphantly above the pit with one hand outstretched, drawing a line of energy from whatever lay below. It was as wide as a bridge cable, heavy with power.

I leapt over Square-Chin and charged at Alexander, whose smile was thick with condescension. Only five feet separated the two of us when Hughes raised his other hand to me, palm out, and my forward momentum halted like I had struck an invisible barrier. Except it wasn't invisible to me. Essence flowed from his outstretched hand like water, cascading over and around me until it enveloped my entire body.

My limbs were stiff, and I couldn't even wiggle a finger, but I could finally peer into the hole. The largest tree root I had ever seen lay beneath us. In the physical world it was a massive brown thing, easily a foot across. The spirit lands painted a different picture. There, it was crystalline, like a wide quartz vein, glistening with essence. The only comparison my mind could come up with on the fly was like watching light pulse through a fiber-optic cable, with bright motes passing north to south.

Hughes laughed exultantly. "I've done it, Pierce! All the power I'll ever need at my fingertips! There's nothing you can do—"

The ground shook violently, and the triumph died on his lips. The light passing through the vein of crystal dimmed in the equivalent of a spiritual brownout, and the luminous cage around me disappeared in a blink. A heartbeat passed, and the only sounds I could hear were the blood pumping through my veins and a confused gasp from Hughes.

Time winked out of existence.

I found myself disoriented and in pain, crumpled against one of the larger gravestones. Standing, I took stock of the groaning bodies strewn around the room. The pit blazed back to life as even more essence flowed through it. But it switched direction, and now the energy flowed to the north. The change in the flow's polarity must have caused a backlash, flinging us around.

The amount of power required to do that was terrifying, and I let out an almost involuntary low whistle of appreciation. The noise brought Hughes's attention to me, his head swiveling to glare in my direction. Surprisingly, when I peered across the veil, I saw a room bright with essence. It infused the stones, and everyone was limbed in faerie fire, lightly dusted with ephemeral shrapnel from the blast.

To the left, Sonia's body lay with limbs akimbo among the broken remains of the stone table. It had cracked and fallen, leaving her a black-and-white discard among a sea of color.

I let out a great huff of frustration. My hand still glowed with the Hunter's Rosary, and I held it between us as I advanced toward his prone form. "I keep having to ask this today. What did you *do*, Hughes?"

"I..." He trailed off, putting a hand to his head in apparent pain. The thin aura around him dimmed as he absorbed it.

Healing with magic wasn't instantaneous, but consuming essence would hasten the process. It wasn't something you could do for yourself too often because it always required external power. You could trade a headache for a head cold, but it was robbing Peter to pay Paul. Lucky for whatever pains he suffered, an unexpected excess floated about the room.

Footsteps echoed down the stairwell, and I glanced behind me to find Taylor and Amanda running into the basement. They stopped after passing through the gate, taking in the scene. Taylor stared at me with open anguish mixed with confusion, but I didn't have time for his hurt feelings.

I strode the last few steps to where Alexander lay and knelt beside him, grabbing the front of his robes with one fist and raising the rosary in the other. "What. Did. You. Do?"

Hughes's eyes snapped back to recognition, and he shoved at the hand holding him with his own, trying to shield himself from my threatened assault. My grip didn't loosen, and I was pretty sure he knew I could take him in a fistfight, so he settled back with a sigh and a groan when I didn't immediately punch him in the face.

"It's a power source, Pierce," he said matter-of-factly.

"I figured that part out, thanks. Have you been outside yet?" The sarcasm in my voice dripped heavily into my reply.

"Out—how could we have gone outside?"

I let go of his clothing, rocking back on my heels. "So...you don't know you've woken the Sleeping Giant?"

"That's a good euphemism, Pierce, but—"

"No. Literally. Hobbomock is awake. Whatever you did here was an alarm clock, and you've got a groggy god on your hands." I stood and offered my hand to Hughes.

He looked at it dubiously, but after trying to lever himself up, he grabbed it so I could pull him to his feet. I obliged, but as soon as he stood, I slapped him with an open palm so hard across the face it echoed through the entire chamber. He staggered and fell to one knee, holding his hand to his cheek with shock written large in his eyes.

"What was that for?" he cried.

Adrenaline still sang in my veins, and a manic grin spread across my lips. "First, I have *always* wanted to do that. Second, you deserved it." I put out my hand again. Perhaps surprisingly, he took it, and I hauled him to his feet once again. "Now. Tell me everything."

Chapter 19

The walls around us shook, which was disconcerting because we were *in a basement.* I headed toward the stairs with Hughes in tow, Taylor and Amanda watching silently as we passed before they turned to follow.

Maslow's Hierarchy of Needs didn't work to help me understand my priorities, so instead, I applied Corbin's Hierarchy of Crisis. Which I made up on the spot. Hughes might have been responsible for deaths of multiple people, but the world seemed fit to shake itself apart while we watched, so step one was getting out of the building.

We hit the street, and it was pandemonium. Only our select group was likely to see what was happening in the spirit lands, but everyone felt the tremors and shakes. The cityscape around the Green wasn't massively tall, but we still had to line up with the street to gaze north at the towering form of Hobbomock.

"Dear God in Heaven," Hughes breathed into the dumbfounded silence that had overtaken the group. "What is that?"

I scoffed. "You know your history; don't pretend you don't understand what that is."

"You can't be serious," Hughes replied. "There's no way we could have—"

"Awakened an ancient god by doing something stupid? I'm a firm believer in that being a possibility." Step two of the triage was finding out how Hughes and his cronies had fucked this up so badly. "Why don't you fill us in?"

Hughes frowned at me but launched into as brief a description as he could, clearly still trying to maintain whatever secrets of his craft he had used in the process.

The Hand had been aware of the vein beneath the Crypt for some time, though no one had the audacity to mess with it. Records going back to the early 1800s held curious references, right around the time they built the church. The "power source", as Hughes referred to it, was known to the leaders of the settlement as a sacred site for the Quinnipiac.

As their tribe waned, the settlers wanted to make a final effort to assimilate the locals. The church leaders pushed for the Church on the Green to be built on this exact spot, hoping to incorporate their beliefs into the town's religious structure. The building was already slated for construction, but they could sway the decision on exactly where to lay the foundation.

So, there it sat, undisturbed, for many years until Hughes took control of the Hand and made a plan to investigate the provenance of the site. After he found the vein, he determined it responded to infusions of essence, and he could feel it "opening." His story cascaded quickly and ended with today, where they unleashed the culmination of their efforts to feed essence into the vein until it revealed its secrets.

"Waking the giant was not our goal, Pierce," Hughes said, as he finished his abbreviated tale. He seemed almost grumpy about it as opposed to horrified, which was about par for the course.

"How are you going to fix it?" I asked.

"Me?!" Hughes exclaimed, taking a step back from me. "We used all our stores to open the vein. What do you expect me to do about this?" He gestured at the giant in the distance.

"I know you have a high opinion of yourself, but I would have hoped 'awakening a god' would lead to a *mea culpa*. Maybe an apology and some effort on your part to un-fuck this whole thing."

"This situation may have to play itself out. Perhaps he'll go back to sleep—" Hughes started to say, but a loud crash interrupted him. We all turned to the steps of the library across the street. An enormous piece of cornice had fallen from the edge of the roof, shattering into many smaller bits and cascading down the stairs after leaving large gouges in the stone of the steps themselves.

"Besides being woefully incorrect," I said, swallowing heavily, "we don't have the time to waste."

"Really, I—" Hughes didn't have a chance to equivocate another syllable before I was on him, grabbing the front of his shirt and leaning in so no one else could hear me.

"I get it, Alexander. You're a coward. But this isn't something you can sit out of. Now, let's move." I raised my voice to carry to Taylor and Amanda. "Release Amanda from her oath, Hughes, so she can help."

Hughes narrowed his eyes at me before closing them, his mouth moving in a silent recitation. A cobalt shell appeared around Amanda's body, changed to mist, and wafted away. She shook herself, like waking from a daydream.

"I'll do what I can," Amanda said, nodding to me.

I faced the giant, whose head poked above the cityscape. He wasn't standing yet but lay in the same prone position as before, propped up on his craggy elbows. I had one hope, that he wouldn't move quickly. When I woke after a long slumber, I might be disoriented and groggy. He had slept for hundreds of years at least, and I gave a silent prayer he was a slow riser.

"We need a better vantage point," I said to the group. Hughes's compatriots had followed us out of the basement after recovering from being thrown around themselves, and there were faces I didn't recognize. We had no time for introductions. I had to assume they would follow Alexander's lead.

Taylor raised his hand, and I shot him a look.

"This isn't class, Taylor," I admonished. "Spit it out."

"We could go up the building on the corner." He pointed at the tallest structure downtown, an office building towering multiple stories above the more modest historic ones.

The ground had stopped shaking, at least for the moment, so it wasn't the worst idea. "Let's make it a quick trip. Taylor, you and Amanda are coming with me. Hughes, you stay here. You'll slow us down."

"I say—" he protested, but I took off at a jog toward 195 Church Street, ignoring whatever else he was going to say.

Taylor, Amanda, and I covered the two blocks easily, but climbing the stairs wasted more time than I liked. It wasn't safe to trust an elevator, given the quakes and aftershocks, so more than a handful of minutes later, we found ourselves on the fifteenth floor. Keycard access was normally necessary, but the fire alarm had been tripped, so the doors were automatically unlocked for safety.

Popping out of the stairwell, we found our way to a corner of the building with a panoramic view of downtown. It would have been breathtaking on any other day, but I was seriously out of breath from the trip upward.

Taking in the scene across the city and into Hamden, Hobbomock was in much the same position as before. I was struck once again by the disconnect between the physical world, where the mountain sat immovable as always, and the spirit lands where his head swung ever so slowly to scan the horizon. His movement wasn't glacial, but he was a being of ponderous stone, so it made sense he wouldn't win any footraces.

"What are we looking for?" Amanda asked, pressing her face close to the window.

"I don't know," I admitted in a low tone. I wished I did. It wasn't about pride or appearing stupid in front of younger practitioners. This was an unfamiliar experience, since I'd never woken a god before, and everyone was out of their depth.

"What's going on with those veins?" Taylor asked, squinting into the distance.

When I saw Hobbomock from the summit of East Rock, thick tendrils of spirit rose up from the land as he did. Now he was stationary again, and those thick cables of energy remained. It was difficult to see from this distance, but they seemed to glow and pulse.

Like the vein below the crypt.

"Son of a bitch," I said aloud, then turned on my heel and pelted down the corridor to the stairs and made my way to ground level, Taylor and Amanda following. We were all panting when we met up with Hughes again, who stared into the distance at the horizon.

"Did you learn anything?" he asked distractedly.

"Let's go find out," I replied, motioning for everyone to follow.

The shakes had stopped while we did reconnaissance, but the ground rumbled ominously as I hit the steps leading into the basement of the church. Sonia's body still lay lifeless and empty among the broken stones. I took off my coat and laid it over her, as if she were only cold and needed warming.

No amount of kindness would bring her back, but I had more respect for the dead than her previous host. There wasn't time for vengeance, but in that moment, looking down at her slight form, I swore Hughes wouldn't get away with his atrocities. But I had bigger fish to fry first.

We arrayed ourselves in a circle around the glowing pit. The motes of light among the stream of energy within the vein still flowed to the north, toward Hobbomock.

"You said this was a power source, Hughes. When you experimented with it, what did you learn?"

Hughes blinked and puffed air from his lips, seeming to settle into an academic mode. "Well, it took anything we threw at it. I could tell there was a threshold of some kind, though our magic didn't get close enough for any number of us to push it over the brink."

"But it never latched onto you?" I asked.

"No, nothing like that. Why, what are you thinking?"

"I've got a theory..." Hesitantly, I knelt and reached out to the vein, running a finger along it. There were no bright flashes, no sudden vortexes, but it was warm to the touch. It was a conduit, not a black hole, and I was thankful for my luck holding so far.

"Sonia's essence, and I'm assuming the method you used to *murder her*, tipped the scales," I said, not trying to hide my contempt for Hughes and his actions. There were a lot of shuffling feet and not much else. "You should try to tip them back."

Hughes gave me a perplexed look. "Come again?"

I stood and dusted my hands on my pants. "We don't have a lot of time. If Hobbomock shifting halfway to sitting knocked part of downtown loose, what do you think happens when he stands up? Goes for a stroll?"

Hughes opened and closed his mouth but no words came out. He nodded, then shakily lowered himself within reach of the vein.

He wet his dry lips and gingerly reached out to touch it. Nothing happened until he extended his essence into it.

He gasped, and his body went rigid, grip tightening on the root, like a man being electrocuted by high-voltage. The light pulsing through the conduit slowed but not to a significant degree. Guttural sounds forced their way out of Hughes's mouth, and I didn't wait more than an extra moment before pulling him forcefully away from the contact. I didn't expect to be taken along for the ride, but it wasn't a zero percent chance. The odds were still in my favor.

"Tell me what happened," I demanded.

A small whimper escaped his lips, but he got a hold of himself again. "It's a torrent. Everything is being pulled to the giant. I would have been lost if…" He looked up at me with surprise.

"Don't thank me. I didn't do it out of the kindness of my heart."

"Of course. Nonetheless, I don't think there's a good chance even the group of us will reverse the flow at this point. The spirit is hungry, and I fear we've set a course of action which can't be stopped. At least not until we learn more."

"That sounds a lot like 'I'm not going to try harder', Hughes."

His eyes flashed with anger for the first time since his plan had gone so far off the rails. "What do you want from me?"

"How many people did you kill to make this happen, Hughes? Three? Four?" My gaze traveled among Alexander and his cronies. "How many would you sacrifice to stop it? Hm? Or is it only okay to murder people when you don't know their names?"

"You want me to throw my life away, when we aren't even sure what will put the giant back to sleep?"

"I *need* you to give a shit that *you* caused this calamity and do something about it."

Hughes huffed loudly at me. "Well, unless you're planning to kill me yourself, I'm not doing it, Corbin. There's got to be another way—"

The ground rocked, and we were all thrown off our feet. My head collided with one of the gravestones, and my ears rang, stars dancing in front of my eyes. When I rose again, half of the remaining members of The Hand were gone, fled during the confusion.

I glanced around and found Taylor standing at the edge of the pit, tears rolling down his face. "It's my fault."

"What?" I asked dumbly.

"If I hadn't agreed to help them, you would have found this place, stopped them." He turned to me, a manic look on his face. "Tell me what I have to do."

I closed my eyes and shook my head to clear it. Taylor was young and stupid, but despite not being entirely wrong, he shouldn't be the one to potentially sacrifice himself for The Hand's mistakes. "Jesus Christ, Taylor. Don't make me want to forgive you." I sighed loudly and tilted my head back. Giving myself a moment to breathe, my hands came to rest at my sides.

A familiar warmth, the stolen essence, burned a metaphysical hole in my pocket. Hughes had called my bluff. Short of throwing him bodily into the pit, I couldn't force him to try harder than he already had, and I wasn't willing to take another life to satisfy my aims. Taylor was an idiot, and I was still beyond furious at his betrayal. But this Hail Mary offer to give up his essence to fix a problem he wasn't the direct cause of? It made me pause, and in a moment of reflection, I came to a quick conclusion.

Pickings were slim, and I wasn't willing to let someone else stand in for me when I could put myself in harm's way. I had said I'd make it right, standing under the moon with Harriet. How much more appropriate could sacrificing my life, alongside the spirit of the man I had killed, to protect the rest of the city be?

"Fuck me, this is a terrible idea," I said, before wrapping the rosary around my left fist again. I shoved Taylor aside, ignoring his shocked expression, and stepped into the pit. I opened my senses, collected my essence, and plunged my hands into the fiery torrent of energy flowing to an angry god.

Hughes was right. The pull was intense and tried to drag me along with it. I pushed against it and drew power from the rosary; the coil blazing white-hot and searing into the flesh of my palm. At first, I could barely maintain equilibrium and keep myself present in the moment, but I gained ground inch by inch until the polarity of the flow neared the tipping point again. My veins screamed with energy, and I pushed with all my might against the will of a god.

Then I died.

Chapter 20

"*Aho*, young Raven. That was a mighty stupid thing you did."

My head ached way more than a dead man's had any right to, and my vision was gone, replaced by solid, blinding white. I shut my eyelids, and they did their job, replacing the bright expanse with the orange glow of sunlight filtering through them. No, not gone. I had apparently been staring at an empty sky. Opening my eyes again, I let my vision adjust, and it resolved slowly into light pinks and rose gold pastels. It wasn't a sky I was familiar with.

Wait. I *did* know it, but I wasn't used to seeing it with this set of eyes. I tried to look with my inner eyes to peer across the veil, and...nothing happened. *Oh, shit.* I levered myself onto my elbows, and the first sight to greet me was a figure in plain clothes. His face was thin, with skin the color of sandstone and similarly weathered. Despite that, he didn't appear old, only aged. He crouched in front of me and must have been the person I heard as I woke. Scuffed work boots, jeans, and a flannel shirt open over a tank top completed a weirdly casual look for my unknown companion.

I cleared my throat and wet my lips before croaking out a response. "Where am I?" Despite the sinking feeling in my gut telling me I already had the answer, I needed confirmation.

"I'd have thought it was obvious, but you're in the spirit lands, Raven." His voice was a kind baritone, with a hint of amusement.

"I was afraid of that. Why do you keep calling me Raven?"

He shrugged and offered me a hand, helping me to my feet. "It's your name, isn't it? It's what Corbin means. I like this version better. Besides, I haven't seen Raven himself in a while, so I figured it couldn't hurt."

Once I was standing, I got a better look at my surroundings. If I didn't know better, I'd have assumed I was still on the Green. The trees were familiar, if more thickly grown, but all the buildings were gone. There were no roads, only thin paths cutting their way through the copses. But it was eerily familiar. These weren't the spirit lands I was used to, overlaid against the "real" world. I had gone deeper.

I guess that's what happens when you die. Vertigo hit me, and I nearly keeled over, but strong hands caught me before I toppled. A few breaths later, I steadied myself, then nodded, and he let go of my arms.

"I haven't gotten used to being dead yet. Thank you—" I stopped myself, unsure of who I was addressing. "Uh, you seem to know me, but I can't say the same."

"Keitan," the man said. "And you're not *dead*-dead, if it makes you feel any better."

"That's good—"

"Not yet, anyway," he continued, which stopped me mid-sentence and dropped a stone of anxiety into the pit of my stomach.

I eyed the figure across from me while regaining what little equilibrium I could, and recognition struck my mind like lightning. Keitan was a spirit from Quinnipiac lore. According to legend, he was the one who put Hobbomock to sleep with a spell, after the tribe called on him for help.

"I'm not sure what I expected a Great Spirit to look like, but after Hobbomock, this isn't it." Running my mouth at an ancient spirit might not have been the best idea, but I had a lot going on.

Luckily, Keitan only chuckled. "Gotta move with the times. What? I need to wear a deerskin loincloth to get some respect?"

"No disrespect intended, sorry." I shook my head to clear it. "Why are you here?"

"I live here. Why are *you*?" he countered.

I opened my mouth to reply but gaped like a fish instead. The pain in my brow was receding but still present, if distant. The last memory I had was grabbing the vein of energy flowing to the waking giant and pushing into it.

My throat was dry, and I cleared it before answering. "I was trying to reverse the flow of power, to put Hobbomock back to sleep."

Keitan nodded. "Not a bad idea, all things considered. It took a lot to get him to go down in the first place. Too bad you leaped before you looked." He tsked at me. "But that's pretty typical of you wannabe-hero types."

"It almost worked. I didn't have a lot to go on, so I accepted the risk."

"Yeah, it's not like you could have sought some helpful *manitou* to guide you." His words were casual but held a gentle sarcasm.

"You're here to give me a hard time because I didn't seek you out?"

He laughed aloud, and it was a pleasant sound instead of mocking. "I'm here because someone was drowning in the river. I stayed because it turns out you've got some powerful medicine, and I'm curious. The ball busting is because you hurt my feelings. A little anyway."

"River?" I asked, dumbly. As if by magic, a crystal-clear river suddenly flowed to my left. The surface sparkled and danced, similar to the vein of essence that had dragged me into the spirit lands.

"How do you think you got here? Hobbomock reeled you in like a trout on a line." He smiled and strolled to the edge of the river, sitting cross-legged in the soft grass. "I don't go around plucking mortals off the street. Hell, I don't get around much outside of the spirit lands these days. Not a lot going for us on the other side."

My brain fog lifted enough for my good fortune to smack me in the face. This was Keitan, the legendary spirit who had taken care of this problem once before. Maybe he could help me, but first I had to contend with the whole "being dead" problem. I sat next to him on my own patch of earth. "You said I wasn't 'dead-dead'. What did you mean?"

"Oh, that," he said airily. "Well, you sure as hell would've been dead if I had let you get carried off. But you won't be able to get back to the physical world by yourself."

"Can you help me cross over?"

Keitan sucked his teeth and tilted his head in a gesture of uncertainty. "Might." He waited, staring at me. "Then again, might not. Do you know why Hobbomock went on a rampage the first time?"

"The stories say it was about him not receiving the proper devotion from the tribe."

"A little vague but close enough for being as removed as you are from it. I remember it like it was yesterday. *Manitou*, like us, want to be acknowledged. We love to be revered, receive offerings, that kind of stuff." He sighed wistfully.

"You keep saying *manitou*, spirits. Are you not gods?"

Keitan laughed uproariously for a good minute, even falling over to the ground before recovering and wiping tears from his eyes. "Is the mountain a god? Is the sky a god?"

"No—"

He cleared his throat. "That was a rhetorical question. You're interrupting."

"Sorry—" I began to say, then closed my mouth sheepishly.

"Is the...never mind, you messed up my groove. No, we're not gods. We're what the Creator made us, playing our parts. Hobbomock sure is huge, though, so I get why you'd think that. Big man like him wants big offerings. You wouldn't *believe* the amount of shellfish I had to feed him to put him to sleep originally. Took years to restock the bay."

"That sounds...bad?" I ventured, hesitantly.

"Anyway, I'm getting off track. I could help you, but the tribes are fewer now. Who's going to pacify the giant if he wakes up again? Not many other white folks with medicine are as interested in keeping this kind of peace as you are, little Raven. Maybe I should let him step all over your fancy city."

"He's going to hurt a lot of people."

"Shame. Maybe your friends should have thought of that before they woke him up."

This wasn't going anywhere, and the twinkle in his eye said he was playing with me. I didn't know exactly how time worked this deep in the spirit lands, but I doubted I had much of it. "You did it once, to aid your people. Clearly, I'll do anything, given I'm already mostly dead. What do you want from me in exchange for your help?"

"Ooh, Bear was right. You're a bright one."

"Bear?" I asked. I could hear the capital letter and expected he wasn't talking about the regular fauna.

"Worry about that if you make it out of here. What do I want?" He spread his arms wide, palms up. "What have you got?"

"I don't have time for games, if that's what's happening."

"Whoa, now. We're just negotiating. It's been a while since I had a supplicant looking for my assistance. I don't even know the exchange rate."

I stood, suddenly looming over the seated figure. "If there's one spirit here, maybe there are others. Thank you for saving me, but maybe I'll try my luck elsewhere." Turning, I took a step away from the river toward what appeared to be a small path through the trees.

"These are my woods, Bird-man. Best of luck if you want to go it alone. I suggest you sit down and consider my question, though. You're right, there isn't a lot of time."

My body tensed, and I twisted around, back toward the spirit. The playful light in Keitan's eyes had died, replaced with a flinty stare. There were limits to his good humor, it seemed, and attempting to leave pushed them too far. I spun and sat again, considering him.

I hadn't considered my appearance since waking and looked down to observe I wore the same clothes I had been on the other side. My leg bag was still there, though it was empty when I patted it. "I'm afraid I don't have a lot that would be useful to you. Left my wallet in my other body, it seems."

"It's what's on the inside that counts," he said, holding his hand to where his heart would be. Did manitou have hearts? Keitan took a tobacco pouch out of a pocket with a set of papers and started rolling a cigarette as he spoke. "Tell you what, you're in a bit of a crunch, so I'll make you a deal."

He paused, waiting for some kind of response, but all I said was, "Go on."

Keitan grinned. Clearly, I'd passed some kind of test. He wasn't a faerie, whose exactness with language was supremely important. If it was an accord with the fae of legend and I'd have said "okay," then that would be me accepting the offer. Even half-dead, I wasn't that much of an idiot.

"I want two things from you. First, a piece of your medicine."

That was a hard ask, if I understood him correctly. I assumed he meant taking a portion of the essence that fueled my magic. It would have been one thing to give him some essence, like I did with Scratch. It was another for him to remove a "piece" of it. "How much?" I asked.

He shrugged. "Not so much that you'll miss it too badly."

"For how long?"

Keitan smiled, nodding slightly in some kind of appreciation for me understanding his request. "Forever."

The blood drained from my face and settled into a knot in the pit of my stomach. He wasn't done yet, though. He had said he wanted two things. "What else?"

"Second, you dedicate yourself to the earth."

I tilted my head in confusion. "Don't I already do that?"

"More than some, not as much as others. Ruffled your feathers, eh? A little pride there? Well, get humble, Corbin. You want my help? You're going to serve the land."

"What does that mean, exactly?"

"It's pretty open-ended, if I'm being honest. Times aren't great on the other side, man. You know that. You've seen it. You're going to work to make things better for the land, more than what you're doing now."

I compressed my lips into a flat line, deep in consideration. "What happens if I don't do it? Do I just die here?"

"You're asking if I'm giving you a false choice." He slapped his knee excitedly, then stuck the cigarette in his mouth. He popped a match, which had come from nowhere, against his thumbnail. It flared brightly and obscured my vision. When it cleared, he blew a smoke ring in my direction. "Good catch. But no, for the sake of argument, if you don't accept my deal, I'll help you cross the veil, for a much cheaper and less permanent price. But you're on your own putting the giant down."

My heartbeat counted the moments as I contemplated his offer. On the one hand, I could take my chances with Hughes and company, see if there was a way to pool our powers and put the giant back to bed. But on the other, I had an offer of aid from the spirit who had done it the first time.

Too many innocent lives hung in the balance, and I had wasted enough daylight messing around with this conversation. I held my hand out and waited. Keitan's eyes lit up, and he eagerly reached past it to grasp my wrist, and I grabbed his in return.

Silver welled up from my chest, flowed down my arm, and into Keitan's. The transfer was quick and painless, if a touch uncomfortable.

"Speak your oath," he said.

The power in my palm mingled with the tawny of Keitan's. It was already harder to do than before, though I didn't have an opportunity to experiment and understand the extent of what I had given up. I had nothing prepared, but after another moment, the words came, and I spoke with a clear voice. "I, Corbin Pierce, vow to serve the land." Simple was best in situations like this. It was open-ended and vague, but I'd have to deal with those repercussions later.

Keitan nodded with apparent approval, removed the cigarette from his lips, and pressed it to mine. I took a drag and inhaled the fragrant smoke, breathing it out easily into the sky above. The energy passed back into my body, settling deep into my bones with the weight of the surrounding forest. I gasped as my joints popped with the tension. We broke contact, and I shook my hands to loosen them again.

The manitou clapped me on the back and then snaked an arm around my shoulder. "Now, here's what you're going to do."

Chapter 21

Pain was the first sensation I experienced once I opened my eyes in the crypt again. The second thing I noticed were three sets of eyes staring at me with varying levels of concern. Taylor's were filled with tears, Amanda's were curious, but Hughes's were downright creepy. It was like he saw an interesting bug and was deciding whether or not to stick a pin in it.

I'd never woken up in a hole in the ground before, and it wasn't a circumstance I wanted to repeat. Granted, the whole dying thing made the entire situation less palatable in general. My throat was dry to the point where swallowing razor blades was a better alternative, but I cleared it anyway.

"What are you all looking at?" I croaked into the silence. My left hand was on fire, and when I flexed it, bone crumbled to the floor. I examined my palm. The pattern of the rosary had made a bright red indentation on my skin. It burned, and my range of motion was diminished, but I could still move it.

"We thought you were dead," Taylor said, reaching down and offering me a hand.

He pulled me to my feet, but my head swam, and I nearly toppled over. I leaned against him for support, turning my gaze on the rest of the spinning room. Everyone else had gone. No other members of the Hand remained standing beside Hughes. Maybe they lost their appetite for changing the world when their attempt went so awry.

My brain offered a popcorn of memory, an old movie featuring an unlikely hero, and a smile grew across my face. "Only mostly dead."

Amanda and Taylor both glared at me but clearly didn't get the reference. There was no accounting for cinematic taste.

"Hughes wanted us to leave you here but wouldn't go without Amanda when neither of us agreed," Taylor said, despite the death stare Hughes gave the back of his head.

Abandoning me, or his pawn, I would have expected. Refusing to desert his student while she was in danger was a surprising point in Hughes's favor. "I guess there's a decent bone in that body of yours somewhere, Alexander."

"Very funny, Pierce. Call it my sense of morbid curiosity. It appears you had worse luck than I did in reversing the flow."

My balance was slowly returning, and I staggered a few steps toward him. The grin on my face grew, my cheeks stretching uncomfortably high. "Oh, I wouldn't say that. I met an old friend of Hobbomock's on the other side."

Hughes's voice held all the understatement of the stodgiest English professor. "I beg your pardon?"

"I've got a plan, but first we need to keep the giant in one place. He's going to move soon. How long was I dead?"

"I thought you weren't—Uh, never mind." Taylor checked his phone, and I could follow his mental math as he rolled his eyes upward. "Twenty minutes?"

"It felt like a lot more than that. Good, we've still got a little time before he goes on a walkabout. Amanda, do you have any quartz crystals on you?"

"Why would I have those?" she asked with a sour expression.

"Because you're learning magic from this jerk." I thumbed at Hughes.

Amanda glared at me but produced two quartz points from her purse. They were large enough to double as blocky daggers, each measuring at least six inches long and a few inches in diameter. "Happy?"

I nodded, then dug into my leg bag to produce two similar crystals of my own. "Just because I don't like him doesn't mean he's never right." I turned to Hughes. "I have to take care of something. While I'm gone, work with the kids to store as much of this ambient leftover essence as possible. We're going to need it."

Hughes cleared his throat. "Excuse me, who died and put you in charge of this escapade?"

Faster than he could backpedal from his words, I was on him. Inches from his face, I jabbed at the air toward Sonia's inert body. "She did. You don't have to like it, but I have a solution and you're going to help me fix this mess you made. So, you get to bleed a little for it, or so help me gods, I will throw you bodily into that pit and you can bleed a lot."

Hughes's face was a mask of indecision, but eventually he landed on something that appeared to be acceptance. A shred of account-ability had to be lurking in there, somewhere, and maybe he found it.

"Fine," he spat. "What else do we need to do?"

My grin was all teeth, a predator's smile. "You're not going to like this part one bit."

"You want what?" Rick's eyes widened in disbelief.

The Owl Shop wasn't exactly full of patrons. If you added me to the total number of people in the store, you'd have two, including the owner. Given the earthquakes and panic, Rick had greeted me with a baseball bat as we stepped into the building. He had grinned sheepishly, stashing the bat behind the bar while muttering "looters" under his breath.

"As much tobacco as you can fit in this." I laid the heavy-duty, black trash bag on the counter.

Rick didn't twitch a muscle but continued to eye me suspiciously. "Things are falling apart around here, Corbin. I understand 'smoke 'em if you've got 'em', but this is a little ridiculous."

"Trust me when I say it's even weirder than you can imagine. But this is important, Rick."

"I've extended you a tab before, but this going to be more than—"

The platinum credit card clicked heavily as I pressed it onto the gleaming wood. Rick quirked an eyebrow but picked it up to examine. His eyes went in and out of focus before he pulled a set of reading glasses from his pocket and popped them on.

"Where'd you get this? There's no way—"

I tossed the handwritten note where the card had been, smiling mischievously. Rick sighed and scooped that up as well, looking from it to the credit card and back.

"You're kidding me," he said flatly.

"It's legit. Call him if you need to, but I'm here on an errand for his nibs."

He tossed the note onto the bar, and I shrugged with a smug pride. The note was my idea. Rick knew about Hughes and my contentious relationship. There was no way he'd have believed Hughes agreed to let me rack up what was surely going to be thousands of dollars on his card.

> Rick,
> Yes, this idiot has permission to use my credit card to purchase a ridiculous amount of tobacco from your establishment. Nothing else, though, not even a breath mint.
> Regretfully,
> Alexander Hughes

He had written his phone number on the bottom in case Rick was feeling less than enthusiastic. Rick turned away and picked up his phone, clearly not trusting the equivalent of a bar napkin contract. I tapped at the counter and waited, knowing what the outcome would be.

Why a giant bag of tobacco? We needed Hobbomock to stay put while we enacted the rest of the plan. Keitan told me something that had been mostly lost to time. Hobbomock was the name of the spirit, but *hobbo-mack* meant "food for the pipe." Tobacco was already sacred, but to Hobbomock, it might be enough to satisfy his desire for reverence and keep him calm and immobile. The key word was "might."

Now it was about getting enough of it to make a sufficiently giant-sized offering, and I didn't know of anyone else with as much stock or patience for my bullshit as Rick. It also had to be good quality. Ransacking a smoke shop for their cheapest bulk tobacco didn't have the same feel to it as sacrificing a pile of the finest leaf Alexander's money could buy.

Rick conversed with Hughes in muffled tones, a note of surprise in his voice. My gaze wandered the store, and another aftershock from the latest quake sent tremors through the glass cases. He came back to the counter and sighed heavily. "Well, I'm not seeing any other business today, so why the hell not?"

"I'm in a bit of a rush," I said, grinning nervously at him.

He grabbed the bag off the counter while giving me a sidelong glare and walked into the employee-only portion of the establishment, where the kitchen and stock rooms were. "Keep an eye on the place," he called over his shoulder as he passed the threshold.

I sat on a stool at the bar and made another call, this time to Harriet. "Hey…I need your help."

"What'd you do, cousin?" she sounded exasperated, and a scraping sound came through the speaker. "I had a bad feeling you had some responsibility for the ground shaking."

"Is everything okay at the shop?"

"Mostly, but you owe me for the statues that jumped off the damn shelf."

"I'll work it off later. Look, I'm in a bit of a hurry," I said, echoing what I had said to Rick earlier. "We have to keep Hobbomock from moving so I can put him to sleep. Keitan said I'd need your help."

"Jesus Christ, Corbin." I imagined her holding her fingers to her temples, it sounded like I was already giving her a headache. "Hobbomock? Keitan? I don't care what kind of rush you're in, you need to explain what the hell is going on."

I made the explanation as brief as I could, though I didn't skip the part where I died. Other than a moment of stunned silence where I thought I'd lost the connection, she took it well. I was sure she'd have more questions than the ones she had already fired at me when I finished. We went back and forth for a few more rounds before I could get to my request. "So that's why I need your help. Keitan said you know the right songs, and the giant is more likely to accept our offering if we do things the right way."

"This is about as far from the 'right way' as I can imagine, Corbin," she said. "I'd want to organize a proper ceremony! How long do we have?"

"We're leaving for Sleeping Giant as soon as I'm done here. So, they'd have to be there in half an hour?"

"You're crazy! I couldn't get anyone from the tribe there in that time. If you want it done correctly—"

"Correct *enough*, Harriet. We can't wait for perfect."

She blew out a long breath, and I waited in silence until she replied. "Of course I'll help. Let me get my gear, and I'll meet you there as soon as I can. I can't make any promises; you usually can't rush this kind of thing."

"Thank you...cousin."

"Ah, don't thank me yet. He still might crush us both."

She hung up, and I went back to anxiously tapping my fingers for the next ten minutes before Rick returned with the sack over his shoulder like a weird Santa Claus. No one had entered while he was gone, so I had nothing to report. He grunted and tossed the bag at the base of the stool. I grabbed the tie at the top and gave it a heft. It was lighter than it looked but still probably clocked in at close to fifty pounds.

"I hope you don't mind, but I gave you all house blends. You said tobacco, not cigars, so it was the fastest way. Since you're in such a hurry."

He went behind the counter and started ringing me up.

"What do I owe you?"

"*You* don't owe me anything, but Hughes," Rick said as he swiped the platinum in his card reader, "isn't going to like this. Tell him I gave him a deal for bulk."

I saluted Rick hastily with two fingers, then lifted the bag to my shoulder and made for the door.

"Hey, Corbin!"

I turned, and Rick was coming around the end of the bar to press the credit card into my free hand.

"You get to deal with Alexander, not me."

"And I almost got away with it." I winked at him, and before he could take the last word from me, the bell rang as I walked out the door.

At least I had been smart enough to drive my car the short distance from the Green to the shop because lugging an enormous bag across the lawn would have been a right pain in the ass. I placed it carefully in the trunk. It wouldn't do to have the plastic split and leave my offering scattered in the crevices of my car.

The return trip was, of course, short, and I parked on Temple Street outside of the church to pick up my passengers. There was a lot more to the plan, but we had to get to the park first. Amanda, Hughes, and Taylor sat on the steps outside the church and came trotting over as soon as I slowed to a stop.

"Shotgun," Amanda cried, which led to some dirty looks exchanged between the other two. Luckily, Hughes didn't dispute this unwritten law of the road and got into the back seat with his co-conspirator. I took off with enough vigor that the tires screeched from the weight the vehicle carried. It wasn't a fast car, or a good car, but it would get us where we needed to go.

We zipped around in a quick set of turns to put us in the right direction out of town. From where we were, the quickest way to not-so-Sleeping Giant State Park was to take the highway, but it consisted of multiple bridges and overpasses. Despite my desire for a quick trip, I had even less interest in being caught on the highway because of damage from the earthquakes. Instead, I turned us around and sped down Route 5 at a much higher than recommended speed to make up the difference.

Once we were on our way, I finally noticed that the giant was slowly shifting his weight and rising to his feet. It was hard to gauge how much time we had left, but I could feel it slipping through my fingers as I clutched the wheel. No one spoke as we went. Everyone's attention was on Hobbomock and his ascent.

There wasn't as much destruction as I feared, but most people seemed to be already at or heading toward their homes. Likely to assess any potential problems and touch base with their families. I expected to see a million "marked safe from the New Haven earthquakes" on social media if we all survived this.

I sent a prayer to anyone who would listen and told everyone to ignore the giant and keep their eyes open for hazards in and around the road as I leaned on the gas like a maniac. Faster than I expected, mostly due to my lead foot, we arrived at the parking lot on the east side of the park. The geography in the physical world had shaken, not changed, but I wanted to set up closest to where Hobbomock's nose would be when standing.

The white trail led us to Hezekiah's Knob, but this wasn't a pleasure hike to stop and enjoy the view. We even passed by Hobbomock's feet, though the landmark was lower on the trail than we wanted to be at for what I had planned. It occurred to me this would be significantly more complicated if both of his feet weren't in roughly the same area. I'd have sent Hughes and Amanda to one and handled the other with Taylor, but I was thankful we should be able to take this first step together.

Hauling the tobacco also took a toll on my back and shoulders, but I'd worry about paying that bill later. We came upon a flat enough expanse of rock for what I needed. I asked everyone to grab kindling wood and large sticks, then I set myself to building a fire.

My companions brought me enough to make a modest blaze. Well, Taylor and Amanda did. Hughes didn't seem to understand what "physical labor" was and despondently picked up a handful of sticks before bringing them over as his contribution. I rolled my eyes and removed a lighter from my pouch, said a silent blessing that my materials were all dry enough to burn, and flicked the wheel to make a small flame. I lit the end of a twig and used that to catch each side of the leaves aflame.

The base flared brightly but smoldered after that. I cursed under my breath, crouched on my hands and knees, and blew into the bottom of the pile. Quickly, the pile caught again, and in moments, the fire was on its way to a tiny blaze. I fed it as fast as I dared, larger and larger branches until the heat radiated through to my chest.

The stones beneath our feet shuddered, and a corner of the fire collapsed, spraying embers into the air. It wasn't at risk of going out as much as catching the surrounding woods on fire, but it seemed contained for the moment. Looking up, Hobbomock turned his head, scanning the horizon, shifting his weight from leg to leg in a human gesture that bounced us all like pebbles across the rocks. I wanted to wait for Harriet, but I feared we'd run out of time.

"We have to do this now!" I cried, stumbling toward the bag of tobacco. Untying the closure with shaking hands, I plunged my fist inside, coming out with a large mass of cut leaf. I sprinkled what I held into the fire, and wisps of fragrant smoke rose into the air. But it wasn't enough. The tendrils dissipated a few feet above the flames. Throwing moderation firmly out the window, I stuffed handful after handful into the hungry maw of flame. Everyone else gathered around me and followed suit, packing it around the edge of the construction and piling it inwards once we had ringed it.

Clouds billowed up as the tobacco smoldered and burned. My eyes stung, and my throat ached from breathing in as much of the smoke as I did to build this unwieldy pipe. But when I looked upwards, Hobbomock had his nose in the air. I didn't know if stone giants had nostrils, but I imagined him sniffing the air.

"Great Hobbomock!" I yelled, straining my vocal cords. "We bring this offering in peace!"

Nothing happened for a moment, but then the eyes of an angry giant fell on me.

Chapter 22

Never had I wanted so badly to not be perceived. I was no introvert, but I suddenly understood why friends of mine wished for a cloak of invisibility on the regular. The weight of Hobbomock's stony gaze was oppressive, his mostly human features considering the ant who had set an offering ablaze for him.

Hastily I threw more and more tobacco onto the edges of the fire, the updraft swirling the smoke high into the sky. There was no guidebook for this, no magical tome of "how to train your giant", so I crossed my fingers and knelt, showing as much deference as possible. I only hoped whatever counted as his eyesight was sharp enough to discern the difference in my posture.

The silence was broken by the crack and pop of wood in the fire. Then the drumming began. Before her head crested the rise in the path, I knew Harriet was going to be pissed at me. She walked purposefully toward us while pounding a steady rhythm on a skin drum with her beater. We locked eyes, and I nodded, smiling.

"I told you not to start without me," she said, moving to sit by the fire. Harriet raised her chin, and a song that I didn't recognize rose from her chest. What I had done so far didn't seem to have pleased the awakened spirit, but now that Harriet was here, I prayed she was enough to tip the scales.

And we waited.

Slowly, Hobbomock turned one hand up to hold his palm out, stone eyelids closing in a gesture of acceptance. I motioned for Taylor to take over piling more cut leaf into the flames. Harriet stared upward with a reverence on her face I hadn't seen before. I don't know what she saw, but I imagined it was hard to *not* perceive the giant when you were this close.

This was where everything could fall apart, in more ways than one. Keitan had explained the need to keep Hobbomock from shifting his feet. "He's still connected to the vein running to the church," he had said. "Everything else is broken, and you'll need to fix that. But if he severs the last connection, I don't think any amount of medicine you've got will hold him down again. So, keep him from moving, but that's only the easiest part."

Easy. Right. With Keitan's aid and the assumption that Harriet would help, I had come up with the plan for the burnt offering, but after that, our situation got more complicated. The physical manifestation of the veins holding Hobbomock to the earth were tree roots but in the spirit lands were a vibrant quartz.

"Amanda, give me the crystals. Things are about to get complicated."

She did as I asked, and I stowed them in my pocket before gesturing for everyone to follow me as I charged back down the trail toward the giant's foot.

When we reached the dip in the trail closest to it, I veered toward the trees. The rest of the group followed. I moved through the brush until I stood in the spiritual shadow of Hobbomock's leg, standing like a monolith. "We do this part together," I said, huffing, "then we split up. Get ready to join with me." I strode to the stone and laid my hands on it, palms slapping against the rock.

The power pulsing through Hobbomock was intense, and for a second my stomach clenched in panic, worry overtaking me. Was this going to be too much? *You're not doing it alone this time*, I reminded myself.

Taylor was the first to touch my shoulder, sending his essence flowing into mine. The warmth bolstered me, and I wove his copper threads into mine. Amanda was next, placing her hand on my other shoulder, sending her cobalt to join us. Last, Hughes slapped his palm squarely between my shoulder blades hard enough to make me wince.

It came to me suddenly that I had never seen Hughes practice before, and the rich vermilion that plaited itself deftly with the rest of us made me shiver. He was strong, probably more so than I would have expected, but I guessed that came with age and experience. Together, our energies became a brilliant weave of metallic wires, and I reached down into Hobbomock's connection to the earth.

The flow was a torrent, and I wrestled with it like a boa constrictor in a river. Wrapping the rope of our energies around the vein, I released one hand to grab the first quartz point from my bag and stab it into the ground. Then I *pulled* as hard as I could, directing it all into the crystal. Without warning, it exploded into dust, peppering us with tiny shards of stone. Hobbomock cried out, which was a terrible sound. The grind of stone against stone made my skin prickle and hair stand on the back of my neck.

But the flow of essence which had been going from the earth upwards was now reversing course. The scintillating motes of energy ran downwards, away from the giant. Sweat broke across my brow as I released the threads of energy, each of us slumping to the ground.

I dropped to a knee, catching my breath, but we couldn't spare the time to rest. If a bug had ever bitten you on the ankle, your first response other than saying "ow" was to swat at it. Well, we had heard the "ow," and a shift of air pressure told me something might be coming our way.

"Move!" I yelled. "Back to the fire!"

We ran up the path toward the campfire, which still emitted plumes of tobacco smoke. As we reached the flat part of the stone, a rush of air made me duck and raise my hands above my head, warding off flying bits of trees and dirt. The giant had shifted position, and one hand had, indeed, come lower to investigate his legs.

Tremors bounced the red-hot coals of the fire, shaking a few loose which tumbled down the stone. I ran to stomp them out. It wouldn't do to have a forest fire chasing us through the rest of the plan. It was going to be hard enough as it was without making things even more complicated.

I motioned for everyone to gather around the fire, where I fed it more tobacco as I spoke. It wasn't likely to help, Hobbomock wasn't stupid, but I wouldn't pass up the chance to buy us more moments if it did.

"This is where we split up," I said, shoving handfuls into the flames. "Hughes, you and Amanda stay on this trail for about ten minutes until you hit the junction with the green trail, then text me. We'll coordinate go-time."

"What exactly are we doing next?" Hughes asked.

Perhaps I had been too light on the details, but in my defense, there was a lot going on. I relayed the next part of the plan in as few words as possible given we had a hike ahead of us and a giant of uncertain temperament towering overhead.

Hughes goggled at me. "A lasso?"

"What, never wanted to be a cowboy, Alexander? I'd say more like a whip, but that's my penchant for fictional archaeologists showing," I scoffed, then took one of the three remaining crystals and pressed it into his hand. "You'll need this. Just go with whatever is the strongest imagery for you. Don't overcomplicate it."

Hughes nodded, if a bit uncertainly, and gestured for Amanda to walk with him.

"And keep up the pace, Hughes. Now isn't the time to dawdle."

"You worry about yourself, Pierce," he shot back.

"Fine," I replied. "Harriet, you're coming with me and Taylor."

"Hold your horses, Corbin." Harriet raised her hands in protest. "I know this park like the back of my hand, and there's no way I'm pacing the two of you running through the forest. He might think he'll make it," she said, pointing at Hughes, "but I know my limits. I've got a better idea."

"All right...what's the plan?"

"I stay here and feed the fire until I run out, then I'll take the car around to meet you at the head."

"It'll be dangerous, even if he doesn't move his feet."

Harriet made a dismissive noise. "Pfft, you let me worry about it."

I nodded and offered a hand to Harriet, which she grasped. "Be safe. I'll see you on the other side."

"One way or the other, eh? Don't die a second time today, if you can manage it," she said with a grin, then turned to the fire and raised her voice in song again.

I took off on the trail with Taylor at my heels. The air held a tense quality. Hobbomock was still for the moment but in the way an animal caught in a trap waited and tested its new boundaries. I kept the more complicated route for myself. Hughes didn't know the trails the way I did. We set a brisk pace as we descended from the Knob and after a few minutes of hiking found the orange trail. We turned and pressed on.

Hobbomock scanned the ground, his broad head panning from side to side. The last time his displeasure manifested, he changed the course of the Connecticut River. I had no doubt he could crush us into a thin layer of slime, this side of the veil or not, if he found us. The lack of canopy, given the season, meant we needed to stay low, but I had to compromise between visibility and speed.

Five more minutes and we came to another junction, this one with a north-south trail that would take us where I wanted. My original idea was to space ourselves across Hobbomock's torso, where he would lie if we finally got him to the ground. It wouldn't do for us to fell the giant, only to be crushed by his ass as he sat back down on the earth.

Not if, when, I told myself.

We took the crossover trail north for a minute or two until we found the green blazes heading west; it was our waypoint and where we needed to wait for Hughes and Amanda to be ready.

A sound I could only describe as ponderous echoed through the woods. The trees creaked and groaned around us. Despite the difficulty of making out exactly what was happening at that large of a scale, I finally realized Hobbomock was crouching to get a closer look at the vermin messing with his morning routine. I held up my hand, stopping my forward momentum and signaling Taylor to pause, then pressed my finger silently to my lips.

His massive hand came to the hill we had just run down, and with a crunch, he closed his fingers around a fistful of rock and earth. Trees cracked and broke on this side of the veil, and a shock-wave ran through the ground beneath us. Hobbomock lifted the handful like a crane and casually tossed it in our direction. The physical effect was a landslide, as the boulders he threw in the spirit lands collided with the land. It was a tidal wave of debris, and all I could do was yell, "find cover" before diving off the trail toward a dense stand of trees.

A rush of air blew past my face, half shielded by the trunk I pressed it against. The scree and dirt rained off the trail and buried my legs to the ankles. The cacophony of sliding dirt and rocks continued for a few seconds then petered out. I ran back to where the trail had been, now partially covered by debris. There was no sign of Taylor, and calling out for him would have alerted Hobbomock we had not only survived but would've also told him exactly where we were.

I hadn't shut my inner eyes since this whole escapade began, but I extended my senses, searching for life. This entire park was bright with essence, but something farther down the trail caught my attention. I loped ten feet along what remained of the path and dropped to the earth, digging and throwing clods of dirt and rocks aside.

Taylor's face finally broke the surface, and a wracking cough spewed brown sludge from his mouth. I grabbed him by the shoulders and pulled him halfway to a sitting position. He turned and hacked again until he was breathing clearly, if raggedly.

"No time for dirt naps, Taylor," I whispered, pointing at the giant. "We have to do this now."

He glared at me with wide eyes but nodded and pushed himself the rest of the way free. I pulled my phone out and checked for a message from Hughes, but nothing waited for me.

CORBIN:

WHERE ARE YOU?!

HUGHES:

Almost there.

I closed my eyes and breathed, pushing frustration aside until I could think clearly again. Opening them, I caught Taylor's gaze and placed a finger to my lips. He sidled over to me and put his mouth close to my ear.

"What do we do now?" he whispered.

"We wait."

Patience, as always, was not my strong suit. But luckily, I didn't have to contemplate my poor life choices long before Amanda texted me, "Here."

CORBIN:

Respond to this text, and once it's read, count ten seconds. Then we take him down.

My heart raced as I watched the "typing" dots play on my screen.

HUGHES:

We'll go on ten.

And then I began. *Ten. Nine. Eight. Seven. Six.*

"Taylor, link up with me," I said.

Five. Four. Three.

Taylor's hand found my shoulder, and his essence poured into mine.

Two. One...

I coiled my energies and formed them into a bright whip, longer than any physical manifestation could have been. The hand that almost buried Taylor was visible above the trees, and I swung my arm in a broad arc, sending the woven construct far into the air. It seemed impossibly thin, a strand of spider silk against the massive form. The silvery rope found its way around his neck, meeting with Hughes's red equivalent. If Hobbomock hadn't crouched lower, I doubted our magic could have reached above the clouds.

A grunt of surprise burst forth from Hobbomock's lips, and he raised his hands toward his neck. But we were smaller and faster. I didn't know if Hughes had any chance of hearing me from as far away as we were, but I screamed, "Now!" at the top of my lungs. Wrapping the end of my line around my fist, I *pulled* with all my might, bolstering myself with Taylor's help. The goal wasn't to root him in place but to take advantage of what I hoped was a universal truth. No one enjoyed being pushed around by their neck. I wasn't sure if a stone giant would feel a razor thin garrote, but our future depended on it.

He had already twisted around, trying to find us from his crouch. We heaved against his massive form, and the whip grew as taut as a bowstring. Hughes's line did the same, and inch by inch, Hobbomock leaned backward toward us.

We kept pulling, and I tensed, waiting for the moment when I would find out if this part of my mad plan would succeed. In a handful of moments or forever, it was hard to tell, the line went slack.

"Get out of the way!" I yelled, drawing our essence back and shoving Taylor to the side of the trail. A long time ago, I had seen a huge old tree felled by a woodcutter. He had spent an hour examining angles and the surrounding area until he had lined everything up perfectly. When the tree finally came down, it started with a single crack and then the silence was deafening as the enormous oak plummeted to the ground.

We stood together in the copse of trees, watching. Slowly, ever so slowly, Hobbomock pitched backwards. He fell in slow motion, or so it seemed, the creaking and cracking of tree limbs and trunks the only sounds.

I shoved Taylor toward the dirt and knelt myself, curling my forearms over my face in an improvised shield. "Stay down!"

This was either going to work perfectly or we would both be dead.

Chapter 23

There was a muffled "whump" and then a concussive blast blotted out the world and bowled me over, sending me tumbling ass over teakettle. I rolled down a hill, encountering every rock and root on my way, eventually coming to a halt when I slid up against a tree trunk.

I could barely describe how everything hurt, though some of it faded quickly as I righted myself. My head swam, and I braced myself against the tree I had collided with. Rustling leaves alerted me to movement on my right, but it was Taylor getting to his own feet in a similar shambling state.

"What the fuck was that?" he asked, brushing his pants and coming over to me.

"We felled a giant. I forgot to yell 'Timber', I guess."

Getting my bearings, I found another trail at the limit of my vision. The blue blazes told me we had been thrown wildly off track, but given the size of the giant laying next to us on the hill, I shouldn't have been surprised. I pulled my phone from my pocket and cursed; the screen had cracked in more than one place. Thankfully, it responded when I pushed the button to wake it up, and I texted Amanda.

CORBIN:

The screen itself began to discolor, a faint blue edging the display. Having broken my phone before, it was only a matter of time before it became a useless brick. I rattled Amanda's number off for Taylor, who made note of it, then stuffed it back into my pocket. We took off at a halting jog up the trail toward the stone tower.

We made our way through the brush and onto the clear path, following the blue blazes west. Despite our injuries, we ascended as quickly as we could, groaning from our bumps and bruises. My ankle protested disconcertingly, but I laced my boots tighter and made it a problem for later.

It wasn't long before we passed the stone tower, which still stood, but not unscathed. Fresh cracks spidered through the foundation, mortar falling from new gaps in some of the large stones. We didn't need to climb to the observation platform to see Hobbomock spread along the valley below us. He shifted uncomfortably, unable to move his feet to help reposition himself. We were still on the clock and headed down the other side of the trail.

Hughes knew to meet us on the giant's chest, which was a much more perilous thing to consider once I'd laid eyes on the expanse of him. But I had made the plan, and we scrambled along the track until it hit another crossover trail, taking it directly south until we came to the giant's shoulder.

I had noted before how strange it was looking across the veil and seeing the giant while still observing the natural world as it was. This was even stranger. When Hobbomock fell, he cratered into the earth across the veil. He had merged with the hills and valley, so our next steps would be both on the ground and on the stone of his flesh. The worry of how the hell I could climb a spirit-giant, which I had imagined being like a mime ascending a ladder, faded. It was replaced with the terror of having to navigate the shifting landscape of a giant's torso blurring with the surrounding forest.

Small stands of trees were flattened as if hit with a microburst, still alive but bent at almost ninety-degree angles to the ground. Much of the woods showed damage, similar to how it had been when tornados had passed through the state some years ago. Broken trunks, dropped branches, and shifted earth.

I leapt as gently as I could into a space where the ground was solid and coincided with the first flat part of the giant's chest. Kneeling, I placed my palm on the stone and listened with all my senses. The giant was in distress but not afraid. Gods only knew what could make a being like this fearful, and it wasn't me. Nonetheless, I spoke calming words into the air. "We're not here to hurt you. Not that we could if we wanted to. You'll rest easy soon."

Patting the stone, I stood and was almost knocked off my feet again by another tremor. Hobbomock might not have been bucking like a horse to get us off, but he didn't seem to enjoy being tickled by the equivalent of ant feet. He was clearly still trying to rise but not having much luck. Without being able to move his feet, he'd need to roll over or do some weird kip-up, and neither of those was likely now. We still had time, but eventually he'd figure something out.

Movement on the other side of the giant caught my eye. Hughes and Amanda appeared through the trees, his arm around her shoulder as they took steady steps toward us. We made halting progress across the expanse of Hobbomock, meeting over where a stone heart might have been. I knelt, as much to gather us together as to keep myself mostly upright against the shifting skin of the giant.

Quickly, I relayed the last part of the plan to the group. Keitan had told me there was only one way we were going to put Hobbomock back to sleep, and my companions might not like it.

Hughes was the first to lodge an official complaint. "I beg your pardon. Why did you spend all that money on tobacco then?"

"To keep him from leaving. Also, because I knew it would piss you off. But now we're going to give him what he wants," I repeated.

"I believe we're running short on everything, Pierce," Hughes said through gritted teeth. His leg was bleeding at the calf. Amanda had done her best to use a bandage ripped from her shirt to bind it, but from the look of it he'd need some stitches when this was all over.

Hobbomock took that moment to shift his weight from side to side, and we wobbled but kept our feet. I glared at Hughes. Self-sacrifice was not on his bingo card, but we didn't have any other options.

"He's not going down easy," Keitan had told me, when we discussed how to put the final nail in the coffin. "You're going to have to give him something. He won't drink a sleeping potion or anything like that. He might be thick, but tricks aren't going to work this time."

The "something" was a giant-sized offering. We wouldn't be sacrificing our lives, but we'd have to feed him a portion of our medicine, similar to what Keitan had required of me for his help, only bigger. The spirit wouldn't let me accept the burden by myself, either. He had clicked his tongue at me. "What use would you be, to me and the land, if you didn't have any medicine left?"

Keitan had warned me that this part wouldn't be easy, but I knew how to push this man's buttons. "This is it, Hughes. We're all that stands between a rampaging giant and the rest of the city."

"This is a bait and switch, Pierce," he complained. "I agreed to help you because I do have some personal responsibility—"

"Some?!" I interrupted. All right, maybe he was pushing my buttons instead. "This is *entirely* your fault. And these *children*—"

"Hey!" Amanda and Taylor cried in unison.

"These *students*," I amended, "are willing to give up theirs because it's the right thing to do!"

They both nodded along with my statement, looking at Hughes with imploring eyes.

"We need your help," Amanda said, grabbing the hand Alexander had draped over her shoulder. "We don't know what happens if we can't fix this."

"Exactly!" Hughes cried, seeming to feel she proved his point.

"But the risk can't be worth it, can it?" Taylor asked.

I glanced away from the heart-to-heart developing in front of me, and Hobbomock's gaze locked with mine. He had craned his neck up and glared at the small group of people, to him the size of insects, standing on his chest.

I cleared my throat. "Guys?"

"You no clue what you're talking about," Hughes said, his voice rising in pitch. "The power you've wielded is nothing compared to what you will develop with years and practice."

"Guys?!" I repeated.

"You coward! How can you even consider—" Taylor yelled back at Hughes, but I interrupted again.

"GUYS!"

They all finally turned to me and took in what I saw. The silence was near-complete. The only sound was the wind through the trees shaking the dry leaves that hadn't fallen yet.

"Well, shit," Taylor said, with a level of understatement I found impressive.

A sudden rush of air alerted me I had missed something. I looked up. One of Hobbomock's hands descended rapidly toward us. He was quiet for a stone giant and had moved his palm close like you had to do to catch a fly. It was hard to gauge if we had time to move, but I doubted it.

"Everyone, get close!" Hughes cried, and Taylor and I dove near his feet. The sun disappeared behind the eclipse of Hobbomock's massive fingers, and he swatted us against his chest like flies. Hobbomock's hand had gathered trees as he lowered it, and they bent around us like a wooden cage, pressing closer and closer.

The impact, even lessened by the veil, should have been enough to crush us. But pain didn't come, only a weird darkness half-made of spirit. A glow surrounded us, pressed against the gigantic palm like a bubble. Hughes's essence was a deep red, but even as I took it in, small cracks formed in its exterior. Amanda had fallen to her knees next to us. Alexander grunted under the strain, his posture that of Atlas holding the world on his shoulders.

"We have to do this now!" I said. "No more bullshit. Either you help us, or you're the one who lets the giant loose on the world, provided we survive long enough for anyone to find out."

Hughes panted and eyed me with more than a modicum of hatred. I didn't care; we were too far along for him to bail now. We both knew it.

A heartbeat sprang to life nearby. No, it wasn't a heartbeat unless it had arrhythmia. "Thank you, Harriet," I sighed under my breath. The drumming had returned. They must have found their way around to this side of the park. Harriet's singing picked up in volume, and the beater drove a heavy rhythm.

Hobbomock's hand didn't move, but from the surprise on Hughes's face, I could tell the pressure had eased slightly. I took the final quartz point out of my pocket and held it up, then placed it tip-down on the ground. I placed my hand over the end, motioning for the others to put theirs atop mine.

"Swear an oath with me now," I said into the stillness, looking at each of them for a nod. "I offer this piece of myself to the land, to the stone, to Hobbomock's keeping."

We repeated it in unison as our essence merged through the crystal into the rock below. I gathered our energies together again, weaving them like a tapestry over our stacked hands. Keitan had been specific that we would need to make connections to each of the elements, helping to bind him to sleep again. It was a combination of sincere offering and a rag soaked with ether. We had to give enough of ourselves to appease him and then use the link to tie him down.

I poured power into my left hand, the one the rosary had scarred. My seared flesh ached with the accumulating essence, and I slammed my palm down over the top of the woven mesh of essence above our joined hands.

The crystal, like the ones before it, exploded, biting into my other palm and shooting outward, striking each of us as the pieces flew and bounced. Nothing happened for a long few seconds, and I looked at each of my companions in turn.

Then the pain came.

My chest burned like I had swallowed a red-hot coal, and I fell over, clutching at my shirt, breathing gouts of steam into the air. *That can't be good*, I thought to myself as my vision blurred. As I lay on my side, I caught the convulsions of the others. Taylor spat blood onto the earth. Amanda gasped and wheezed, coughing all the air from her lungs, and Hughes's forehead was suddenly slick with sweat, beading and falling to the ground.

The sounds of agony swelled, and thick ropes of essence exploded from our chests, weaving together and plummeting into the small hole where I had pounded the crystal into the dirt. It drew and drew until there was nearly nothing left of me.

Our tapestry grew and spread, covering the land. It hugged the earth like a blanket, settling into the restless form of Hobbomock. The shadow cast by his hand fell to the side, our construct tucking him in up to and over his neck, then his head. It must have reached all his extremities and stretched to the edges of awareness because Hobbomock finally went still. The shift was palpable, the difference between the stones gathering themselves for action and finally being at rest.

After an eternity, the embers in my chest faded. I sucked in lungfuls of clean air. I had never experienced relief so intense. I rolled onto my back, taking deep breaths. *At least the screaming stopped*. Then I passed out where I lay.

Chapter 24

I swam in and out of consciousness. The light above had faded to dark, but the next time I hit awareness, an orange glow permeated my eyelids. Later still, and one side of my body was warmer than the other. When I finally opened my eyes, light danced on the underside of the canopy Hobbomock had bent over us.

"You could make a hell of a wigwam out of this," a familiar voice said next to me.

"Harriet," I whispered, but even that was too much for my throat. I rolled onto my side and coughed, hacking painfully until whatever fit had possessed me passed. Pushing myself into a seated position, I groaned and looked about. Taylor and Amanda huddled on the other side of what turned out to be a small campfire. No one was dressed for the evening chill, and my body shivered lightly as the ground leached the warmth from me. I returned my attention to Harriet and gestured toward the fire. "This you?"

She nodded solemnly. "Wasn't sure when you'd wake up. The young ones recovered first. Well, not recovered, but they're at least more alert than you two old men."

I laughed at the jab but glanced over to where Hughes still lay. His open mouth twitched slightly from whatever danced inside his head. "How long was I out?"

"It's been a few hours. No signal out here right now, and enough people back in the city need paramedics more than you two." Harriet fished a flask out of her pocket and handed it to me.

I uncapped it and tipped a measure of it into my mouth. It burned as I swallowed and winced, sucking air through my teeth. The alcohol numbed my throat pleasantly after the initial sting, so I shrugged and took another tipple. The second time was easier, and I thanked Harriet before passing the flask back.

A surprising voice chimed in from beyond the edges of light the campfire cast. "Hughes is going to need to go to the hospital as soon as we can get him there." Nour strode in between the gaps in the trees arching over us, two straight sticks in hand. She dropped to one knee by Alexander and began wrapping a splint around his leg. "I don't know if it's broken, but he'll need stitches at the very least."

"What are you doing here?" I asked.

"Harriet called me after you talked to her. She thought it might be a good idea if a medic was on standby. Once I knew where you were going, I headed there after the network was overloaded." She finished tying off the wrapping, then dusted her hands and came over to me. Pulling a flashlight from her pocket, she held me by the chin as she checked my pupil response.

I pulled away and shook my head. "I don't have a concussion."

"Can't be too careful," she shot back but relented and sat next to Harriet. "So much for that stray dog, huh?"

Casting my eyes downward with a sheepish grin, I nodded. "It might have been a little more complicated than that."

Nour waggled a finger at me. "I'd slap you, but you're injured."

I raised my right hand in front of my eyes, fingers together, and bent forward slightly. "Thank you for coming, regardless."

She returned the gesture. "*Aadab*."

"Was that all what I think it was, Corbin?" Harriet asked, tossing more sticks onto the fire.

"How much did you *see*?" I asked with emphasis on the last word.

Her face was contemplative as she poked at the fire with a thicker piece of branch. "When I drummed by the fire he was like a mirage, fading in and out of focus. But when I came here, it was different. More like a weight, a presence. It was amazing, Corbin."

"How did you find us?" I asked, rubbing at the base of my spine. Sleeping even a short while on the hard ground hadn't done me any favors.

Harriet laughed. "Pfft. Like I don't know where Hobbomock's head is in this park. If it worked the way you said it might, that's where you'd be."

"Fair enough." I paused, staring into the firelight. "Thank you. He seemed to care about your song enough to pay attention to that instead of crushing us to death under these trees. It was the moment we needed."

Harriet didn't say anything else, but she didn't have to. No one else seemed inclined to talk either, and that suited me fine. Exhaustion pressed heavily on my eyelids again, and I wanted nothing more than to sleep. But it had to wait until we got out of here.

Pained groaning alerted us to Hughes's return to consciousness. Nour rushed to his side and helped him into a seated position, muttering gentle words under her breath I couldn't make out. Soon enough, he moved himself closer to the fire with Nour's aid and warmed his hands. His face was pale, a light sheen of sweat coated his brow. If I had to guess, I'd say his body already fought an infection from his injury.

It was bad enough having a gash in your leg when you were hiking, let alone being thrown around and covered in dirt. Normally, it would take longer for something like that to set in, but given how depleted our reserves were, we effectively had compromised immune systems. I hoped he was up on his tetanus shot, but only time would tell.

We waited about twenty minutes but then, in unspoken agreement, began breaking down our impromptu camp. Harriet doused the fire, mixing fresh earth into the coals until only steam rose from the hot circle. Nour had Hughes test his splint, but Amanda came over to give him a shoulder to lean on again for the trip out.

Harriet was kind enough to drive us back to my car. I rode shotgun while Amanda, Taylor, and Hughes were in the back. Consciousness eluded me as soon as the car was in gear, and I woke again when we arrived at the east parking lot. I didn't remember how I got home, but sometimes it would come to me in flashes. Despite being bone-weary and developing my own symptoms of magically-induced exhaustion, I got everyone back to their cars.

Eventually, I opened my eyes, and I was on the couch in my study. I hadn't even made it all the way upstairs before passing out again. If the escapade with Katie had knocked me on my ass for a few days, I wasn't sure what I was in for this time. Taking a mental inventory, I had given up part of my essence to Keitan for his help, then spent an ungodly amount of energy in dealing with the giant, culminating in sacrificing a quarter of my magic to put him back to sleep. Pure adrenaline had kept me upright, and even that had been tapped out for the foreseeable future.

I was pretty sure I was fucked for a while. Checking the campus website for their rules on leaves of absence, in between bouts of chills and fever, I finally caught some good news in my inbox. The school was closed for a week as engineers swarmed the buildings downtown, ensuring everything was structurally sound after the quakes.

Giving a silent prayer of thanks to all things good in the world, I surrendered to illness and recovery.

Larceny with a raccoon accomplice had netted me a weekend of bed rest. Knocking a giant out for the next millennium laid me up for the entire week. It would have been nice to enjoy the break, but I was a mostly unconscious lump traveling between my bed and the couch simply for variety's sake.

Taylor had texted me a few times, to continue apologizing for his betrayal of trust, but I ignored the messages after seeing the preview. He had been instrumental in putting Hobbomock back down, but I felt justified in holding a grudge. It was a little petty, but he still deserved it. Hughes might have been the one to blame, but Taylor's help had made my intervention impossible until it was too late. I mulled that over often in my half-awake fever state.

One afternoon, and I couldn't have told you which one, Harriet knocked on my door. She hadn't seen me leave the apartment in a few days and brought me a pot of corn chowder she had made. I was ravenous, having eaten nothing recently that I couldn't heat in the microwave with the least amount of effort. Two bowls of it disappeared before I fell asleep on the couch with the barest memory of her patting my shoulder before letting herself out.

I resurfaced near the end of the week, weak as a kitten but feeling clearer than I had since the events at Sleeping Giant. Catching up on the local news, I found Sonia's name in a small article which hadn't made the front page. "Overdose in the Crypt" was the headline, and I cursed Hughes as I read it. Additionally, the crypt itself had suffered a lot of structural damage. It was unlikely anyone would assume changes to the floor plan, like an open pit, were anything other than incidental.

Despite Alexander's help, even saving our lives near the end with his efforts, I had hoped consequences would find him. It should have been obvious they'd have doped her before the sacrifice to cover their tracks, if nothing else. That was a thread I'd have to tie up myself, and despite my infirmity, the fire in my belly made me equal to the task.

A quick text to Amanda on my new phone informed me Hughes had ended up in the hospital. His wound had gotten infected, as I feared. His weakened state worsened it, by her account, and they admitted him to Yale New Haven Hospital for treatment and observation. He was already much recovered by the end of the week, otherwise I'd have left him alone, but I expected him to be released soon, and there was no time like the present. At least I had a captive audience for what might prove to be a hard conversation.

I showered and ate the last of the chowder Harriet had left, dressed in my usual fall attire with an added cross-body bag, and took myself to the hospital for visiting hours. Hospitals always bothered me, despite how important they were. The sterile hallways, chilly temperatures, and often impersonal standard of care made the experience less than ideal. After checking in and finding out where Dr. Hughes was being cared for, I wandered the halls until I found him.

Balloons and flowers filled the place when I entered, and his room had the cheery air of a "get well soon," rather than a "we have bad news, sir," situation. Hughes looked...frailer than I expected. His gaze was sharp, and he held a book in front of him with a steady hand, but he was rail thin. A mostly empty IV bag hung next to him, a narrow line leading to the back of his hand. The hospital gown took some dignity away, which I knew he'd have missed if he could see himself through my eyes.

As soon as I stepped through the doorway, he closed his book with a snap.

"Ah, Pierce," he said, his voice light but even. "I wondered when you'd come. Here to gloat?"

A smile crept across my face; he certainly hadn't lost his temperament. "Not exactly." I sat in one of the visitors' chairs. He had gotten himself a private room, which seemed unlikely but made my life easier. "I came to thank you."

His mouth twisted, clearly questioning my sincerity. "That's out of character for you."

I shrugged. "Maybe I'm turning over a new leaf. I nearly had to beat it out of you, but you made the right choice when it mattered."

"Nothing like a backhanded compliment to brighten my day," he said drolly.

"Seriously, this time. Thank you for your help."

"I appreciate the recognition, but I did it to protect the students, not you."

"Then you still chose well." I nodded, pausing, and changed the direction of the conversation. "Say, have you been keeping up with the news?"

Hughes's eyes took on a suspicious cast, but his tone remained cordial. "I have. Little else to do while I'm recuperating besides watching the news and reading."

"Strange reports about what they found in the crypt."

"Yes," he said flatly and without elaboration.

I drew a small bag out of my kit, and Alexander's eyes widened in shock. The heavy plastic crinkled as I placed the syringe on the table next to his bed. He glared at me, and I couldn't keep the smug smile off my face.

"Where did you get that?" he demanded, reaching for the evidence.

I snatched the bag up again, stowing it safely out of reach. "There was a *lot* happening in that basement. Must have gotten lost in the confusion." The reality was it had rolled near to me after everyone had been thrown around in the crypt. I had pocketed it and left it under the seat in my car until I could store it properly.

"That proves nothing, you'll never—"

I interrupted him with a raised hand. "Calm down, Hughes. You'd probably get away with it, even if I went to the cops and told them the whole thing. The syringe almost certainly has your prints on it, and you might even get named as a person of interest if they fielded an investigation. But I doubt anything would stick."

"Then what's the point of this?"

"Because there are other ways this can ruin you. You might be acquitted, but between the investigation and the campaign I'd launch against your good name, administrative leave is the best outcome you can hope for. Think of your *reputation*, Alexander."

He blew out a frustrated breath, crossing his arms over his chest. "What do you want?"

"First, this pissing match between you and me is over. I need something? You back me. If I have an apprentice and they need to learn a skill you can teach? You do it."

"If this is about Taylor—"

"Fuck Taylor," I spat. "This is about you and me."

He looked at me appraisingly. "Fine. What else?"

"Second, you take an oath that you and your cabal will never harm another human being again. You won't do it personally, direct anyone else directly, indirectly, or encourage it to be done for your benefit."

"I can't make promises for other people, Pierce."

"No, but you *can* for yourself and whatever is in your power to control." I pushed my essence into my palm and held it out, staying in my chair to keep the immediate vertigo from sending me to the floor from the effort. My silver threads were tarnished, thinner than before but still there.

Hughes stared at my hand, then reluctantly reached out with his own. His essence was a lighter red than I remembered. Apparently what we had sacrificed would be evident for all of us. He spoke the words that he wouldn't harm another soul for his benefit or the benefit of The Hand.

"And if I betray my oath, I will wither and my power is sacrifice," I added. He tried to pull his hand back, but I held firm. We were both weak, but I was still stronger than him.

Hughes's lips pursed like he had sucked on a lemon, but he repeated the words. The mingled essence sunk into his flesh. He winced, and the machines monitoring his vitals gave a querulous beep but returned to their normal operation. I stood and walked to the door. My business was done.

"Blackmail isn't a good look on you, Pierce," Hughes called after me.

I turned and leaned against the door frame. "I'll do what it takes, Hughes. It's one of the few ways we're alike."

Epilogue

Nearly a month passed before I would say anything returned to a semblance of normal. Classes continued, though Taylor didn't attend any of my lectures. I would see him in the hall, and we acknowledged each other with the occasional nod, but our companionable lunches were a thing of the past.

The church and the buildings surrounding the Green weren't the only places to sustain damage from Hobbomock's waking. The army of civil and structural engineers swarming a large swathe of the county meant a regular stream of areas were closed to the public while repairs took place. Beyond the official government response, the community had suffered a lot of hits. Insurance adjusters became personae non gratae as people made claims, got denied, appealed, and often denied again.

It was painful to watch. I even participated in some half-hearted protests against the lack of support for the unexpected natural disaster caused by Hobbomock's brief jaunt on this side of wakefulness. Eventually everything settled, for the most part, with the local communities coming together to help each other repair their homes more than any assistance from the companies they paid their premiums to.

I met up with Jake on the Green, and he was happy to hear things would be calm again. We mourned Clyde, Sonia, and the others together with a beer, spilling some out for lost comrades. He didn't ask what had happened but trusted I was right. My work with the charities providing food for the homeless continued, as well as my activism with Nour.

The return to the familiar was a balm for my soul, even if the memories of death from the recent past haunted my dreams. Teddy was a recurring figure, though I rarely remembered much more than his presence. I hoped he looked up from hell and nodded approvingly at my actions, his unwilling sacrifice meaning something in the end.

It was afternoon the day after Thanksgiving; the schools were closed, and the sun was already down. I was pounding away at my laptop in my study, agonizing on the latest round of edits for one of my grant proposals, when a light tapping caught my attention. I stopped what I was doing when it came again, I followed the noise to the window. The old single-glazed windows had another layer of storm glass on the outside, and the claws of a fat raccoon made a racket against that thin protection against the cold.

I lifted first one pane, then the other, until I was face to snout with Scratch. He didn't come inside but rested on the sill as if waiting. "What are you doing here?" I asked.

He sat on his haunches to stare me full in the face, then turned and climbed down the conduit next to the window, paw over paw, and took off at speed toward Whalley Avenue. A thin stream of essence flowed from his tail, like a line-painter on the street leaving a trail behind him, beckoning me to follow.

First, I closed the windows. I didn't make enough money to heat the outside. Next, I pulled on a pair of boots as I made my way to the stairs. My laces flopped about as I crossed the street and trailed the thin line of spirit into the park. It was closed after dark, but that was nearly meaningless when pitch-black came so soon. It was still early enough in the day for no one to question my presence, and I hoofed it along the path until I came to the pond where I had worked with Scratch, training for our retrieval mission.

Scratch sat at the edge of the water, nibbling on something next to what I could only describe as a mountain of a person. Their back was to me, but the width of their shoulders said they were over six feet tall and as broad as a refrigerator. I opened my senses, and they shone like a bonfire, bursting with essence which leaked across the veil. They existed in both places, in the spirit lands and here, like Scratch did. Only *more*.

As I approached, they turned to me and it was a woman, broad-chested and husky. She had a dangerous grace packed into a muscular frame, but the smile on her face reflected the light of the moon and didn't hold any threat. Her clothes were plain, jeans and a flannel, like mine, but she didn't wear a jacket despite the cold. It didn't seem to bother her, and she gestured for me to sit.

Scratch was eating a french fry and looked at me with no apparent concern, so I took a patch of grass next to the woman. We stared out over the pond for a minute, and she fed Scratch more french fries from a small carton. Neither of us spoke until I broke the silence.

"You must be Bear," I said, verbally capitalizing the B.

A chuckle bubbled up from her chest. "Got it in one, little Raven." Her voice was a deep contralto, honey-rich.

I sighed and closed my eyes. "I'm never getting rid of that nickname, am I?" When I opened them again, she looked at me with her head cocked to one side.

"Do you want to?"

I opened my mouth but closed it again, considering. "No? It just feels weird."

"If you're worried Raven will mind, he won't. He's a good sport," she said with a nod.

"Uh, okay. Am I...in trouble?"

She barked a laugh that shook my chest and made Scratch's tail puff up to twice its normal size.

"Far from it, Corbin. I saw what you did with my kin downtown. So, first, thank you. Keitan also told me about your agreement. Call me your...handler. We're going to be working together a lot, you and me."

"I'm not exactly at full capacity. I haven't even figured out what that looks like yet or how much use I'm going to be for a while. But I'll do my best."

Her gaze took on a sly cast. "Oh, we might be able to do something about that. But you'll be plenty helpful even as you are now. Have no fear, you'll serve the land just fine."

I reached over and stole a fry from the container, popping it into my mouth. "So, what's next?"

"I don't know, Corbin," she said, with a glint in her eye. "How far are you willing to go?"

Acknowledgements

Thank you, kind reader, for making it this far. The idea for this book sprang to life based on the indigenous tale of Hobbomock, now the Sleeping Giant at the heart of a state park in Hamden, Connecticut. The challenge when including cultural material from a people that we are not, ourselves, a part of can be challenging. I did my best to represent some of the stories of multiple Algonquian tribes, with the help of some extremely generous native readers.

Special thanks to author Suzie LaVonne, of the Anishinaabe people, and Clan Mother Shoran Piper, of the Golden Hill Paugussett tribe. They were instrumental in providing feedback on the cultural aspects and themes used in this book. I hope that I honored the stories and culture, while providing some entertainment. I did reach out to many more tribal resources, but unfortunately most of them did not have the time to provide feedback. I did my best, as we all try to.

Thanks also to my early readers. My partner, Kat, listened as I read and re-read chapters to them on a daily basis. Authors Tanya Hagel and AJ "Poppy" Alexanders, as well as David Huffman, and Laurie Neilsen, have been my constant friends and supporters on this writing journey.

About the Author

Ben Schenkman likes many things in his life: his 20-pound Maine coon cat, his family, his coffee, and his eclectic hobbies—not necessarily in that order.

Ben also likes to play devil's advocate in his urban fantasy books by exploring the gray areas of good and evil with questions like, "Does the end really justify the means? Or is it all simply black and white?" Ben leaves these questions lingering in the ether to challenge readers' conventional thinking and delve into the complexities of moral dilemmas.

As a writer and a native of Connecticut, Ben draws inspiration from his upbringing and college years in New Haven, where his urban fantasy novels take place. On the days he wants to escape being a writer, he's a massive foodie who goes on daring gastronomic adventures, an overachiever who collects degrees in Theater, Nuclear Engineering, and an MBA, or the manager-slash-performer of the fire dance troupe, "HVBRIS"—all in a day's work, really.

To learn more about Ben Schenkman and his work, or if you simply want to invite him for a coffee and talk about cats, visit https://benschenkman.com today.

Thank you for reading! If you enjoyed this book, please consider leaving an honest review on your favorite platform. Until then, what's next for the author?

Also by

Available Now

My Boss is the Devil — The Devil You Know: Book One
Dueling Shoulder Angels — The Devil You Know: Book Two
Too Many Gods in the Kitchen — The Devil You Know: Book
Three

Coming Soon

My Brother's Keeper